along to add to the cheap... g.
Something told me I'd b... gh
the night. Not that I was... n.
He handed over the bottl...

"Thank you," I said. "You didn't need to do that."

"It's no bother," Claire answered. I knew she meant nothing by her comment. It was just her way of communicating. Her gaze soon left me and flicked to London. She moved into the house and took off her coat. "Look who's here." She made a show of glancing around. "What? No boy toy?"

I suppressed a groan as London and Claire got off to their usual start. They were like fire and ice at the best of times. It was usually harmless, but occasionally, things grew out of hand. Especially when there was alcohol involved. And, of course, alcohol was going to be the key ingredient of the evening.

"How's married life treating you, Claire?" London asked. "I hear they've just invented a new mop."

Claire feigned some laughter as she guided Thea into the house. Instead of ignoring London, she came back at her with another thinly veiled slight I hoped her daughter didn't understand. I sighed and rolled my eyes. The insults were already flying. I guessed it wouldn't be a dinner party without them.

Richard looked uncomfortable and fixed his gaze on me like he was waiting for me to intervene and pull the dueling duo apart. There was no way I was getting involved.

I gave Richard a shrug. He was a soft-spoken man who seemed the opposite of Claire's type, but they got married a year ago and hadn't had any problems that I knew of. I couldn't handle attending their wedding, but I'd seen plenty of happy snaps on social media to suggest he was a great stepdad to Thea. Maybe he was just the type of man Claire needed, considering her disaster of an ex left without a word.

I directed London and Claire toward the dining room, letting them continue their exchange while I headed to the kitchen. Richard and Thea decided to follow me. Richard asked for Brad along the way. I couldn't help but smile at his attempt to avoid the potential drama.

"Brad's in the living room," I told him.

"Thanks, Maia," he said with a relieved look in his eye. He guided Thea along on his escape.

* * *

Over the next hour, more guests arrived. My former work friend Hazel, along with her husband, Mike, were next to knock on the door. They brought their three young and bouncy kids with them. Then, our neighbors from across the street, the Thompsons, were last to ring the doorbell, arriving with their two children.

Pretty soon, we were all gathered around our extended dining table, eating, drinking, and chatting like old times. It was the beginning of an enjoyable evening with a small selection of people we cared for. Our wedding anniversary was just a good excuse to invite them over. There were others we could have invited, but I wanted to keep the guest list down as small as Brad would allow. If I'd let him have his way, the house would have been swarming with friends and family.

I glanced at the kids at the separate table we laid out for them. They were making a mess between complaints and giggles, but Abby sat quietly, looking at her plate. She wasn't used to being around so many other children. It was my fault, of course. For her entire life, I'd kept her away from other people, thinking it was the safe move. All I'd done was turn her into a shut-in like me.

Brad cut into my thoughts by tapping on his wine glass with his fork. It was a good thing, too, as I was on the verge of breaking down into sobs. I turned from the kids and Abby.

"If I could have everyone's attention for just a moment, please," Brad said. The roar of conversation around the room came to a stop as all eyes shifted to him.

"I'm not one for speeches, but on behalf of the Fairbankses — Maia, Abby, and myself — we would like to thank you all for coming tonight. It means the world to us that you made it here to help us celebrate our ten-year wedding anniversary. As you all know, things haven't been easy on our family for the last five years. Losing Imy hit us harder than we could have ever imagined. We forgot who we are and what it means to be alive. And without meaning to, we let most of you down at one time or another. For that, we are truly sorry."

I cast my gaze around the room. There wasn't a dry eye in sight. I found saying Imogen's name aloud hard enough, but talking about her death so openly was worse than I could have imagined. Brad was doing well to keep it together.

He cleared his throat and continued. "Tonight, we are not only celebrating our marriage, we are making up for lost time. I know it's not much, but it's a start."

Our guests all beamed as they stared at my husband with admiration. He had told me they would all be happy to hear these words. I didn't believe him, but I saw it now. He was a smart man – one who always stood tall with pride. His neatly trimmed dark hair gave him an aura of respect, and his shining blue eyes commanded the room. I was proud to be married to him.

The dark button-down he was wearing accentuated his athletic build as his hands guided his speech. Those strong, familiar hands had always been a source of comfort for me. It was in these moments that I remembered the man I fell in love with.

"And with this meal," Brad concluded, "we'd like to welcome everyone back into our home and our lives. Here's to a happy future. Cheers!" He took a sip of the wine. The motion took me by surprise. I had thought the glass of wine was purely for show. Brad hadn't had a drop of alcohol for at least two years. After Imy died, he started drinking far more than normal. He was never deemed an alcoholic, but he came about as close as a person could.

I shot him a quick look to see if he was okay, but he ignored me. Maybe I was overreacting. After all, what harm could one sip do?

Every person around the table said "cheers" in return and sipped their drinks. Some of the children even copied their parents with their glasses of soda. Abby just stared at the festivities in confusion. Shame washed over me again. She might only have been three, but this kind of environment shouldn't have been so foreign to her. How lasting was the damage I'd inflicted on her social skills?

I took another sip of wine after saying my cheers. I couldn't let my past dictate my future. I'd let it for long enough. It was time to listen to my husband's words and look forward. We needed to get Abby out into the real world as much as possible. Tonight was the first step of many.

When Abby came along less than two years after we lost Imogen, I had a lot of trouble. The birth didn't go according to plan, and things just fell apart from there. Abby barely slept, and feeding was a nightmare. Every doctor, nurse, or midwife I saw had a different opinion. I felt like I was going insane. Imogen had been such a calm baby. Before I knew it, I slipped into another deep depression and could hardly function.

Brad was there for it all. He tried his hardest to help me, but I could see he was struggling as much as I was — sometimes more. It was no wonder he'd taken up drinking every night. I regularly walked in on him passed out in the living room. Brad never drank that much. Ever. For him to have reached such a point said it all.

London's loud laugh cut off my thoughts. I forced myself to concentrate on her as she told a story I'd heard a hundred times. I knew it word for word, but the distraction was what I needed.

* * *

As the evening progressed, familiar dynamics emerged. Old arguments, both friendly and heated, resurfaced. Some things never changed. Little digs were made between compliments, but there were more laughs than feigned expressions. I was confident people were having a good time, but my smile was increasingly strained as the night wore on.

I caught Brad's eye across the room; his brow furrowed as he gulped down more wine. How many glasses had he had? I'd lost track. I should have done a better job of stopping him at one. But I'd been so distracted by my own anxiety. Surely, though, he could have seen how stressful this night was going to be for me and how badly I needed him to support me through it all? This was his idea, after all.

Without wanting to, I retreated from the room and into myself. Every conversation became twice as much effort to process. The volume of noise seemed out of control, and I couldn't look away from the mess. Oh, God, the mess. It was everywhere. I wanted to scream and tell everyone to get the hell out of my house.

As if detecting my self-contained tension, Hazel clapped her hands together and grabbed everyone's attention.

"How about we play a game?"

"A game?" Claire asked.

A sigh of relief escaped me as the room quietened for a moment.

"Yes. I've got a good one." She glanced around to make sure everyone was listening. "Two Truths and One Lie."

A few murmurs flowed across the table. "That could be fun," London said.

"How does it work?" Claire asked.

"Simple," Hazel started. "We go around the table, one at a time. When it's your turn, you have to say two truths and one lie.

Then, we all have to guess which of the three is the lie. No help from spouses."

More murmurs and smiles were swapped between the adults.

"But my teacher says lying is wrong," said Jackson, one of the Thompsons' kids. We all shared a laugh as his mother explained that we were just playing a game. Jackson still seemed stressed out by the idea but soon got distracted. Abby was still staring at us with the same blank stare she'd had all evening. Not that a three-year-old would know what we were talking about. Still, she wasn't her usual self. I knew she was struggling with the number of people in her space. What was it going to be like when I'd be forced to send her to preschool next year? Brad had made it extremely clear he didn't believe in homeschooling.

"I'm in," Hazel's husband, Mike, said, rubbing his hands together.

I shared a look with Brad, who shrugged at me and took another swig of wine as he grinned. "Sounds fun." There was a slight slur to his speech. I had no idea what so many glasses of wine would do to him after two years of relative sobriety.

"Okay," Hazel continued. "Let's get these kids off to another room with some activities to keep them busy. That way, we can give good answers."

Everyone agreed that the game would be even better without the kids around. My stomach twisted at the thought. Even though Abby would only be in the next room, I couldn't stand the idea of her being alone with the other children. She wouldn't cope. But I couldn't intervene and make her the odd one out. She needed this, and so did I.

The other mothers and I gathered the kids into the living room without being asked. We put on a movie and instructed the older kids to keep an eye on the younger ones as best they could. Abby was the baby of the group and didn't know what to do. I placed her down on the floor with some coloring books and crayons and asked if one of the girls closest to her age would sit with her. Thea volunteered and gave Abby a warm smile.

"Mommy's just in the next room if you need me, okay?"

She nodded but didn't say a word. She looked so young and helpless. As if on cue, Imogen entered my thoughts. She was only four years old when—

"Are you okay?" Claire asked, squinting.

"Uh, yeah. Just making sure she has everything."

"She'll be fine," Claire whispered. She knew what was going through my head. Well, mostly.

We left the kids to play and returned to the dining room, ready to start the game. Two Truths and One Lie — it sounded like a simple idea. I could handle it. I just had to stay focused.

What could go wrong?

CHAPTER FOUR

We went around the room, taking turns playing the game. It was surprisingly fun. I had forgotten what it was like to spend time with adults. I had forgotten what it was like to enjoy myself.

Hazel came up with the most outrageous lie to start things off, making it easy for us all to guess. "I once wrestled an alligator in Florida." She had never even been to Florida, let alone wrestled an alligator.

London's turn made me laugh louder than I had in ages. Her two truths were stories we'd all heard before that would come across as pure fiction to anyone who didn't know her well. Twice, she recounted a tale of love gone wrong in foreign lands. I swear that woman had lived five lifetimes already. Then, her lie came, and I almost fell out of my chair. "I've never been dumped."

We all called her on it right away. No one was convinced, and London didn't even attempt to defend it. I joined in on the laughter and felt a wave of guilt hit me right away. I shouldn't have been laughing at my friend like that. Her destructive behavior wasn't a joke. She often used self-deprecating humor to cover her true feelings. I'd lost count of the number of relationships she'd had over the years and wished she could find someone and settle down.

A few more of our guests had a turn and kept the mood going. I was silently dreading when the focus would come to me. Would anyone notice or care if I made up an excuse to leave the room just before it was my turn? I knew I wouldn't be good at the game. No doubt I'd screw up or not have anything funny to say.

I thought about taking an extra dosage of my medication. Dr. Corbyn told me it was okay to take an additional dose every now and again when things became too much. I should have done so before everyone arrived. Tonight felt like the kind of night that the chemicals had been made for. I had resisted the urge, though, wanting to get through the night on my own and not rely on a prescription to function. I counted to ten and remembered to breathe.

Richard's turn came and went as the game progressed toward me. I stayed in my seat and decided it might be a welcome distraction from the thoughts that had been gnawing at me all night.

The Thompsons had their turn together, mixing things up. No one guessed their lie, and they finished with a smug look on their faces. They tricked us all quite easily. It was a little concerning.

With the Thompsons done, I was next.

"You're up, Maia," London said before taking another gulp of wine. She wasn't pacing herself. I hoped she didn't take things too far. We were all drinking now. It wasn't a great idea when we had children in the house, but the night rolled on.

"Honey?" Brad prompted, gesturing with his wine glass, making sure I was focused on the task at hand.

"Sorry. Uh, let me see," I said, stalling for time. I kept my entries light and delivered them all at once. "I went sky diving once. I've been to every continent. And I once owned a pet snake."

"Oh, good ones," Claire said as she eyed me up and down. She stared at me through a narrowed gaze while holding a glass of wine up high.

"You hate snakes, and you're not much of a traveler," she said. "But I could never picture you jumping out of a plane."

19

I gave her an innocent shrug.

London leaned close to inspect me. "I don't know, either. God, you little devil."

Everyone laughed and looked at Brad. He focused on taking another gulp of wine and did an excellent job of holding a neutral yet tipsy expression.

"Well, someone needs to call it," Hazel said.

"Be my guest," London replied, waving Hazel off.

"You know what? I will. The pet snake. That's the lie."

I shook my head. "It's the continent one. I once had a pet snake for a day, and I went skydiving when I was in my twenties."

"Dammit," London said. "I knew that. You made me drink all this wine so I'd forget."

"Yeah, right, *I* made you," I said, laughing along with everyone else. And for once, I felt normal. This was what things were like in the old days.

Hazel blew a puff of air out in defeat as I took a bow.

I shared a smile with my husband. Maybe this was a start to our new beginning. I'd never forget the past, but tonight was showing me that anything was possible.

"Brad's turn," London said before taking another sip of wine.

"All right," Brad said as he rolled up his sleeves. He took another hefty gulp of wine, finishing his glass.

"This looks serious," Richard cut in.

"It is, Richard," Brad said louder than he needed to. The wine was spurring him on.

"Here we go," Brad said. "I've never seen *Harry Potter*." That elicited a few flabbergasted questions from around the table. "I once stole a bike," he continued. This time, there were more chuckles than anything else. Then, he stared into the distance and chuckled to himself before he delivered his last statement. "I once killed a man."

Laughter erupted in the room, resulting in Mike spilling his wine. I could understand why. The idea of Brad — the man who hated squashing spiders — being a killer was too ridiculous to consider. London wiped tears from her eyes, struggling to contain herself.

I got caught up in the fun and couldn't stop laughing. That was until I stole a look at Brad. His smile had faded entirely. His eyes met mine as he poured himself another glass of wine. There was something cold and dark in his stare that stopped my heart: something I knew I'd seen before.

Something that ripped my mind open and tugged at the edges of a haunting memory I wanted to stay buried.

I tried to grip the edge of the table but missed and knocked my glass. Fortunately, there was no liquid inside.

"Are you okay?" Claire asked me from across the table.

I couldn't let my eyes meet hers and waved her off. "I'm fine," I whispered as the joys of the game continued without me. London called out the killing as the lie.

"Wrong," Brad declared, thumping the table with a fist for emphasis. "I stole a bike when I was a kid, and I've never seen *Harry Potter*."

Hazel cut in first. "That can't be true. Everyone's seen *Harry Potter*."

"Guess I'm a killer then," Brad said.

More laughter filled the room, but none of it was coming from me. Instead, my heart filled with a terror that sat beyond my consciousness. I couldn't comprehend it, but I understood what was there. I slammed my eyes shut and exhaled, remembering the breathing exercises Dr. Corbyn had shown me. It took until the count of ten to get my thoughts back in order.

Brad was called a cheater for supposedly telling three lies.

Needing to leave, I excused myself and whispered that I needed to go check on the kids. Only Claire acknowledged me.

As I walked away, I looked at Brad again and saw more darkness burning in his eyes. Maybe I'd had too much to drink. Maybe the stress of hosting was messing with my brain. These were perfectly rational explanations, but they weren't good enough. I knew what I saw in his eyes.

Was I being crazy? Surely, I couldn't be thinking what I was thinking. One thing was for certain, though. For the first time in a long while, I wasn't sure if I could trust my husband. My breaths came in short and sharp as a silent question echoed in the back of my mind.

Was Brad a killer?

CHAPTER FIVE

I retreated from the buzz of the party to the living room to check on Abby. It was my excuse to leave, but in reality, it was the only reason I hadn't collapsed into a heap.

Brad, a killer? I couldn't stop thinking about the look in his eyes — the look of pure, unwavering madness. But it was insane. I'd had one too many glasses of wine, and my anxiety was playing tricks on me. That was all. My mind had conjured up something that wasn't there.

Before I checked on Abby, I rushed upstairs to our bedroom and took my medication bottle from my bedside table. I hadn't wanted to resort to this, but I had to. I tapped out an extra dose, then swallowed it. I was going to need it to get through the night.

After taking a few minutes to sit and be alone, a cloud of fog enveloped me. The chemicals started working their magic and calmed my breathing.

I made my way downstairs to the living room. My gaze fell on Abby immediately. She was playing blissfully with Thea amidst an uproar of laughter. The older kids were watching an animated film on Netflix, ignoring the younger ones as I had feared they would.

I didn't know if it was my meds or the sight of Abby playing so enthusiastically with Thea, but I was pulled back all the way from the brink. I'd never witnessed her innocence from this perspective.

More often than not, I was always the one playing with her. For the past three years, Brad and I had been her only playmates. Seeing Abby happily interact with her cousin was a delight I had kept from her for too long. How could I have been so cruel?

It was impossible to protect a child from the complexities of the real world. I knew that. It was selfish of me to think otherwise. I didn't deserve Abby. She was a second chance. A precious miracle. One I had to protect at all costs. Her vulnerability became my only focus. Brad supported my insanity and tried to keep our family functioning. Some days, I wished he hadn't.

Thinking I was doing the right thing for my daughter, I avoided play dates. I kept Abby home as much as possible. Claire invited us to her house, and the Thompsons always invited her to birthday parties for their children, but I would never let her go. I never took her on trips to somewhere as every day as a park. I was so determined to keep her safe.

Without meaning to, I deprived Abby of a life worth living.

I was frozen at the edge of the living room. The consequences of my actions sat in plain sight and pulled me down like gravity.

Abby's laughter softened the commotion in my head. My disordered thoughts slid back to where they belonged. At least for now. Watching the kids, a sense of gratitude washed over my soul. Everything would be okay.

I took a moment longer to enjoy the wonder before me. Thea was so good with Abby. She was doing such a fantastic job that Abby still hadn't noticed me in the room. That was a big deal. They looked almost like sisters. Thea was like the older sister she had never had. The older sister she should have had.

Brad wasn't with me on the day it happened. He was at the office in Syracuse, like always, earning money so I could stay home with Imogen. He wanted me to look after her full-time and never have to worry about going back to my job until I felt like it. But I wished he had been there. He would have kept Imogen safe. He would have stopped that evil lowlife. Things would have been so different.

A little over a year after Imogen was taken from me, I found out I was pregnant with Abby. From the moment the doctor confirmed the pregnancy, all I could think about was how I would protect my new baby. Nothing bad could ever happen to her. She would become my second chance at happiness. I would gladly die to keep her safe.

Abby ran up to me with a huge smile. She practically leaped into my arms as I squatted down to her level. "Mommy!" she said in her squeaky voice. I held on tight and gave her a big hug. In an instant, she absorbed most of the anguish from my head.

"Where's Daddy?" Abby asked. It was well past her bedtime, but I couldn't bring myself to take her away from the fun she'd missed out on for years.

"Daddy is playing a game."

Curiosity lined her brow. "A game?"

"Don't worry, sweetheart. Are you having fun?"

"Yeah!" Abby jumped from my grip and rushed back to Thea.

I stood and placed my hands on my hips as I watched the kids play. They looked so innocent that I couldn't help thinking about Brad again. That look on his face was as plain as day. There was something malicious behind it. Was there a sliver of truth to what he'd said?

I once killed a man.

I shuddered at the mere idea. I was just stressed from the evening. Brad, a killer? Not possible. I knew him better than anyone.

We were in our twenties when we met, both of us teeming with hope and ambition. We fell in love, eventually got married, and started a family. Brad was always there for me. And even after Imogen's horrific end, he stuck by me. He saved my life. No matter how awful I was to be around, he never gave up on us.

Despite his support, Brad couldn't understand my level of pain compared to his at the beginning. After all, he wasn't there when it happened. He didn't have guilt following him like a shadow wherever he went. And my only way to cope was to turn my shame into anger and take it out on him. He was the last person who deserved to be treated that way, but I couldn't stop myself. Then, when Abby came along, I put him through hell again with postpartum depression. It was amazing he still loved me.

He's a good man.

So why couldn't I shake the possibility that Brad may be guilty of killing someone? The idea was senseless. We were playing a game. That's all. And yet . . .

"He's not a killer," I whispered.

"What?" asked Peter, one of the Thompsons' older kids.

"Nothing," I smiled. "What movie are you watching?"

Peter stared at me for a second, then shrugged and wandered off. I exhaled and backed out of the room to return to the party. With any luck, I'd find my senses along the way.

I took a detour to the kitchen to see if there was anything I could bring out for our guests. It would help to sell why I had to leave so suddenly. But I didn't stop in the kitchen. Instead, I went beyond the room and continued on autopilot to the foot of the steps that led to our bedroom upstairs. I wanted to bail on the party and hide under the covers in my bed.

Laughter roared through the house from the dining room. I was missing out on the fun again. How much time had I wasted standing there? I shouldn't have been this out of sorts over an anniversary dinner. Everything was going so well until Brad had said that. Just my luck that Hazel suggested we play some damn game.

Pulling myself together, I rejoined the group. There was no point in ruining the night for everyone else. I needed to be a good host.

26

As I reached the entry to the dining room, I saw that the game of Two Truths and One Lie was over. Our guests had left their seats and were now scattered around the room, conversation flowing easily. The night had become even more relaxed than when I'd left.

Claire was showing Richard a photo frame of our family. She pointed to each person in a black-and-white photo, speaking in hushed tones. They saw me standing in the room's threshold and placed the frame down. Claire gave me an awkward smile and moved away from the picture.

It didn't take me long to work out what the problem was. Claire, along with everyone else here, had known Imogen. She was probably pointing her out to Richard. He never had the chance to meet her.

I've not had professional photos taken since then. Every photo of Abby on our walls, I took myself. I couldn't bring myself to take her to a studio for a session or allow someone to come to our home. Plus, something about the idea felt disrespectful to Imogen.

I brushed my dress down as I sat in my chair. Brad stared at me for a moment with half-shut eyes and asked, "Is everything okay, honey?" He overemphasized the last word. And not in a good way.

I faced him with a trained smile. "Yes. I was just checking on Abby and the kids."

He nodded without blinking as he sipped yet another glass of wine, and the twinkle in his eye reminded me of what I had noticed during the game. Was he interrogating me just now? I turned away before I gave Brad a reason to think I had a problem. Not that there was anything wrong. I just needed a good night's sleep to remind myself how wrong I was about him.

London's heels clacked against the hardwood floor of the dining room as she stumbled toward me. Her cheeks were flushed, and loose strands of her blonde hair swayed as she teetered.

"God, I think I've had one too many," she said, slurring. She was holding a half-empty glass and took a sip as she plunked down on a seat beside me. Some of her wine spilled on the table.

"Glad to see you're enjoying yourself, London," Brad said with a sneer.

"Of course, Bradley," she replied. "That's why you invited me here. For some cheap laughs, right?"

"It's not like that," he snapped.

"Calm down, killer," she muttered.

My heart raced. I knew London was only joking, but her words hit me all the same.

"Bradley the killer. It makes perfect sense. You've got that serial killer look in your eyes. Say, where's your best pal, Fletcher, tonight? I would have thought he'd be here, huh?"

"He's busy," Brad fired back with venom. Brad and London weren't close, but they were usually a lot more civil toward one another.

"Okay," Hazel said, taking London's glass. "I think it's time we got some coffee in you."

"Whatever," London said. "I've had enough of this night. Some asshole stood me up, so what's the point?"

"Don't worry about it," Hazel said, looking at me with a shrug. She guided London to the kitchen as she continued to mumble and complain. I should have been the one taking her to sober up, but I was feeling less than useless.

"Same old London," Brad muttered, staring at me like he was expecting a response.

I didn't want to say anything mean, but he was glaring at me. I wanted to look away, but I couldn't. Eventually, I said, "Yeah, I guess."

He looked at me for a moment longer and took another gulp of wine. Only hours ago, he was concerned about me. Now, all I felt from him was indifference. Was I imagining something that wasn't there, or was the alcohol bringing out his true self?

Richard stepped in between us to ask Brad a question about football. I seized the opportunity to work my way into a conversation between Claire and the Thompsons. Within a few seconds, I was just standing with them, half-listening to the second half of a story.

Laughter and conversation filled the background as I stared back at my husband. An uneasy feeling settled into the pit of my stomach again.

My husband is not a killer. I repeated it like a mantra, hoping it would dissolve the wild doubts that were festering within my mind.

My husband is not a killer.

CHAPTER SIX

I had let Abby stay up too late. What was I thinking? I should have put her to bed by eight at the latest, but it was now well after nine, and I could hear her still running around with Thea, fueled by nothing but junk food and excitement. On a normal day, Abby would be fast asleep by now, but Thea's presence and the party food had given her extra energy. The party was still in full swing, and I was struggling to find a gap in conversations to break away.

Finally, I saw an opportunity and made my move. As I did, I realized Brad wasn't among the scattered group of people. He was probably in the toilet or grabbing yet another glass of wine. I walked to the kitchen, half expecting to see him there, but it was empty. There was, however, a horrendous mess that would be hell to deal with in the morning. I shuddered at the thought and headed to the living room.

It was definitely time to collect Abby for bed.

Getting Abby's attention was harder than usual. I called out her name several times, but she ignored me. She clearly knew why I was there and that I was going to spoil her fun. A full minute passed before she acknowledged me.

"It's time for bed," I said.

"No," she argued. It took me a second to register her defiance. I was accustomed to a little angel who did whatever she was told.

But Abby had tasted the good life and didn't want to go back. I couldn't blame her.

"Two more minutes," I warned, then headed to the dining room to see if Brad had returned. He still wasn't there.

Where was he? What was he doing?

It didn't matter. The bigger issue was how I was going to get my three-year-old daughter to bed. She was hyped up and not interested in anything I had to say. If I was a good parent, it wouldn't be a problem. I felt so hopeless.

I walked back to Abby and bribed her with a candy-related promise I hoped she'd forget by morning. She happily accepted the offer. I scooped her up into my arms, trying to ignore the bags under her eyes. I knew I'd pay for this tomorrow, but it would be worth it. She'd had a fun time.

Bypassing some of the louder guests, I carried Abby through the kitchen toward her bedroom upstairs. Just as my foot landed on the first step of the stairwell, Brad came down. He kissed Abby on the forehead and whispered, "Goodnight."

"Night, Daddy," she whispered back.

I resisted asking him where he'd been despite my curiosity. The last thing I needed was for him to think I'd been watching him. I wasn't. At least, I thought I wasn't.

Brad continued on to the kitchen before I could say anything.

Abby went down faster than I expected, but right before her eyes drifted off, she told me for the tenth time how much fun she'd had. Her delight only sent more guilt my way. What kind of parent had I been to her? I thought I was protecting her, but in reality, I'd made things harder for her. With any luck, I could turn her life around and arrange some play dates with Thea. The only way Abby would develop some resilience to the challenges of the world was by letting her experience both the good and the bad. It wouldn't be easy.

I stayed for a minute, watching her tiny chest rise and fall. Then I decided it was time to head back downstairs, but something caught my eye.

The light was on in Brad's study. There was no reason for it to be, so I went into the room to hit the switch. But as my hand reached around the door frame, I started thinking. I was sure it hadn't been on earlier.

Was this where Brad had disappeared to? None of our guests would have ventured up here. They'd all been using the downstairs bathroom.

"It doesn't matter," I told myself. I switched off the light and left. I had guests to talk to, and I needed to check in on London and see how drunk she was. Hazel's attempts to sober her up earlier had failed. She had refused to switch to coffee and continued drinking wine.

I made it halfway back to the stairs and came to a stop. Curiosity tugged at me. I couldn't return to the party just yet. Not until I'd taken a look around Brad's study. His light had been left on for a reason.

I knew what I was doing was a mistake, but I couldn't ignore that stare Brad had in his eyes during the game. It was like he became another person. No amount of kidding about could conceal it. But if Brad truly had killed a man, why would he make a joke about it? Had the wine dragged something from his mind that he wanted to stay hidden?

The thought kept me frozen in place. I had to make a decision: go back to the party or listen to my crazy brain.

Apparently, I was going to listen to my crazy brain. I turned back and hurried to Brad's study. There had to be something in there worth seeing. Why else would he feel the need to sneak off during a dinner party to use his study? It wasn't a work night, and he only checked his emails during the day as a matter of policy. Whatever sent him in there had to be important.

I entered the room before I lost my nerve and flicked the light on again. Taking a breath, I scanned the space and tried to determine if there was anything out of place. This wasn't my study, but I did clean it once a week. Brad sometimes worked from home for his accounting firm, so the only object that caught my eye was his computer.

As carefully as I could manage, I took a seat in his leather office chair. The desk was in perfect order. Nothing was out of place. I looked through his desk drawers and didn't find much. All I saw was Brad's watch sitting in one of them. It was a Garmin and had a crack in the middle of the screen. I'd asked him why he hadn't thrown it away, but he got defensive and insisted he was going to have it repaired. It felt like a waste of money to me. I couldn't even remember when he'd bought it.

My head started pulsing. Most likely, it was from my meds swarming my mind with their usual fog and exhaustion. I pushed through it as best I could and closed the drawer.

Annoyed that I'd found nothing, I raised the laptop lid. The screen was blank, so I wiggled the wireless mouse sitting on the wooden desk. The large piece of furniture was a family heirloom. Brad's father had left it for him when he died of cancer before Imogen was born. Brad's mother had disappeared long before then, so Imogen never met his parents.

My mother and father no longer lived in the country and had taken up residence in Spain. We rarely saw them anymore. Abby essentially had no grandparents.

The thought of family made me aware of the betrayal I was committing by invading my husband's privacy. He didn't like me using his work computer. He said it had a lot of sensitive information stored on it. I didn't doubt him. He was concerned I'd accidentally install a virus if I used it, so I often avoided the thing. But I needed to do this. If I didn't look through his computer, it would become an obsession for me. I'd let Brad's dark stare control my every waking thought.

The screen on the laptop came to life and presented me with a lock screen. I had to enter a password to get into the system. Fortunately, Brad kept it written on a piece of paper he had taped to the bottom of the laptop. It wasn't that we were hopeless with passwords. Brad changed the password once a month.

I carefully lifted the computer and saw the latest iteration of the password.

!m0g3n.F@!rb@nk17

It was a complex password of Imogen's full name, followed by the year she was born. Brad insisted on changing it once a month, using different variations of the letters and symbols each time. Despite it looking odd, it was a nice way to honor Imogen's memory. I typed it in, hit enter, and was met with an error message. I must have made a typo, so I tried again.

Another error — incorrect password.

"What the hell?" I let out. Checking the note under the computer again, I hadn't made a mistake, but to be certain, I took a pen and piece of paper from one of Brad's mini notepads and wrote the password down. Maybe the wine I'd had tonight was getting to me.

Taking my time, I entered the password slowly, making sure I jotted it down as it was written. I hit enter and got the same damned error message.

"Why?" I asked the empty room. But then it dawned on me. Maybe Brad had changed the password. If he'd done that, though, why hadn't he written his new one down?

My rambling thoughts were interrupted when I glanced up from the screen to see a figure standing in the doorway. I gasped. My heart pounded in my chest until I realized it was Abby.

I snapped the laptop shut and almost leaped from the chair. "What are you doing, honey?" I asked. She seemed confused.

"Thirsty," she mumbled. Abby had a decent vocabulary for a three-year-old, but when she was tired, she spoke like a caveman.

"Come on, baby," I said, scooping her up. She was getting heavier by the day, but I loved to carry her around. I wished she could stay this small forever. But she'd grow up. And one day, she'd be old enough to know that we'd kept her locked away from the world for years. I hoped she could understand our reasoning. *My* reasoning. I kept thinking if I said "we" or "our," it would ease my guilt, but it wasn't Brad who had done this to her. It was me. He'd tried countless times to get me out of the house with Abby.

"Whatcha you doing, Mommy?"

"Carrying you."

"No, in there." She pointed toward Brad's study as we walked. "Daddy's room."

"Oh, nothing, sweetheart," I said as I rested her head against my shoulder. I prayed she wouldn't remember it in the morning. I took Abby to the bathroom and filled up a plastic cup with water. I helped my daughter have a few sips, then carted her back to her bed. For the second time, I told her I loved her and to go to sleep. She gave me a beautiful giggle and said, "Love you, Mommy," before rolling over as I tucked her in.

I left Abby's room with a clearer mind, knowing I needed to return to the party. Whatever it was I thought I saw in Brad's eyes wasn't real and wasn't worth compromising what we'd rebuilt.

As I rejoined the group of adults, I was relieved to notice the Thompsons gathering their children to leave. I'd reached my social fill for the night. Hopefully, other people would take that as their signal to leave soon too. I shuffled in by Brad's side and thanked them for coming. We waved them off together.

"What took you so long?" Brad asked, half squinting as I closed the front door.

"Sorry?"

"With Abby. You were up there for a while. Is she okay?"

"Yeah. She just needed a bit of convincing to go down. I guess she was enjoying herself too much." He returned my grin with one of his own, but before I turned my head, his smile faded.

CHAPTER SEVEN

Our second-to-last guest left just after midnight. London was still here, but she wasn't going anywhere. I'd placed her on the sofa in our other living room to sleep it off. Despite our best efforts, she kept drinking until I had no choice but to lay her down on the plush couch and trick her into falling asleep. Anyone who hadn't left took that as a sign to grab their things and go.

I should have been furious at London. She was supposed to support me through the evening. This was my first real social gathering since Imy was taken from us, and London had spent the night drinking and complaining about her latest fling. But I was too tired to care. Too tired and focused on Brad.

Brad and I headed to bed after checking in on Abby. I usually did this a couple of times in the night. It was a habit I couldn't shake. When Abby came along, I'd insisted she sleep in our room until she was two. Frustrated, Brad eventually convinced me to put her in her own bedroom, but I still woke at all hours to go check on her.

"What a night," Brad muttered as he changed for bed. He was slow on his feet. He'd slowed down on the wine after I put Abby to bed, but the alcohol in his system was combining with fatigue.

I was in our ensuite, brushing my teeth, mumbling in agreement. I spat a mouthful of toothpaste into the sink and said, "I'm sorry about London. If I had known—"

"It's fine, honey," he said, cutting me off. "London is London. She had too much to drink. I guess I did as well. It's just . . ." He trailed off.

"What is it? I thought you had a nice time?" What was he going to say? Did he notice me watching him?

"I had an enjoyable time," he said. "It was just harder than I thought it would be. I shouldn't have been drinking like that. I'm sorry if I said anything stupid. I was just trying to cope with it all, you know?"

Relieved, I left our ensuite and walked up to Brad, placing a hand on his chest. "I get it," I said. "Trust me. Tonight pushed me in all directions to my damn limit."

He gave me a crooked smile. One I'd seen a thousand times in the past. But it disappeared five years ago. I hadn't seen it since.

Brad slid a fresh undershirt on. "I guess throwing a dinner party for our anniversary might not have been the smartest way to get back to normal. Maybe we should have started with something smaller. But it's done now."

"It was hard," I agreed. "But for Abby's sake, I'm glad we did it. She got to stay up late and play with her cousin."

"That's right, she did," Brad said, smiling. He pulled me into a hug and kissed me on the forehead. "There's hope for us yet."

I breathed in Brad's scent and tried to forget all about the strange looks he'd had on his face tonight. The stress of hosting a party while also having me to worry about had probably messed with him. That's all it was.

I held him tight, absorbing a warmth from his chest that made me feel whole again. Things could only get better from here.

Then I remembered Brad's study. I'd left that piece of paper on his desk with his old password written on it. And it was in my distinctive handwriting. The second he found it, he'd wonder what I'd been up to.

"I should check on London," I said as I pulled away from Brad.

He grabbed me by the wrist and said, "She'll be fine. It's not like this is her first time passing out drunk." He dragged me in and wrapped an arm around my waist. He leaned in and kissed my neck, making his intentions clear.

"Happy anniversary, honey," he said. "Ten years."

Crap.

I looked at our closed door and wracked my brain for a reason to run to his study and destroy a sliver of paper that might cause an argument. Nothing came to mind. What the hell was I thinking, leaving it there? I'd let myself get distracted by Abby.

Just as I was about to wave off Brad's attempts with a valid excuse of being exhausted, I realized how I could use the situation to my advantage. It sounded dirty, but if I had sex with my husband, he would fall asleep ten seconds after we were done. With all that wine he'd had, he'd be out like a light, leaving me plenty of time to grab that damn bit of paper. It was our anniversary, after all.

"Ten years," I said with a grin. Then I did what had to be done. It wasn't like I didn't enjoy sleeping with my husband. I was just drained from the night.

Fortunately, Brad got down to business, and the whole thing was over in about ten minutes. He was normally more attentive to my needs, but not tonight. Fine by me.

As I tiptoed to the door, Brad was already asleep. I rolled my eyes. He didn't even bother to cuddle me after. Usually, he brought his A-game. But after however many glasses of wine he'd consumed, I wasn't surprised.

I twisted the doorknob as slowly as possible. The hinges groaned, and I made my way through a small gap and left the door open only a few inches. We always left a light on in the hallway so Abby could find the toilet during the night.

I tried to potty-train Abby too early and ended up making the process take far longer than it should have. We got there in the end, but it had no doubt added to her anxiety levels. I'd thought she was ready at the time. She seemed to be a fast learner: she crawled early, walked early and she definitely talked early. I liked to pretend that Imogen's spirit was there, guiding her little sister. It was silly, but the idea always brought me comfort.

I didn't know where she got it from, but Abby was a talker. Well, more of a singer. When no one was around, she loved to sing in her squeaky, out-of-tune voice and mostly sang the same three songs over and over. It was adorable, but some days I longed for silence.

It had been different with Imogen. One thing she'd do early, and the next, she'd drag her feet and take her time learning. I saw a lot of Imogen in Abby's eyes, yet there were just as many distinctions between them. I would give anything for them to have met and been true sisters.

Our hallway was carpeted, allowing me to sneak along to Brad's study without making much noise. It was how Abby had crept up on me before. Surely she wouldn't remember me being in there in the morning? If she was going to recall anything from the evening, it would be the fun she had with Thea.

I made my way into the study and left the light off. All I needed was the scrap of paper and nothing else. I didn't know Brad's new password, and I didn't want to. He was my loyal husband of ten years. We didn't keep secrets from each other. Well, not normally. I guess I currently had one given what I was doing. And there was another I had kept from him. Two nights ago, I swear I saw a man staring at our house. I hadn't told Brad about it. I didn't want him to worry.

Thoughts of secrets made me wonder why Brad had changed his password without writing the new one down. He would've had a valid reason. Maybe he'd simply forgotten to do it. It wouldn't be because of anything sinister, would it?

"Stupid," I muttered. For God's sake, he's an internal accounting auditor. Brad must have left the light on while under the influence of too much wine. He didn't mention anything about his study when we came to bed together and didn't even look in that direction when we walked by it.

Inside his study with both hands out, I fumbled in the shadows until I found the edge of the desk. There was enough light coming in from the other end of the hallway for me to see what I was doing, but my eyes were a little blurry.

I made my way along Brad's desk, trying to remember where I'd left the note. It should have been next to his laptop.

"Dammit," I muttered. The simplest thing, and I couldn't manage it.

After thirty seconds of fumbling around in the dark like an idiot, I gave up on being subtle and retreated to the entrance to turn on the light. Brad was dead to the world, and it would be quicker and easier than whatever it was I was attempting.

I found the switch and gave it a flick. My eyes squinted as I adjusted to the sudden brightness. The dull headache I'd been experiencing flared into something worse. With any luck, Abby would have a big sleep-in and not get up at sunrise.

I put the problem to the back of my mind and focused on the task at hand. I just needed to get the note and destroy it. Then I could sleep. I reached the desk again and searched, but there was nothing there. The note was gone.

I patted the desk frantically and lifted the laptop in case the piece of paper had slid under it.

Nothing.

I shoved the big office chair out of the way and searched the floor. Maybe the heating had blown it off the desk. But there was no note to be found.

I rechecked the desk and looked under the laptop again only to find more desk. Brad kept the room immaculate. I didn't know if it was an accounting thing, but there wasn't a single bit of mess or pile of paperwork strewn about the place. The note should have been there, plain as day. Which meant only one thing.

Someone had taken it.

CHAPTER EIGHT

Eventually I had to give up on the note and return to bed, but I couldn't sleep. Too many possibilities were running through my brain. I wondered if Brad had found the note after I returned to the party — my attention *had* wandered to London for a while. Maybe he'd taken that opportunity to discover it. But if that were the case, he should have said something. He had acted like nothing was wrong and pressured me to have sex with him. Though, Brad was always trying to get me to sleep with him. He probably figured that our anniversary guaranteed he would get lucky. But would he really want to have sex with me if he knew I'd been snooping in his study?

My thoughts swirled, and a growing nausea accompanied them. The headache I'd been ignoring threatened to become a full-blown migraine, and it was already after two in the morning. At this rate, I'd be lucky to get any sleep.

I should have been exhausted and down for the count. Unfortunately, taking an extra dose of my tablets always came with a certain amount of brain fog. The medication helped calm my thoughts, but it often left me feeling disoriented and out of control.

I couldn't make sense of what was going on for the life of me. Had Abby woken up again and gone into Brad's study, thinking I'd be there? Did she, by chance, find the note and take it?

Unlikely.

Did I even write the note? I ran over my movements in my head. Yes. Yes, I did. I picked up a pen, pulled a slip of paper from one of Brad's small notepads, and wrote down that damn password. I could see it in my mind.

!m0g3n.F@!rb@nk17

The throbbing in my temples increased, forcing me to shut my eyes. I needed sleep if I wanted to function tomorrow. Granted, it was a Sunday, but I still had a list of chores to complete. Plus, we'd planned to drive Abby to a park out of town in the afternoon. Not the park from five years ago — we didn't go there. Ever. It would be a different park, one I thought would be nice to visit. After all, I had agreed to take Abby out of the house more. Brad had been pushing me to do so more and more.

On the rare occasions when we actually left the house, it was only if Brad came along. And if he couldn't attend, if I had to take Abby to the doctors or on an errand that couldn't be avoided, it took everything I had in me to not freak out.

A few months ago, Brad had convinced me to bring Abby to a theme park of all places. Despite him being there, it didn't end well. As soon as we arrived at the gate, I spotted someone there who looked off. I couldn't explain it, but this man seemed out of place. He reminded me of a person I never liked to think about, so we left. Abby complained and cried. Brad told me I was being ridiculous and got angry, but I didn't care. We had to go.

That style of parenting had to end, though. Abby needed to learn what the real world was like. Sure, it wasn't always a safe place, but constant fear wasn't the life I wanted for my little girl.

I needed a change of scenery to clear my head. Sleeping next to the snoring man I was having paranoid thoughts about wasn't helping.

I wasn't as cautious when I left our bedroom this time. If Brad woke up and wondered where I'd gone, he wouldn't find me snooping in his study. I'd be downstairs in the kitchen, most likely eating a snack. Nothing out of the ordinary there.

I had never been a great sleeper. Even with the tablets, I still struggled to get in enough hours each night. When Abby was born, her sleeping and feeding problems only made my habits worse. It wasn't uncommon for me to get up during the night for hours at a time to check on Abby or read a book beside her bed as she slept. I didn't know why I felt the need to be so careful earlier when I poked around in Brad's study looking for that elusive note. He was so used to my irregular behavior that he always slept through it. I guess panic got the better of me.

In the kitchen, I poured myself a glass of water and found a bottle of aspirin I kept above the fridge. After fumbling with the childproof lid, I swallowed a few pills and glanced around the space. Dirty plates were stacked on the counter, crusted with remnants of the meal we'd eaten. The sink was overflowing with used wine glasses and silverware, and crumbs were scattered across the floor. The mess mocked me. And there was a bigger one in the dining room. I doubted the kids had gone easy in the living room either. But a disordered house was a small price to pay for the overall good time we'd had, especially Abby. If it weren't for the whole your-husband-might-be-a-murderer thing, I would have called the night a success.

London groaned from our second living room. It was a tiny area of the house, more of a reading nook than anything else. Instead of shoving another TV in there, we installed some shelving and filled it with books and a sofa.

Both Brad and I were avid readers, and we wanted to instill that love in Abby too. I went through at least one novel a week, whereas Brad took longer. I couldn't imagine my life without books. They'd done a lot to get me through Imy's death and the days that followed. They had provided me with an escape that TV shows and movies couldn't compete with. If London weren't here, I'd already be reading by now, despite the headache.

London groaned some more, persuading me to go check on her. It seemed like a smart idea to make sure she hadn't vomited on anything. It wouldn't have been the first time.

As I entered the room, I did my best to be quiet, although I was confident I could roll a marching band through the house and she wouldn't notice.

London was tossing and turning like she was in a fight for her life. Sweat coated her brow, and there was a look of distress on her face that had me concerned. I kneeled beside her, unsure what to do.

Was it a good idea to wake someone who had passed out in a drunken stupor? Could I even rouse her?

"No," London whispered. "I can't."

I held a hand over my mouth and prayed that her nightmare wasn't as bad as it seemed. I had never seen her like this before.

"Please," she begged. "Don't do this."

What was going on inside her head? I couldn't take it anymore. Call it mother's instincts, but I needed to wake her. When I reached out to intervene, London rolled over and fell off the sofa, crashing into me. I broke her fall, providing her with a soft landing. She let out a small scream and opened her eyes wide.

"Hi," I said.

London blinked with a wild, drunken gaze. She tried to scurry away but soon stopped when she recognized me. "Maia? What are you doing? Why are you in my house?" Her voice was rough, like she'd swallowed gravel. Her eyes darted around the room. "Wait. I'm still at your place, aren't I? Oh, God."

I stared at her as the truth dawned on her features. She knew why she was still here.

London rubbed her face with both hands. "I had too much to drink, didn't I?"

"Yeah."

"I'm so sorry, Maia," she mumbled, not meeting my gaze. She probably had a headache worse than mine.

"It's okay. You had your reasons, just like we all do."

"No, I got plastered because some asshole stood me up when I was supposed to be here for you. I'm a terrible friend."

"No, you're not. I was only hosting an anniversary dinner. I should have been able to handle it."

"Please don't defend me, Maia. It only makes me feel worse."

"Too late. Already done," I said, offering her a smile.

London chuckled and shook her head. "I don't suppose you can tell me how I ended up on the floor. I mean, I assume I was asleep on the sofa."

"You were, but I think you were having a nightmare. I was about to wake you, but you beat me to it and fell off. You landed right on top of me."

"You're joking?"

I shook my head.

"Wow. Must've been some dream. I'm sorry for landing on you, among other things."

"It's okay. I'll live. Do you remember what you were dreaming about?"

London stared into the distance, her expression darkening for a moment before she forced a smile. "Uh, no idea. Probably nothing. You know how it goes."

I thought about pressing her, but she clearly didn't want to talk about it. Something told me this wasn't the first time she'd been dragged out of a nightmare in a ball of sweat and confusion. Instead of prying, I offered her a glass of water and some aspirin.

"That would be amazing. I owe you."

"You can buy me a cup of coffee on Monday," I said.

"Consider it done. It's the least I can do. God, I can't believe I got drunk. I'm such an idiot."

"Come on," I said, pulling her out of her self-loathing. "Let's go to the kitchen and talk. You'll have to excuse the mess, though."

"I can handle a mess. Tell you what, I'll help clean it up in the morning."

"Oh, you don't have to do that," I said, linking my arm with hers. I should have been upset with her, but I'd learned some time ago that no one was perfect. If Brad could handle everything I'd thrown at him, then I could be more understanding of people's flaws.

I owed a lot to my husband. If our roles had been reversed, I wasn't sure I'd have been strong enough to do the same for him. I'm sure I would have tried my hardest, but I wasn't sure I'd cope as well as he did. Hopefully, I'd never be tested like that.

Maybe I needed to find some way to repay his kindness. I could start by forgetting the whole password thing. If he had found that note, he clearly had thought little of it. Or maybe he hadn't wanted to upset me.

London gulped down a glass of water with the aspirin. "Oh, God, please let that help," she said, catching her breath before pouring herself another glass. "Quite the mess, isn't it?"

"Yep," I sighed, taking it all in again.

"You know what that means?"

"What?"

"People had a good time. And I'm sure they had fun seeing me fall to pieces. Especially Claire."

I chuckled. London always had a way of coming up with these strange little pieces of wisdom, even when she was being self-loathing. "You didn't fall to pieces. But you're right. Everyone enjoyed themselves. Abby sure did."

"Oh, really?"

"She was playing with Thea for hours. I've never seen her so happy." I tried not to think about how I'd sheltered Abby from the world, but London saw right through me. Of course she did — she knew me too well.

"Hey, it's okay," London said, placing an arm around me. "I know this was a lot to handle being the first time since . . . but you did a good job. Or at least you did with the parts I remember."

"Thank you," I chuckled. "I tried."

She rubbed my back, giving me that look I'd seen so many times over the last five years. It was meant to be sympathetic, but it just felt like pity. It always reminded me how pathetic I was — and still am. I moved away from London's embrace. "I should start tidying this up now." I grabbed the nearest dish.

"Not a chance. You need sleep. Now march your butt upstairs and go to bed."

"What about you?"

"I'll be fine on the sofa. Just wake me in the morning so I can help you clean. Throw a wet sponge at me or something."

"Okay," I said as I left. Going back to bed was the right move. Sure, I'd rather stay up and chat with London, but if I did, we'd be up until sunrise. I needed to get some rest before Abby woke up.

London followed me and guided me to the stairs. "Whatever's keeping you awake, Maia, can wait for another day, okay?"

There was something odd about the tone of her voice. I wondered if her advice was generic or if she knew about my problem with Brad. No way. London knew I was a terrible sleeper, so it couldn't be more than her trying to help me go to sleep, could it?

A twisted thought invaded my mind — what if London was pretending to be drunk so she could sneak around my home? I scoffed at the idea and continued upstairs.

I needed sleep. The longer I stayed awake, the less objective my thoughts became.

CHAPTER NINE

I fell asleep quickly after returning to bed, forcing my concerns about the note and everything else to the back of my mind. Sometimes, all I needed to sort myself out was to get up for a few minutes. That and chatting with a friend always helped.

Yet, despite falling into a deep sleep, I had a dream that could have been on par with the one London was having.

I was on a mountain, hiking alone. I heard a voice carry up from a chasm, begging and pleading. All the while, I was drawn to the same cliffside like a moth to a flame. No matter how hard I tried, I couldn't stop walking.

On the edge, my feet were half over the point of no return. I looked down into the abyss. It was like staring into the mouth of a swirling vortex made of teeth. Two hands gripped me by my ankles and dragged me over. But I didn't scream. I just accepted my fate with a sense of calm.

The fall seemed endless, like I was floating. A peace washed over me. Then, a burst of raw energy hacked through my chest as I collided with some jagged rocks.

I bolted upright in bed, drenched in sweat. Sucking in hard breaths, I grabbed my temples. A bright light stabbed at my eyeballs. For a few seconds, I couldn't tell which way was up, but I soon discovered it was morning. My head throbbed. It was like

I hadn't gotten a minute's rest. Just another great night in a long list of bad ones.

Brad was beside me, out cold and still snoring. He rarely noticed my nightmares these days. He'd grown accustomed to them. Or maybe he no longer cared. The sight of his blissful ignorance sent a rage to the pit of my stomach. I resisted the urge to smother him with a pillow. I got like this when I was at my lowest. Rage swirled in my mind, and I couldn't justify why.

Brad had done nothing wrong. I had to remind myself of that. Any bad thoughts that were in my head right now were simply thoughts. I was just tired. He wasn't a killer. He wasn't some secret psychopath. I had nothing to support the idea other than a missing note, a changed password, and a concerning look on his face that I'd seen when I was already on edge.

There was a knocking at our door. Tiny hands I knew all too well: Abby. We taught her to knock on closed doors so she didn't end up barging in on anything inappropriate. But she hadn't quite grasped the concept and usually came in straight after knocking.

"Hey sweetie," I said through a croaky voice as Abby walked in, clutching her stuffed bunny. She'd had the thing since she was three months old and had worn down its fluffiness.

"Hi, Mommy," she replied, looking surprisingly rested.

I glanced at the time on the clock on our wall and saw that it was just after eight in the morning. Abby had slept in for a change. All that playing had really worn her out. I should let her stay up late with Thea more often.

"Is Daddy asleep?" Abby asked.

"Yes, he is. Do you think we should wake him?"

Abby grinned widely and gave me a big nod.

"Me too." I shoved Brad a few times. He snorted and groaned before waking up. He glared at me with confusion and asked, "What is it? What's wrong?"

"It's morning, honey, and your daughter is awake."

"Oh, hey baby," Brad said, smiling at Abby through bleary eyes.

"Daddy!" She squealed as she charged at him and dove into our bed. He caught her mid-jump and let out an exaggerated whine when she landed on his chest.

"Good to see you, too. Did you have fun last night?"

"Yeah!" Abby said louder than my ears could handle. "I played with Thea lots."

"Oh, did you? Tell me all about it."

Abby told her father all about her perfect time with her cousin as best as a three-year-old could. Brad gave her his full attention.

Brad and Abby were close. He treated her like his little angel. A child that could do no wrong. That meant I was usually left to be the bad guy when it came to discipline.

After Brad finished hearing Abby's every detail of Abby's night, we headed downstairs to have some breakfast. I was already dreading the giant mess waiting for me to clean up, but it could wait until after we'd all had something to eat.

When we reached the kitchen, I found the room spotless. "What the heck?" I let out. "Did you do this?" I asked Brad.

He shook his head. "Not a chance. I didn't wake up once last night. Slept like a baby."

"No kidding," I muttered as I did laps of the kitchen in disbelief. Confused, I moved through to the dining room and found it to be just as tidy. London was in there, straightening up the last of the chairs.

"Morning, sunshine," she said, beaming.

"You cleaned up for me?"

"I told you I wanted to help."

"But you did everything."

She shifted closer to me and whispered, "I owed you."

"Well, thank you. I don't know what else to say."

"There's nothing to say. I spoiled everyone's evening, so I thought it would be a smart move to clean up the mess."

"You didn't spoil—"

"Hush, hush. Let's not drag this out. What's done is done."

I smiled and pulled London in for a hug. "Thank you for helping me in your own special way. And, I have to ask: how did you pull this off? You were pretty drunk last night."

She tapped her nose. "A magician never reveals her secret. But if you must know, I have plenty of experience handling a hangover. The trick is to have a shot of vodka in your orange juice."

She wasn't kidding. There was a half-empty glass of what looked like orange juice on the dining table. I'd read somewhere that alcoholics avoided hangovers by continuing to drink the day after a big night. Was London's problem with drinking worse than I thought? Was I supposed to say something? Or would that be a touch ungrateful, considering she'd gone to the effort of cleaning up for me?

"Morning," Brad said to London. "Don't tell me you did all this?"

"Guilty as charged. Think of it as an apology for whatever it was I did last night. Or if I said something stupid."

Brad stared at her for a moment, looking like he was about to say something. I wondered if he remembered London calling him a serial killer. The thought sent a fresh shudder down my spine.

"You weren't that bad," he finally said. But his words felt less than genuine. "Plus, I've seen worse. Thank you for sorting out the mess."

"Any time, Bradley," she said.

He flashed a smile and headed back to the kitchen, taking Abby with him. "Who wants waffles?" he called out.

"Me!" Abby yelled as they left.

"There goes my clean kitchen," I said.

"Was bound to happen," London replied with a shrug.

I stepped closer to her. "Would you like some breakfast?"

"No, I better run. On to the next disaster and all that."

"London," I tutted.

"I'm kidding. But seriously, I need to head home for a long bath and a nap. That should recharge me enough. I have plans for tonight."

"Tonight? Tell me you're kidding."

"You know me, Maia. I'm like a shark. I can't stop moving."

"Okay, but if you change your mind, we'll be here."

London gave me a quick hug, then finished her special orange juice. She gathered her things and said, "I'll be in touch. We should catch up tomorrow. Just the two of us. Like old times."

"I'd like that," I said. She knew if we went to a café or anywhere, I'd be bringing Abby along with me.

"Perfect," London said before I had time to check. "I'll text you tonight."

"Okay, but—"

London's cell phone rang, cutting through the air with a loud shrill. She pulled the device from her two-thousand-dollar handbag and held her phone up as if she was screening the call. Her forehead wrinkled. She looked up at me, then back to the screen. She hesitated before she picked it up. "I'll call you back later," she muttered to the phone.

"Is something wrong?" I asked, unable to avoid the question.

"Nothing, darling," she said, waving me off. "Anyway, I should get going. Have a nice day with the family."

"I will," I said, hoping I had done nothing to upset my friend.

She put on her designer sunglasses and yelled goodbye to Brad and Abby. Then, she disappeared out the front door.

I watched her uneasily. Who was on the other side of that call that she didn't want me to know about?

CHAPTER TEN

I walked into the kitchen and found Brad making waffles while Abby tried her best to help. She was wearing an oversized apron that hung past her feet and was assisting her father by awkwardly stirring the ingredients. I took in the sight and felt a warmth inside me.

I used to do a lot of baking with Imogen. It was one of her favorite ways for us to spend time together. We'd bake oddly shaped cookies and give them to Brad, who'd make a big fuss about how wonderful they tasted. I hadn't baked with Abby yet. Something about it felt wrong, as if I was betraying Imogen's memory.

As I watched Brad and Abby make waffles, the usual thoughts came to haunt me — ones I couldn't stop. Imogen would never have the chance to be a mom and spend time baking with her children. She would never know what it was like to stare into the eyes of her own child and feel at peace with the world.

I dug my nails as hard as I could into my palm. The pressure and pain soothed my guilt for a moment, but I knew it wouldn't last. Still, any relief was welcome. I wouldn't let my twisted thoughts spoil our day.

It reminded me I needed to take my meds. Typically, I had one dosage of three tablets with each meal three times a day. And if there was something I feared would cause me too much anxiety,

I took an extra dosage beforehand. I'd questioned Dr. Corbyn about it because it seemed like a lot, but he was concerned that any reduction in medication would have negative consequences.

With the stress of the anniversary dinner over, I could relax and try to accept the positives from the night. That way, I could focus on the future. The past would always be in my mind, but I couldn't let it define the rest of our lives, especially Abby's. Today, the normalcy would continue with a trip to the park. I didn't care how tired we all were. We were going, and I wasn't going to freak out about it.

I took a seat in the kitchen and continued to watch Brad and Abby have fun making a messy breakfast. It was a good thing London had to leave. Her beautiful cleanup of the room was disappearing.

Brad started serving some of the waffles. But before he had finished a full batch, he pulled his cell phone from his pocket. His eyes scanned the screen hastily. He was entirely absorbed in it, as though it was more important than anything else. I was sure it could have waited.

As he peered at his phone, his smile faded and was replaced by a look of uncertainty. The concern on his forehead sent a flutter to my stomach. What had him so rattled?

"Uh, can you watch these, honey?" he asked me. "I need to check on something." He rushed out before I declined.

"Is anything wrong?" I asked.

Brad didn't stop. "No, no. Just a damn work thing."

"On the weekend? Tell them to wait until Monday."

"I'd like to," he called back, "but this looks important. I better go sort it out now." He left the kitchen with his face buried in his phone.

"Daddy?" Abby asked after he was gone, but Brad ignored her.

"He'll be back in a minute, honey," I said. "He just has to do some work."

"Okay," she said, but the damage was done. I ran my fingers through her hair and pulled her to my side for a hug. She gave my legs a squeeze and started playing a game with her rabbit.

I tended to the waffles and finished cooking the batch. Then I turned off the gas and told Abby to climb onto her special stool in the kitchen. We often ate from the breakfast bar at the end of the bench out of convenience.

I served the rest of the waffles, and filled two glasses with orange juice for Brad and myself and half-filled a colorful cup with apple juice for Abby. Brad was still upstairs, so I spread some Nutella over Abby's waffles and sliced them into bite-sized portions. I should have been getting her to practice cutting her food on her own, but not today.

The meal was ready, but Brad was still up in his study. What was he doing?

"Start eating, baby," I said to Abby. "I'm just going to go check on Daddy."

"Okay," she said with a loaded fork. I heard her stuff her mouth full before I had even left the kitchen. She let out a little contented noise a second later.

I headed upstairs, keeping my footsteps as quiet as possible. I wasn't trying to sneak up on Brad, but the hairs on my skin prickled. This wasn't like him. His job rarely came home with him. Only when it was close to tax time did he get extra busy. Weekend problems like this were almost non-existent. He mainly dealt with companies that operated nine to five during the week and hated doing any work outside of those hours.

Brad was muttering to himself from the study when I reached the top of the stairs. I could tell from the flurry of typing that he was on his laptop. I went to call out to him about breakfast being ready but found myself biting my tongue instead. Maybe I needed to listen in and learn what all the fuss was about. It couldn't be anything to do with the weirdness of last night, could it?

I shook my head. Of course not. He was dealing with something for work. I was just hungry and not thinking straight. "Honey, breakfast is ready," I said from the top of the steps.

"Okay, I'll be there in a minute. Thanks."

With a hand on the railing, I contemplated going into the study with some follow-up questions. Normally, I'd be in there by now, making sure everything was okay. We didn't keep secrets from each other in this house — at least, I thought that was how we operated.

Brad muttered some more. I could just make out what he was saying. "How the hell did he find this?"

What was he talking about? I was dying to know, but I knew I shouldn't have been snooping on him.

"Mommy," Abby called from the kitchen. I almost tripped over my own feet as I rushed down the stairs. I prayed Brad was too wrapped up in his problem to hear me creeping at the end of the hallway.

"What is it?" I asked Abby once I'd walked into the kitchen. I looked around for any sign of danger.

"I missed you," she said, looking up at me with Nutella smeared over part of her face.

I exhaled. "I missed you too, baby."

"Is Daddy finished?"

"Still doing some work, honey."

"I'm here," Brad said from only a few feet behind me. I almost leaped out of my body and let a small startle escape me.

"Sorry," he said. "I didn't mean to sneak up on you like that." He had that same uncaring look from last night on his face. But then it faded and transitioned into a happier one.

"No problem," I blurted. "I thought you were still upstairs. Did you solve your issue?"

"For now." He walked past me and sat down at the breakfast bar next to Abby.

"Come on, Mommy," Abby said a second before stuffing her mouth with another bite of food.

I smiled at my husband and daughter, then took a seat in my spot. As we ate, Brad gave Abby a smile but didn't offer one to me. Did he know I was listening in on him? There was no way to know without asking him, and I sure as hell wasn't going to do that.

Whatever he was doing up there, I had to find out.

CHAPTER ELEVEN

After breakfast, I told Brad I'd clean up the kitchen so he could take a shower. I also reminded him to dress warm so we could head out to the park like we had promised Abby.

When Brad headed upstairs, I put Abby in front of the TV in the living room with her favorite animated show. I needed her distracted so I could go upstairs myself and rummage through Brad's study again.

I couldn't help myself. It was a terrible idea, but I couldn't just sit there, living my life, knowing something strange was going on with my husband. Sure, I could've been an adult and asked him about it, but that would've been the responsible and sane thing to do. I needed to take another look in his study and reassure myself that whatever this situation might be was all in my head.

With Abby occupied and Brad taking a shower, I made my move and went upstairs. Brad wouldn't hear me while the shower was running. There wasn't a second to waste.

With no better ideas, I found myself at his laptop again. I knew I wouldn't be able to get past the damn lock screen. Not unless I took a stab at guessing the password. I thought about the previous one I'd tried, *!m0g3n.F@!rb@nk17*, and got an idea.

"No, it couldn't be," I muttered to myself. But my fingers started typing out a few variations of my idea. Finally, one worked:

@bbY.F@!rb@nk22. I was met with Brad's desktop. "Yes," I said louder than I should've.

Before I began my snooping, I thought about the implications of Brad's new password. What made him change it from Imogen's name to Abby's? He'd always used a variation of Imogen's name for his password. Had it become too painful for him to keep entering the name of the daughter we'd lost?

"It doesn't matter," I whispered, hoping the words would get me back on track.

The shower was still running, and I could hear the faint sound of Abby's TV show playing downstairs. I needed to see what my husband had been up to. He wasn't the kind of man who would break the law, let alone kill a person. And yet, his sinister expression last night made me feel just as terrified as I was on the day I lost Imogen.

"It was just a game," I said out loud, doing a lousy job of convincing myself. "Just a stupid game."

I shook my head and got back on track. Once I made sure everything was okay, I could forget this madness. Brad might be up to something as simple as gambling. He'd had a problem with it in the past, but that was years ago.

Oh, God. He wasn't cheating on me, was he? My eyes darted left and right as the room felt ten degrees hotter.

No. Brad wouldn't cheat on me. Where would he find the time, for one? And besides, he loved me. We'd been married for ten years and had been together for even longer. He wouldn't betray my trust like that.

I shook my head at the very idea and opened his Internet browser before I spiraled out of control. I wasn't proud of myself, but I clicked into his search history. My stomach churned as I browsed. Not because of anything that I was finding, but because of the betrayal of trust I was undertaking.

After a few minutes of clicking and scrolling, I came to a sound conclusion: my husband was boring. There was nothing in there but sports, accounting blogs, and news articles. The occasional celebrity gossip clickbait article showed up, but that was about as nefarious as it got.

I wasn't complaining. Boring kept a couple's feet on the ground. And besides, we'd had enough chaos for one lifetime. I continued sifting through Brad's search history, puffing out with tedium as I did so. There was nothing in these pages worth searching for.

The thought of the password was still getting to me, so I lifted Brad's laptop up again to look at the note he had taped to the computer. I expected to find *!m0g3n.F@!rb@nk17*. Instead, I saw something that made no damn sense. Something that stole the air from my lungs.

On the small piece of paper that I had taken the time to study last night, was written *@bbY.F@!rb@nk22*. It was written in Brad's handwriting, just like last night.

"What the fuck?" The laptop slipped from my shaking grip and slammed on the table. The sudden noise sent a jolt of lightning through me. I know what I saw. It had said *!m0g3n.F@!rb@nk17*. Not *@bbY.F@!rb@nk22*. This was impossible.

I closed my eyes as my thoughts carried me away from what I was doing. I blinked rapidly to bring myself back and refocused on the job at hand. I obviously was too tired last night to think straight. And the two passwords looked similar at a distance.

I leaned back and sighed. I was adding unnecessary stress to my life. It was time to turn off Brad's computer and leave. Then I heard it. Or more importantly, I couldn't hear what had been droning in the background. The shower was no longer running.

How long had I been confusing myself with wrong passwords? I needed to close this computer, but I couldn't just shut the lid. It would save everything on the screen and give Brad a damned good idea of what I'd been doing.

"Shit," I whispered as I hurried to close everything down. I wasn't a tech whiz, so it was a slow process. There was probably a quicker way to close all the windows and tabs I'd opened without doing it manually.

"Okay, okay," I muttered as I hit the close tab again and again until I reached the last item. All that was left to do was to click shutdown. Oh, dammit. I slapped my head as I remembered a shutdown closed all the apps and windows. Stupid. Fortunately, I didn't have time to beat myself up. Brad could walk into the room at—

Footsteps approached the study from our bedroom. I was screwed. Brad was going to find me in here. I closed the lid on the laptop as quietly as I could, then slid down under the desk. It was big enough to keep me hidden. As soon as he was gone, I'd be out of there.

As I hid under Brad's desk, feeling as guilty as sin, I listened for his footsteps. They creaked past the room and faded into the distance. A sigh of pure relief escaped my lungs. What was I expecting to find? The murder weapon? A signed confession to something I was imagining?

Then, out of the corner of my eye, I spotted it: the tiny scrap of paper. The one with my handwriting on it. The one that read *!m0g3n.F@!rb@nk17* and not *@bbY.F@!rb@nk22*. I couldn't believe it.

The damn thing must've come off the desk when the heating came on overnight. The airflow had blown the note down under the desk. I couldn't see it before because it had gotten caught partway under the rubber mat Brad had under the desk for his feet. Just my luck.

I took the note and scrunched it into a ball in my fist. It was time to leave this room and resume my life while I still had some dignity left.

But when I stood up from under the desk, I saw Brad staring straight at me with that same darkness in his eyes.

CHAPTER TWELVE

"What are you doing?" Brad asked, staring right at me with a wrinkled brow.

A few ideas rushed through my head: I was cleaning. I was looking for my wedding ring. I thought I heard a noise. But no words came out of my mouth. Instead, I let out an incoherent groan and mumbled, "I don't know."

"You don't know?" he repeated, taking a measured step into the room. Then his eyes fell to the mouse on his desk. It wasn't in its usual perfect position and was too far from the computer. I must've knocked it away in my desperation to dive under the desk. "Were you on my computer?"

"Yes," I answered. I could've lied to him and said no, but my thoughts weren't forming fast enough.

He crossed his arms over his chest. "Why? You know that's my work computer. It has sensitive data on there."

"I'm sorry. I was, um . . . I needed to look something up."

"Why didn't you use your phone?"

"It's not charged. The battery's dead."

"Really?"

Without a doubt, he knew I was lying. It was hard for me to keep anything from him. I might as well come clean. "No, that's not the truth."

Brad walked all the way into the room and sat down in the spare seat he had by the wall. "What's going on, Maia? Something's clearly up. This isn't like you."

"You're right. It's not like me." I let out a sigh. This was going to suck, but I had to do it. What other choice did I have?

"So what's going on?"

"I wasn't spying on you or anything, but . . ." I trailed off.

"But you were going through my work computer?"

"Yeah."

He pinched the bridge of his nose. "I'm sorry, but that sounds an awful lot like spying to me."

"I get that. This must look bad."

"It does. What am I supposed to think?"

That I'm crazy and stupid. That I let my thoughts spiral over nothing. That I'm an awful wife. I didn't say these things out loud. I probably should have. Instead, I stared at the floor and noticed it was due to be vacuumed tomorrow. I should have brought the vacuum cleaner in here. It could've been a half-decent cover.

Brad continued. "You know I don't mind you using my computer, but you have to ask me first. I can't risk it catching a virus. I could get into a lot of trouble if any of the files on there got into the wrong hands. What were you even looking for?"

It was honesty time. There was no other choice. "Maybe you can tell me."

"Tell you what?"

"Oh, I don't know. How about you tell me why you rushed off halfway through making breakfast to use your computer? And don't say it was for a work emergency."

"It wasn't exactly an emergency, but my boss had a question that needed answering. Do you want me to show you the email he sent me?"

Email. Damn. I hadn't thought to check his email.

Brad pulled his cell phone from his pocket and unlocked it. He opened an email app and scrolled down the screen in a hurry. "Here," he said, shoving the device toward me. An email with today's date and a time that roughly synced up with him making waffles stared at me. I didn't understand the technical talk in the message's body. There was something about a private healthcare company and other boring things that didn't concern me. The intent was clear. There was something important that required Brad's immediate attention.

My face burned up. It was official. I was an awful spouse who spied on her husband.

"I'm sorry," I rushed to say. "I thought there was something going on."

"Something going on? Like what?"

Honesty time was over. I couldn't tell him what I was really looking for. How do you break it to your husband that you were searching through his computer to find potential evidence that he once killed a man without sounding insane? I went with the lowest common denominator. "I thought maybe you were cheating on me."

His jaw dropped. "You're kidding? So not only did you think I was cheating on you, but that I was using my work computer to what, organize it?"

"It sounds silly when you put it like that."

Brad shook his head. "Never in our entire relationship have I so much as thought about cheating on you. What the hell made you think I would do such a thing?"

"It's just that you came up here last night during the dinner party to use your study. And then you rushed off during breakfast to do the same thing. I thought something was going on. But I know you wouldn't do that to me. You're perfect. God, I'm so stupid. I'm sorry." I let the tears flow. They weren't forced, either.

Brad stood and moved past his desk to me. He wrapped his arms around my body and pulled me in tight. "Shh, shh. It's okay. I'm not mad. I just wish you had asked me instead. You know I would do nothing so pointless as cheating on you. I love you, Maia. You and Abby are my world. I would never do a thing to compromise that, got it?"

I sobbed into Brad's chest, feeling about as low as a partner could go. What damage had I caused with my paranoia? Brad would never cheat on me, and yet there I was thinking something as extreme as him killing a man.

"Come on," he whispered. "Let's head downstairs and sit with Abby."

"That's a good idea," I said with a sniff. Anything to pull me away from this embarrassing situation. He guided me up and out of the study. But as we left the room, I remembered the scrunched-up note in my hand. I still had one unanswered question for Brad: why did he change his password and not tell me?

"Can I ask you something?"

We paused in the hallway. "What is it?" he asked.

"Why did you change your password?"

"Change my password? What are you talking about?"

I shook my head. "It was always Imogen's name and birth year. Now you've changed it to Abby's. I'm not upset or anything. I just wanted to know why."

Brad looked me in the eye and said, "I changed that password a week ago."

"But you usually write it down under your computer."

"Yeah, I do. I forgot to update it until this morning. That's how you were able to log in to use it, right?"

"Ah, yeah. Exactly," I lie.

He stared at me with pinched features and asked, "Are you okay?" His eyes cast over me the way they had back in the first year we lost Imy. His gaze was consumed with doubt.

"I'm fine," I said, brushing away from him. As we walked downstairs, a little voice in my brain said it all still didn't add up. I should've ignored it. But I wasn't about to listen to my advice. Instead, I glanced back at Brad as he came down after me.

Why had he been so upset about me using his computer? It didn't matter. If there was anything on his laptop worth finding, he was going to erase it the first chance he got.

CHAPTER THIRTEEN

Brad

What the hell was Maia doing on my laptop? She knew better than to use my work computer. I've always made myself clear on that. I guess that's not what I was really upset about, though. Her using my computer wasn't that big of a deal. I had enhanced security for my most important files. The ones I can never allow anyone else to see. Especially not her. And they weren't protected by some password that got changed once a month. They were secured via an authenticator app on my cell phone. It was a good thing I had that extra layer of security in place.

But something had changed with Maia. And it all started last night when we played that damn game. Well, before then, really. Most likely, when I made the idiotic decision to drink.

I hadn't touched the stuff for two years, but the pressure of the evening and keeping Maia in check was too much. I needed something to keep my mind off things and had figured wine was the answer. It went about as well as expected.

At first, I'd thought I was being paranoid or that Maia was stressed out from the evening, but she'd seen my face after I'd said that stupid joke. The one that conjured up a memory I wish I could burn from my brain. I couldn't stop it from twisting my features. I had risked so much with those words. What the hell was I thinking? Was it my guilty conscience shining through, protected from rational thought by the cloud of alcohol? Maybe. It didn't matter. Maia had stared back at me with a familiar look of horror.

As I walked Maia down the stairs, I could feel the tension in her step. She looked over her shoulder at me with genuine suspicion. I'd have given anything to know exactly what was going through her head.

Her snooping through my computer was unexpected and was a sign I needed to get things back on track. I couldn't afford for it all to go off the rails. Not now. Not after everything I'd done to keep this family whole.

"Have you had your medication?" I asked Maia.

"Not yet," she said in a sharp tone. She hated to be asked, but I had to check. She couldn't miss a single dose. Especially right now.

"Why don't you go take them now while I make you a coffee," I said. A hit of caffeine would help clear her head before we sat down to watch TV with Abby. If I acted normal and pretended the laptop situation wasn't a problem, maybe I could keep things under control. I had overreacted before. That much was obvious.

"That would be nice," Maia said, smiling at me as she sniffed. I grinned in return and glanced away before my eyes betrayed me. She left the kitchen and headed for the stairs.

I once killed a man.

Why did I say it? Maybe I was trying to ease my guilt and find absolution for that night. I didn't know. Whatever it was, I was certain Maia was now walking a dangerous path. I couldn't ignore any odd behavior from her. She was digging through my computer for a reason. But how much did she know? And what was she searching for? I needed to go into my study as soon as possible and double-check it all.

I made my wife a strong black coffee with a creamer, just the way she liked it. The steam from the coffee filled the kitchen with a robust aroma that put me at ease, if only for a moment. I made one for myself while I was at it, adding milk and sugar. After last night and the extra strain I had put on myself, I needed the energy. Instead of drinking, I should have been watching Maia to see how she handled herself.

"Did you have fun last night?" Maia asked as she returned and collected her coffee. She blew on the vapors rising from her mug.

"Yeah, I had a blast. It was great catching up with everyone again," I said, forcing a smile. "It's been too long."

Maia's eyes fell to the floor. "I know. I'm sorry."

"I didn't mean it like that, honey. Listen, the last five years are what they are. We can't change any of it. But what we can do is focus on the here and now. Dwelling on the past won't help. Will it?"

She shook her head at my Hallmark-card advice. I knew my words wouldn't sink in beyond a surface level. Not with her spiraling thoughts. But I had to try. I couldn't let her uncover the truth. I couldn't let what I had done be for nothing. I could, however, steer her away from it and make sure she forgot what I had said last night at the party.

When everyone laughed at me, I had no choice but to run with it. If I'm lucky, Maia won't pursue this any further. Something told me, though, that I had already pushed her to dig deeper. I wasn't going to be able to sweep this under the rug.

With our coffees in hand, we made our way to the living room and sat down with Abby. I prayed that some time out of the house with our daughter would make Maia focus on what was more important. If not, if she couldn't let this go, I didn't want to think about what I'd be forced to do.

CHAPTER FOURTEEN

Maia

We sat on the couch with Abby in the middle. It was her favorite spot, no matter what. She loved being close to us, and on most days, I didn't feel worthy of her unconditional affection, especially with the guilt that followed me everywhere. Today was definitely one of those days.

As Abby watched her show — one we'd seen a hundred times before — Brad and I pulled out our phones, starting the endless scroll through social media. It was a terrible habit we both needed to break, but in that moment, it was one I was grateful for. With Brad focused on his screen, I could pretend to be looking at mine while I did my best to watch what he was doing. I wasn't an expert, but I was certain he could delete things from the cloud on his phone and have it sync up with his computer. He could clear an email or wipe his search history, and I'd never know.

I pretended to scroll through Instagram while keeping one eye on Brad's screen. He was just watching a sports video on YouTube with the sound on low. I couldn't help but wonder if it was all for show. Did he know I was watching him?

"Mommy, look," Abby said, tugging on my arm and pointing at the cartoon. I'd been asked to watch this scene so many times I could recite it word for word.

I forced a chuckle as Abby giggled. When it was safe, I subtly checked on Brad again. I didn't even know what I was supposed to be looking for, or if my suspicions had any merit. Abby giggled as the credits rolled on her show. "Last one," I told her as the next episode started. I should have turned the TV off already, but I was too burned out to provide an alternative. Thankfully, it was almost time to fix Abby's hair and help her get dressed for our afternoon trip.

Brad didn't look up from his phone as he watched a video of a man throwing random objects into an industrial shredder. Apparently, he was done with sports for now. He'd spend twenty minutes watching something like that, but if I mentioned an interesting makeup tutorial I'd seen on Instagram, his eyes would glaze over. There was a time when we'd both laugh at funny parenting videos together, but not anymore.

Abby's show ended after the cartoon animals resolved their problems and learned valuable lessons that were clear from the start. If only life were as simple.

"Okay, baby," I told Abby, "time to turn it off."

"One more?" she begged.

"No, honey. We need to do your hair and get dressed."

"Why?"

"So we can take you to that park we talked about."

"Park?" she asked, her eyes lighting up. The late night must have pulled the conversation from her mind. I was certain I had told her about it.

"A fun one," I said. "Daddy and I thought it would be nice to go for a drive and see this special place."

Abby let out an excited cheer and leaped from the sofa. I stood as she grabbed my wrist and pulled. "Come on, Mommy."

"I'm coming," I said. Brad was still staring at his phone like he was in a trance. "Come on, Daddy," I added, giving him a gentle shove.

"Sorry, what?" he said, snapping out of his daze.

"Time to get ready for the park."

He peered down at himself with open arms. "I'm ready. Just need my jacket."

"Perfect. You can make us all an early lunch then. Thanks, honey."

Brad sighed. "No problem."

Abby laughed some more as she dragged me out of the room. I glanced back at Brad and wondered if I should leave him alone. It wasn't like I could keep watch over him twenty-four seven. I also couldn't go sneaking around his study for a third time. If he caught me in there again, I wouldn't be able to cry my way out of it.

I did what I was supposed to be doing and focused on Abby. I took her to the upstairs bathroom and gave her hair a brush. She had such thick, beautiful curls. Any girl would kill for them, young or old. I brushed out the knots and tied her hair into a ponytail. I didn't have the brainpower for anything fancier.

With one task completed, I walked Abby to her room to find some clothes for her to wear. As we made the brief journey, I glanced toward Brad's study. The door was still open. Had he taken this opportunity to creep into the office to cleanse his computer of anything malicious? It didn't matter. I knew this was all unfounded paranoia and nothing more. The dinner-party game had corrupted my thoughts.

I shook my head and continued into Abby's room. It was in a bit of a state, but I'd tackle the mess tomorrow during my cleaning rounds.

"Can I wear this, Mommy?" Abby asked, holding up a pink cotton T-shirt with a worn graphic of a cartoon tiger on it. One I recognized instantly. I took the tiny piece of clothing with a twisted brow.

Abby didn't have any pink tops.

I held the T-shirt in two shaking hands. Before I could put it back down, water gushed through the shirt from behind, darkening the material like it was being submerged in a bucket. In an instant, it was heavy with the liquid and started spilling all over me. I flung it away and scrambled backward, colliding with the wall. A picture above my head rattled, but didn't fall.

"Mommy," Abby giggled. "You're silly."

My breath heaved in and out as I stared at the pink T-shirt across the room. There was no water on it. It was completely dry. I checked my hands and body — they were also dry. And as if that wasn't bad enough, the shirt was no longer pink with a cartoon tiger print. It was aqua colored and had a cartoon dolphin on the front instead.

I held my hands over my face for a moment and pressed my palms around the sockets of my eyes. I removed my hands from my face and did what I could to dismiss what my mind had conjured up.

Imogen's favorite color was pink. I know that's a cliché, but my little girl absolutely loved the color. She wore it constantly, and the pink shirt with the tiger was the one she wore when she drowned. When Abby came along, I couldn't let her wear anything close to pink. It would always send me spiraling. And stopping a three-year-old girl from wearing pink was no easy feat.

"Mommy?" Abby asked, moving over to me. "Are you okay?"

I gazed at her gleaming eyes and forced a smile. How could I explain to her what had just happened? Abby stared at me, expecting a response, so I gave her one. "Mommy was just playing a game, sweetheart."

Abby smiled in return, but I could see a hint of confusion in her eyes. This poor girl. She had me for a mother.

I closed my eyes and tried to focus. We were supposed to be getting ready to go to a park. That's right, a park. It was no wonder

I was hallucinating. What the hell was I thinking? How was I going to manage such an outing now? I could tell Brad I was too tired. He wouldn't be upset. He looked like he wanted to stay home. But what about Abby? She'd be devastated.

I opened my eyes and saw Abby grabbing a different T-shirt. She threw it across the room just like I had done with the aqua one and giggled. Lucky for me, she was still at an age where everything could be reduced to a silly game. Her innocence pulled me from a nosedive and reminded me of what was at stake.

I guess it was settled. We were going to a damn park.

CHAPTER FIFTEEN

After too long, I pulled myself off the floor and helped Abby get dressed. Once she was ready, I turned my attention to quieting the barrage of thoughts that were swirling in my head. Going to this park would be harder than I thought. My meds would struggle to keep up.

With Abby ready, I asked her to hang out on my bed while I got dressed and did my makeup and hair. She brought some plastic ponies into my room and played with them, doing all the voices as she reenacted scenarios from the TV show the toys were associated with. As I listened to her play, stabs of guilt ran through me. She was supposed to have an older sister by her side, showing her the ropes as they played together.

Abby smiled when she caught me watching her. "Mommy? Can we go to the park now?"

"Soon," I said as I straightened my hair. I was taking longer than necessary, hoping to delay the inevitable. Brad was probably getting impatient. I could picture the frustrated look on his face. Then again, he had likely returned to watching industrial shredder videos on YouTube or some other dumb thing like "Top Ten Train Derailments." No matter how long I lived, I'd never understand the things he did in his spare time.

With us girls finally ready, we headed downstairs, hoping to find the sandwiches Brad was supposed to have made for us. He didn't disappoint — two perfect club sandwiches and a PB & J for Abby were sitting on plates at the breakfast bar, along with some fruit slices to share. Each of us had some water to drink. After last night, water was exactly what Brad and I needed.

"Thank you, Daddy," Abby said as she climbed onto her stool and settled into position.

"You're welcome, angel," he replied.

"Thank you," I added, patting Brad on the shoulder. I appreciated his efforts, especially after he caught me hiding under his desk before. I hated the feeling of mistrust I now had for my husband, but I couldn't help it. It burned in the background whether I wanted it to or not, and it wasn't fair to him in the slightest. After all, I still had nothing concrete to tell me he was a killer.

We ate our lunch in relative silence. It would have been easy to use our fatigue as an excuse to skip the park, but I'd made my little girl a promise. I was sure we could get through the afternoon with nothing awful happening. It was just a trip to a park, for God's sake. But for Imogen, five years ago, it had been more than that — it was the last trip she'd ever take.

"You okay, honey?" Brad asked, pulling me out of my thoughts.

"Uh, yeah," I replied, wrenching a smile.

He pulled back, narrowing his gaze. "Are you sure?"

"Yes. Thank you again for making lunch. These are delicious."

He stared for a moment longer with an analytic eye, then said, "You're welcome." Did he think my behavior was just stress or something else?

When we finished eating, I took our plates and cups to the dishwasher. Then I grabbed some snacks and asked Abby to find her water bottle for the park. It was always best to be prepared when taking a three-year-old anywhere. You didn't want to be caught out of the house with a hungry kid.

Before we left, I headed to Abby's room to grab a spare change of clothes for her and threw them into the cute backpack I liked to take with us. It had once been Abby's diaper bag and had only been used on the rare occasions when we actually left the house.

We never planned on having another baby after Imogen passed. It just happened. It was a blessing I didn't deserve, but I couldn't imagine life without Abby. She didn't know it, but she was the one holding this family together. Without her, Brad and I would have been divorced by now. I would have driven him away.

As I loaded up the bag, I felt a small lump in the front pocket and investigated. Hopefully, I hadn't left any food in there. I just wanted to get this excursion over and done with. Cleaning out a backpack before we took off would only delay things further. The thought reminded me of times when I've had no choice but to take Abby places. We were forever late to every appointment, meeting, or event. It had been the same with Imogen. It amazed me how something as tiny as a baby could take up so much of your time and energy.

I opened the front pocket of the bag and reached inside with a cautious hand. If it were old food, it would be disgusting. But instead of food, I found a scrunchie. I pulled out the mustard-yellow hair tie that belonged to Abby. Imogen had one just like it that was pink. It had been my favorite thing to tie up her hair with, back when all I could do with her short hair was make a small ponytail.

Imogen's hair had taken a long time to grow after she was born. For a good while, I had to make it clear to people that she was a girl. Her slow-growing hair made people so unsure, especially those who didn't know us. It shouldn't have bothered me, but it did. Then again, it was the least of my problems as a first-time mom. I didn't know which way was up, but people were drawn to you when you only had one child. The number of strangers who approached me with unwanted advice was astonishing. And because Abby was also an only child, they assumed she was my first and felt compelled to impart their wisdom on me.

With the scrunchie in hand, my eyes misted over as I swallowed the sob that threatened to break free. I should have felt grateful for having had such a beautiful little girl, and especially now that I had another, but if I could go back to the time when Imogen was born, I would do so in a heartbeat.

"Mommy?" Abby's voice asked, pulling me out of my spiraling thoughts. She must have followed me into her room.

I wiped my eyes and sniffed before turning to face her. "Yeah, baby. What is it?"

"Are we going to the park now?" she asked, her voice tinged with a moan.

"We are. I was just making sure we had everything we needed, that's all, sweetheart."

"But I want to go now," she replied, looking up at me with those gentle eyes.

"We'll get there soon enough."

"Okay," Abby said, her excitement deflating. I gave her another smile and placed the scrunchie back in the backpack's pocket.

"Mommy?" Abby moaned again. "Are we going?"

"Yes!" I snapped.

She recoiled. Realizing my mistake, I reached for her and said, "I'm sorry, Mommy didn't mean to get angry."

Her eyes welled up as her bottom lip quivered. Then the tears came. I did my best to console her and apologize, but I'd unleashed an anger on her she hadn't deserved.

What the hell was wrong with me? Abby just wanted to have fun. I patted her head and guided her along as we prepared to leave. She had stopped crying and was happy again. Hopefully, she'd stay that way. I was determined to take her out for a nice day. No matter what.

As we headed for the stairs, we passed Brad's study. The door was closed — something he never did. After catching me snooping around in there, he might have developed some trust issues. Fair enough.

Nevertheless, I rounded up Brad so we could leave. The three of us headed to my navy-blue Toyota Grand Highlander. I hadn't driven the oversized SUV in at least a few weeks. The only time I left the house was when something couldn't be dealt with online. I had to stop doing that and use any excuse possible to take Abby places.

Brad held out his hand for the keys to drive. I handed them to him, breathing a sigh of relief. I hated driving. Although I should have been the one volunteering after getting caught in his study, driving put me on edge. I needed to get over it, though. If I stopped ordering everything to be delivered to us, I would need to drive places with Abby. Did she even know what a grocery store looked like? Probably only from what she'd seen on TV. At this rate, she'd grow up ill-prepared for the world and end up like me. No one wanted that.

Of course, a voice in my head whispered that I shouldn't drive so that I could keep Brad from using his phone. It was a dumb thought, but it came to me all the same. He might have explained himself well this morning, but I still couldn't ignore some of the behavior I'd witnessed.

I helped Abby into her booster seat and made sure she was buckled in tight, checking she was secure three times. The only reason we'd shelled out for this enormous car was to keep Abby safe. A Toyota Grand Highlander wasn't necessary for a family with only one child, but I pushed Brad to spend the extra money on the vehicle after Abby was born. He wasn't too happy about it at the time.

With Abby secured, I climbed into the front passenger seat as Brad played on his cell phone. We'd been in the car for two seconds, and he'd already pulled it out, scrolling through some website looking at God knows what.

"Are we going?" I asked.

"Yeah," he said, not raising his eyes from his phone. His finger hovered over the engine start button, but then stopped. "Oh, crap."

"What's wrong?" I asked.

"I just remembered. I was supposed to send a quick email for work."

"Can you do it on your phone?"

"Yes and no. There's an attachment I need, and it's on my computer."

"Can it wait?" I asked, not hiding my impatience. Some days, his timing was atrocious.

"It could wait, but it's all I'll be thinking about while we're out. You know me. I just need three minutes to head inside and get this sorted. Then I'll be able to concentrate on our trip."

I sighed and looked away. "Okay."

"Thanks, honey," he said, taking out my keys from his pocket. He then scurried out the door and half-jogged to the house.

"Where's Daddy going?" Abby asked.

"He'll just be a minute, baby. He forgot something."

"Silly Daddy," Abby giggled.

"Yes, silly Daddy," I muttered, shaking my head. I contemplated pulling out my cell phone to pass the time, but settled on staring blankly into space instead. Then I noticed something out of the corner of my eye. In the driver's seat sat Brad's unlocked phone. He'd left it behind. My hand reached out toward the device on autopilot, but I froze halfway there.

After everything that had gone through my head in the last sixteen hours, I couldn't help it. I knew what I was thinking was wrong, especially with my daughter sitting here. Brad was entitled to a little privacy. But that damn question I had about my husband came to me again, sending a flurry of anxiety through my chest. Was my husband a killer? Was he capable of something so evil? Maybe the answer was inside his cell phone.

CHAPTER SIXTEEN

I wasn't going to search through my husband's cell phone. It was wrong on so many levels. And besides, what secrets did I think I would find on there? As I'd discovered, Brad was just a normal man. One who worked hard to provide us with a beautiful home and a comfortable life. Going through his phone would simply jeopardize our relationship. Plus, he'd left it behind and unlocked. If there was anything on there worth seeing, he wasn't trying hard to hide it.

The logic was sound. There was no argument to be had. But apparently, it wasn't enough to stop me. I was going to look through Brad's phone while he wasn't around. There was something wrong with me. I knew it, but I couldn't silence the idea any more than I could stop myself from thinking he once killed someone. Maybe once I'd done this, the thought would leave my mind for good.

There was only one obstacle in my way, and that was my wide-eyed angel in the back seat. Abby had a perfect view of me and might notice if I picked up her father's cell phone and started using it. I needed to distract her.

More guilt flooded my system. Was I really going to deceive my child just so I could betray my husband's trust for the second time in one day? Apparently so.

"Are you excited about the park?" I asked Abby.

"Yeah," she almost shouted with a massive smile.

"It's a bit of a drive to get there, so why don't you take a nap?"

"But I'm too excited," she said.

She wasn't lying. I could see it in her eyes. She was bouncing in her seat. I'd need to think of another angle. An idea came to me soon enough. "Do you wanna play on Mommy's cell phone while we wait for Daddy?"

"Yes, please," she begged, her legs kicking.

I occasionally let Abby experiment with some age-appropriate apps on my phone. It could be a big help when I was waiting anxiously in a doctor's office and had neglected to bring along enough activities to entertain her. It happened more than it should have.

I unlocked my cell phone and handed it to Abby, loading up an app I knew she enjoyed playing. She hadn't worked out how to get to the other parts of my phone. Fortunately, she wasn't like her untrustworthy mother.

With little time on my hands, I picked up Brad's cell phone while Abby was distracted popping virtual balloons in the backseat.

Brad had set his phone to remain unlocked unless he pressed the button. He was constantly leaving it around the house unlocked. It drove me nuts, only because I thought about how it must drain the battery. I was one of those people who liked to keep their phones charged up at all times. You never knew what was going to happen when you were out of the house. The thought of a dead cell phone sent a bout of nausea to my stomach every time. It never used to, though. In the past, I'd be happy scrolling social media with less than three percent battery left.

With Brad's phone in hand, I opened his email app and was careful to only look at messages that had already been opened. And that was all I found in there. His emails were organized as well as his study. Not a single one sat there unread. They didn't reveal a lot. I couldn't understand half of what I was skimming through. There was too much boring technical jargon.

Frustrated, I went to his web browser and went through his history again. I wanted to double-check it was the same as what I'd found on his computer.

A few minutes went by. I'd gone through the list again in his history. From what I could tell, it was the same as before. Relief washed over me. Again, I found accounting blogs, sports results, and news reports. Brad was clean. I could finally put this irrationality to rest.

Deciding I was done, I cleared away the tab and any new browsing history I'd now left on his cell phone. The device was ready to be placed back where I had found it. But there was one more item in his browsing history I'd almost missed. It was a news article right down at the bottom of the list.

Brad had visited the link late last night, around the time I was downstairs with London when I was struggling to sleep. But the time made little sense. He'd told me he slept like a baby, that he didn't wake up once overnight. Why did he lie to me? I swear he fell fast asleep after we'd had sex. I must have woken him up when I'd left.

I tapped on the link.

An old article came up on a news site from four years ago.

Local Brookfield Terrace Man Missing

Why was Brad looking at an old news article about a man from our town who had gone missing years ago?

Before I could read the story, I saw the front door to our house open. Brad came through, holding my keys. I lowered his cell phone and closed the tab and browsing history. There was no time to share the article to my phone. He was already locking the door and would be in the car in no time.

Before Brad turned around, I got his phone back to the site he'd had it on and placed it where I found it. I held my hands in my lap, and my heartbeat throbbed in my ear. He hadn't seen me. I was in the clear.

"That's Daddy's phone," Abby said from the backseat.

Oh, come on. The one second Abby looked up from her game was when I was placing Brad's cell phone back into position.

"Mommy was just checking the weather," I said, trying to sound casual. "And it's time to turn that off, sweetheart." I turned in my seat and held out a hand for my cell phone as Brad approached the car.

"Five more minutes?" Abby begged, copying words she didn't quite understand yet. She had no concept of how long five minutes actually were, but she loved to say this to us whenever she wasn't ready to give something up.

"Come on, baby. Daddy's back now. We're about to leave."

"Please," she begged with round eyes and thrashing feet.

"No. I need my phone so I can tell Daddy where we're going."

"Use the TV," she said, pointing to the GPS screen on the dashboard. Some days, this kid was too clever for me. Today was certainly one of those days.

Brad opened his door and climbed in. I glanced at him for a moment and noticed the confused look on his face.

"What's going on?" he asked.

"Nothing," I said, looking away from him as I reached my hand farther out to Abby. Abby pulled my phone closer to her chest like it was the most precious thing in the world. I guess she constantly saw Brad and me being distracted by our phones and figured there was a good reason for it.

"Why does Abby have your phone?" Brad asked.

"I wasn't sure how long you would be," I snapped.

"Whoa, I said I'd be three minutes. I took five. Sorry."

I shook my head. He didn't know what I was furious about. And until I read that article I'd found on his cell phone, my mood would not change.

I faced forward in the passenger seat and gave up on getting my cell phone back for the moment. A hand covered my eyes as I tried to focus. A wave of fog came over me. Brad was looking at that article in the middle of the night. Was it a coincidence? Was it clickbait? My head was spinning.

Brad's hand found its way to my shoulder. I flinched at his touch.

"Jesus," he said, reacting to my freak-out. "I was just checking if you were okay."

"I'm sorry," I said, avoiding his gaze. "You startled me."

Quiet settled between us for a moment until I lifted my gaze to his. He stared at me with darting eyes and a half-open mouth like he was looking at a stranger.

Brad glanced down at his cell phone and paused. His eyes rolled up to mine. I quickly looked out the window. Did he know what I had been doing?

The engine started, and Brad shifted the car into reverse. Before we left, he told Abby to hand over my phone. Abby continued to complain. Her late night had given her a newfound confidence to be defiant. I couldn't say I was enjoying this new trait. Brad promised to buy her some ice cream on the way back home if she did what he asked. He always went for the bribe. It was frustrating, but I couldn't object. Not when I'd been using the same tactic on her.

Abby handed over my phone in a flash. I took it back and tucked it away. Something told me I would need it today, especially if I was going to find that news article.

Brad reversed out of our driveway while I wordlessly entered the address of the park we were driving to on the GPS.

"The TV," Abby said to me.

"Sorry?" Brad asked, confusion lining his forehead.

I gave him a shrug, pretending I didn't know what Abby was on about. I swear this kid was too smart for me.

I concentrated on the GPS and saw that the park was about twenty-five minutes away. There were probably a dozen parks between here and there, but we needed to be far enough away from a certain one I could never return to. I couldn't be anywhere near that place or something like it. I tapped the start button on the satnav and leaned back in my seat.

"Thanks," Brad muttered, but I sensed a gruffness in his voice. Had he worked out that I'd been snooping through his cell phone?

As Brad drove down our street, I caught him glancing sideways at me several times when he thought I wasn't looking. But he had it all backward. I should have been the one staring at him.

CHAPTER SEVENTEEN

We got to the park sooner than I expected after a relaxing drive through several suburbs southwest of Brookfield Terrace and Syracuse. They all had that small-town charm that flowed from the area. Light traffic also allowed us to enjoy the countryside and rolling hills. It had been a while since I'd visited this part of the area. We were so fortunate to have access to such a beautiful space so close to home, and I had squandered the privilege.

The drive made me forget about the article for a few minutes. But the second we arrived, it all came back to me. I needed to get on my cell phone and find out who this missing man from four years ago was. I was too afraid to locate the article during the drive, not with Brad sitting only a few feet from me.

Abby's legs kicked when she saw the park. It wasn't hard to see why. The park had such an inviting atmosphere. A section filled with colorful play equipment stood near the gravel parking lot we pulled into. There were swings, slides, and things to climb. And from what I'd seen online, it catered to a variety of ages. There was also a large open field with a baseball diamond in the distance that looked like it would be fun to run around on.

"Mommy?" Abby begged. "Are we here?"

"Yes, honey," I said as Brad rolled to a stop and cut the engine. "Daddy will get you out."

I stayed in my seat and beamed at Abby as she jittered with excitement. Brad exited his side of the car and helped her unbuckle herself from the booster seat. She bolted and ran toward the playground the second she could.

My heart raced at the sight of Abby rushing away from me. One of my hands reached out to stop her, but I reminded myself that it was perfectly normal for a three-year-old to rush off toward a set of swings at a park. I dug my index finger into my palm as hard as I could on the same spot from earlier and welcomed the pain.

"Are you coming?" Brad asked me, leaning into the car through Abby's open door.

"Uh, yeah," I said, almost forgetting he was there. He'd already taken the backpack out and was holding it over his shoulder.

"If you think you need to take an extra dose of your meds—"

"I'll be fine," I said, harsher than was needed.

He closed Abby's door with a slam and walked around to my side, shaking his head as he went. His shadow cast a darkness over me that sent a tremble up my spine. In an instant, the news article headline overloaded my brain with possibilities. Brad had visited it in the middle of the night when he thought he was alone. Why?

I had to read that story. And I had to know why he was reading it.

Brad had his spare hand in his jacket pocket as he watched Abby with contentment. I stared up at him and wondered if this man, this father who clearly loved his daughter, could also be a murderer. It didn't seem possible when I saw him like this.

Before Brad noticed me studying him, I exited the car and made sure to bring my cell phone along. With any luck, he would want to pass the time staring at his screen. It would give me the chance to pretend to scroll through Instagram until I found enough courage to search for the article.

But I had worse problems to deal with. We were at a park. I couldn't sit back and be distracted by my cell phone while Abby was running around on her own. The playground might seem like a safe place, but there was no way in hell I was going to relax while we were here. Even though there was no water at this park, that day was always on the edge of my mind.

Brad found a park bench close to where Abby was playing and sat down. I followed and took a seat beside him, but kept some distance between us. I was stuck in an awkward position of needing to be close to Brad, but not so close that he could see what I was doing.

The park was busy. There were kids running around in all directions while parents with coffees in hand chatted away. The weather was on the cooler side, but the sun was shining.

I stared at Abby. She was on a swing set that had three individual seats and had climbed into the toddler-sized one. After rocking back and forth a few times, she tried her hardest to get some momentum going. Before long, she called Brad to be her pusher. He let out a groan as he stood.

I watched him as he strolled to his daughter and wondered just how safe Abby was with him around. As much as I wanted to read the article, I couldn't do so with Brad so close to Abby. What if he were a murderer, and I found out? He could turn on any of us. Abby included. He wouldn't harm her, would he?

"Listen to yourself," I muttered while shaking my head. I was once again letting things get out of hand. Brad would never hurt his daughter. Not in a million years. Even if he had killed a man like he joked he had, he would never harm that little girl. Ever.

"Higher, Daddy," Abby called out.

"That's what I'm doing, honey," Brad said with a smile. "It takes time."

"Higher," Abby urged again.

Brad gave me a chuckle and a shrug. I responded with a grin that faded the moment his attention was back on our daughter. I should have been delighted by their interaction. I only had myself to blame. If I hadn't looked at his phone, I might have been enjoying myself right now.

With Brad busy with Abby, I pulled out my phone. The article was gnawing on my brain, clawing at me to read it. As much as I wanted to know what the article was about, I also didn't want to go through it. What if its contents changed everything?

I shifted my eyes to see if the coast was clear. A second later, Brad glanced up ever so subtly. I swear to God he was watching me any chance he got. Or maybe my paranoia was making me think so.

In a panic, I opened the camera app instead of my browser and started recording a video of Brad and Abby having fun. He seemed to accept what I was doing and looked away.

I stared at my family through the screen and wondered how few recordings I had of moments like the one that was unfolding before me. I was missing a joyful time at the park because my mind was elsewhere, thinking irrational things. But what was I supposed to do given the headline of that article?

Deciding I'd had enough of a recording to keep Brad off my back, I tapped the stop symbol on the camera app and got started on looking for the article. I couldn't put it off any longer. In my browser, I entered the search terms.

Brookfield Terrace man missing

The top result came up and looked like what I had seen on Brad's phone. I hovered my thumb over the link as a tremor ran through my body. Once I had read this article, there would be no going back. I might stumble down a path that could destroy everything Brad and I had built together. I didn't have to do this. It could have just been some random article and nothing more. I was better off deleting my search history so I could concentrate on Abby instead. I could force myself to go back to a state of peaceful oblivion and pretend that everything was okay.

"She's having a blast," Brad said, as he sat down beside me.

I almost dropped my phone as I twisted away from him with wide eyes. He came out of nowhere.

"Are you okay?" he asked, leaning closer to me.

I locked my phone and flashed him a reassuring smile. At least I tried to. "I'm good," I said.

"Are you sure, honey? Because you don't look okay. I'm not trying to be rude or anything, but I can see how much you're struggling with this."

"With what?" I asked, sitting up.

"You know, being at a park with Abby? We both know why this is a big deal. And more so right after we had guests over last night. If you weren't ready for today, you should have said something."

"I'm fine," I said in a hushed voice.

Brad glanced around at the other parents and children who were enjoying themselves on this Sunday afternoon. "No one is listening to our conversation, Maia. Just answer me honestly."

I shook my head and turned away from him. "I said I'm fine."

"Okay. My mistake. It just seems like you might be struggling a little. I'm sorry for giving a crap."

Brad huffed and mumbled to himself. He pulled out his cell phone and rushed to occupy himself with social media. Typical. But I knew that in less than a minute, he would say something else to me again. In an instant, an argument would pop into his head about my odd behavior.

He didn't disappoint.

"It was *your* idea to come here," he said.

I closed my eyes and summoned all my willpower not to react. Brad realized his words were only going to piss me off. But he had to say them. It was like his head would explode if he didn't. I swallowed any rage that was brewing within and prayed it stayed where it belonged. I shouldn't have been so antagonizing, giving him reasons to think I was suspicious of him.

Brad gave up on goading me and went back to his cell phone. I exhaled and almost felt a surge of pride run through me that I hadn't lost my cool more than I usually did.

I looked up at Abby and saw that she had moved on from the swings. She was taking turns with the other children to go down a small slide. There were about half a dozen kids around the ages of three to five using the same section of the playground. The older children were on the bigger equipment.

Abby's face was almost euphoric. Some of her energy transferred to me. It was like the cloud of misery that followed me around had been lifted temporarily. What would it take to keep it this way?

I stood and put my cell phone in the back pocket of my jeans. Someone had to watch Abby with a keen eye. I couldn't sit on a park bench and assume she would be okay playing on her own. Keeping her safe was more important than any possibilities that were waiting for me in that news article.

CHAPTER EIGHTEEN

Brad

I could no longer ignore it. Maia was acting so skittish and distant. She was lost in her thoughts one second, then startled the moment she spotted me looking at her. What was going on in that brain of hers? We'd come so far. We were so close to becoming a normal family again. The dinner party was supposed to be a test to see if she could handle things getting back to normal, but then I made the stupid mistake of drinking. I knew I wouldn't stop at one sip or even one glass. That dumb line was bound to fall out of my mouth. It was like I wanted the truth to come out. As a result of my actions, things had changed.

And Maia was forcing my hand.

I watched her as she stood thirty feet in front of me, keeping a sharp eye on Abby at all times. She was so paranoid about the smallest thing happening to her. I understood why, but I wished she could forgive herself for what happened to Imogen. Lightning would not strike twice. That much I could guarantee.

I pulled out my cell phone again. I should have been enjoying myself, but Maia had put me on edge. I wondered if she'd gone through my phone when I went back inside to sort out my work issue. I had left it there as a test of sorts while I made sure everything was where it needed to be on my computer.

It wasn't my only reason for needing to check my laptop. My boss had been emailing me lately about what he said were discrepancies found in the files we had on our private healthcare network client. He didn't know about the fraud I'd found that had been committed by a particular party. What he had found, though, were breadcrumbs that someone had been sifting through certain blocks of the client's files without permission. I'd been as careful as I could, but my boss was no moron.

"Maybe we've been hacked," I'd said to him one day in the office.

"It's possible," he'd replied.

"Do you want me to have the tech geeks look into it?"

"Not yet. This doesn't come across as a data breach. Just keep an eye on things and let me know if you see something out of the ordinary."

"Will do," I'd told him. He had no idea just how close an eye I was going to keep on it. Fortunately, he trusted me and would never suspect I was the one poking my head where it didn't belong. The sheer size of the data was the only thing keeping me from being caught. For anyone to see what I had been up to would require a lot of extra hours. And frankly, our firm was too busy handling our legitimate work for anyone to bother.

I had a good reason for leaving my phone unlocked with my web browser open in the car. I wanted Maia to believe that I wasn't hiding anything. Little did she know that I'd already cleared my history and populated it with some of the usual things I browsed online. I went and did the same thing on my computer while I was in my study, sending an email to my boss that would steer him in the wrong direction — toward my unauthorized activity.

Maia wouldn't find anything on my cell phone that was out of the ordinary. That was if she decided to spy on me again.

I had been positive she'd taken the bait. It had been written all over her face when I had returned. I guess she couldn't help herself. She'd used the opportunity to break my trust and poke around in my phone. I should have been furious. I should have confronted her about it. But that wasn't why I'd left it there to begin with. I hoped that finding my phone with nothing incriminating on it would put her mind at ease, but apparently, it hadn't. In fact, the opposite seemed to be true. And I needed to find out why that was the case.

"Hi, Daddy," Abby called out to me from the playground. I gave her a wave and beamed at my little girl. She was getting bigger by the day; what I'd give for her to have Imogen as an older sister right now. Abby knows about Imogen on some level. She's seen the photos in our house and has asked questions, but I doubted she understood who Imogen was. I sometimes imagined Imogen playing with Abby in the backyard. They would run around together, laughing without a care in the world. But it never took long for reality to kick in and spoil the illusion.

A thought about Maia's behavior came to me. I opened my Internet browser and double-checked my history. I was positive I'd wiped it earlier. Only the planted history I wanted Maia to find should have been visible. I'd had all the time in the world to do it while she was getting herself and Abby ready.

Everything appeared to be in order. The only websites on the list were the ones I had intentionally visited today. Maia would have only seen—

Oh God.

The article. It was there at the bottom. How was that possible? I'd cleared my history. Twice. I checked the settings and tapped the clear history button again, just like I'd done earlier. That website shouldn't have been there. It made no sense.

"Crap," I muttered under my breath. My mistake was obvious now. I'd only cleared my history from the last hour when I tapped that button back at home. I'd looked up the article for the second time last night when Maia left the room. Again, the alcohol in my system had caused a massive slip-up. I just had to see the article again, didn't I? With my dumb comment at the dinner party dredging up the past, I wanted to make sure there had been no progress or updates on the case. It had been a while since I last did so. That's why I went to my study during the party. Well, for that and to look at something else while I was there.

Thankfully, there hadn't been any changes to the case. But I may have inadvertently pointed Maia toward something I couldn't afford for her to see.

What had I done? How could I have screwed up so badly? I could write it off as a mistake made while being too hung over, but that wasn't good enough. I had to try harder. If Maia had read the article, what would I have to do now to stop her from uncovering the rest of it?

CHAPTER NINETEEN

Maia

Abby kept running around the playground with boundless energy. Staying up late hadn't affected her at all. After gathering some courage, I made my way back to the park bench. Even though it meant sitting close to Brad, I was too tired to stand.

I wondered if it was possible to push a thought out of my head and keep it that way. They say, if you tell yourself a lie enough times, you'll believe it. Maybe I could convince myself that I never saw that news article on Brad's phone and also erase that overwhelming fear I'd felt at the party.

Brad's dark glare had started this whole mess. Until that second, I was feeling mostly positive about the future. Now, I wasn't so sure. I would give anything to go back in time to that moment and leave the room right before Brad had his turn of Two Truths and One Lie. Brad might actually be a killer, but I would gladly live the rest of my life in denial, if it were possible.

Brad was still on his cell phone, scrolling with a frantic finger through something I couldn't make out. No doubt it was accounting-related. Probably a technical article from his industry that would put me to sleep on a good day. I couldn't understand how he enjoyed that kind of work.

Abby rushed up to me, breathless and wide-eyed. "Mommy, this is so much fun."

"That's great, honey," I said. "You look like you're having an awesome time. Are you thirsty?"

Her eyes darted left and right as she thought. "Yeah." She jumped up and down.

I retrieved her water bottle and handed it over. She took several huge gulps of water like she hadn't drunk any in days. The exertion left her breathless.

"Wow, big drink," Brad said, pulling his focus away from his cell phone. "Are you having fun?"

Abby giggled in return. "Yeah, Daddy. The best." Then she turned to me in a hurry. "Can I have a snack?"

"Of course, sweetheart. Let me get one for you." I unzipped the backpack and dug around for one of the snacks I'd brought along for Abby. I pulled out a small container and opened it. Abby reached out her hand to take the food, but stopped when she saw what was inside.

"What's wrong?" I asked as I looked at the sliced banana in the container. I couldn't see anything out of the ordinary.

"I don't like bananas," she said.

"You don't like bananas?" I asked, repeating her words like I was translating a foreign language. Then I realized what the problem was. Abby was right. She didn't like bananas; she never had.

Imogen was the one who had liked sliced bananas.

"Oh, God," I whispered. How could I have forgotten? Imy used to love eating them for her afternoon snack. Not Abby. Brad noticed my mistake almost immediately.

"It's okay," he said. "Let's see what else Mommy's got in her bag of tricks." He took the container and closed it without asking. Then, he grabbed the backpack and put the sliced banana away. Before Abby could complain, he pulled out a small pack of whole-grain crackers. He opened it for Abby and handed her the package.

"There you go, honey."

"Thanks, Daddy," she beamed.

I stared at the ground, feeling stupid. Abby sat between us on the bench and ate her snack. She rushed each bite and was done in less than five minutes, oblivious to the turmoil in my own brain.

"Can I play again?" she asked us.

I nodded, not wanting to speak. Abby bolted back to the play equipment. I watched her go as a sting of embarrassment overtook me.

"Are you okay?" Brad asked for the second time since we'd arrived.

I shrugged. "How could I have forgotten?"

"It was just an honest mistake. It was bound to happen one day. They are so much alike. It's no big deal, right?"

I didn't answer. Brad was one of those people who liked to smooth everything over as quickly as possible. Unless we were arguing, of course, then he just wanted to get out what he had to say and not listen to me. It tested my tolerance like nothing else.

"Right? Not a big deal?" he pressed, leaning closer to me so I could see his smile. He seemed eager to make me happy. More than usual.

My instinct was to turn away, but I could see that he needed a response. "Sure," I said. "Not a big deal." But it felt like one. Abby had never liked bananas. No matter how many times I'd offered them to her.

"Maia," Brad started.

I glanced at him. What did he have to say now? I knew my mistake wasn't his fault, but I didn't want to hear another lecture. "What?"

"Do you think you might need to make an extra appointment to see Dr. Corbyn?"

I crossed my arms over my chest. Of course, that was the first thought he had. "I'm fine. I don't need to see Dr. Corbyn over a box of banana slices."

"I wasn't saying that. It's just you haven't been yourself since the party. It's a lot to deal with at once— the party and now this. I thought maybe it would be a good idea to go in for a quick session and make sure you're not struggling with anything else."

I looked away from him. "Again, I'm fine. I forgot a few things. So what? I'm sorry I'm not perfect like you."

"I never said I was perfect," Brad huffed. "I'm just concerned."

There he went again, making matters worse. I could feel my temper swelling. It was only going to take one more sharp comment for me to snap. I clenched my fists and held them tight to my eye sockets. The pressure calmed me down a bit, but I probably looked like a crazy person. Despite the image, the technique always helped. Enough so that I could give Brad a better answer.

"I'm sorry," I said in a level tone. "I didn't mean to bring the wrong snack for Abby. I'm just so tired."

"It's okay," he said. "It's my fault. The party was a mistake. We should have started with something smaller. I'm the one who should be sorry."

This was unexpected. So much so that I didn't know what to say to him. I swallowed my pride and said, "Thank you. I know I'm hard work, but I'm trying my best here."

"I know you are, Maia. But remember, you don't have to do this on your own. Not only am I here for you, but so is Dr. Corbyn."

"Okay," I muttered.

"Just think about it, okay?"

"I will."

Brad nodded and returned his focus to his cell phone. It sounded like he was being controlling, but this wasn't the first time an extra session with Dr. Corbyn had been the topic of discussion. Maybe seeing my therapist wasn't such a bad idea. I hadn't been feeling myself since the dinner party started.

Abby squealed with glee as she took part in a game of tag with some of the other children. I pushed the thought of therapy and news articles from my brain and absorbed the precious image before me. Everything else could wait.

CHAPTER TWENTY

When it was time to leave the park, I offered to drive. I could've used the opportunity to look up the article online, but I didn't want to do it with Brad so close by. If I drove, it meant I could keep my hands busy and couldn't go anywhere near my cell phone. I was desperate to read the news story, but at the same time, I wanted to put it off for a while longer.

Brad asked me three times if I was okay to drive. He was treating me like an escaped mental patient, staring at me with pity. It could have just been him trying to show his concern, or perhaps he wanted me to feel pathetic and useless.

Maybe I was letting the day get in my head. I didn't know anymore. This extra session with Dr. Corbyn was looking more and more likely. I hadn't seen him in three weeks. I hated attending his practice and only went to keep Brad happy.

As we were about to leave, London sent me a text, reconfirming our coffee plans for tomorrow morning. She'd obviously had her nap and bath and was now wide awake, ready for her next adventure. I wish I had half her energy.

I considered canceling. With all this chaos going on, I wondered if spending time with London was the right thing for me. In her text, she emphasized her desire for it to be just the two of us tomorrow. But she had to know I had no one else to watch Abby for me. My daughter would have to come along. I thought about reminding London of the fact, but I didn't want her to call and pressure me into getting a sitter. I would just bring Abby with me and see what happened.

We left the park at the same time as a few of the other families. I tried to focus on the positives as I drove. We had taken Abby to a park. She'd had a lot of fun, and nothing bad had happened to her. It sounded like an average day for a normal family, but for me, it was a big deal.

I glanced in the rearview mirror at my baby girl. She was fast asleep; she'd run herself ragged today. After also having a late night of partying, she was going to sleep well tonight.

"What's all this?" Brad asked, lowering his cell phone.

I looked ahead at what he was staring at and saw a wall of red brake lights. There was police activity and the clear markings of a sobriety checkpoint.

"Slow down," he said as I approached a stationary car in front. I had to apply the brakes harder than normal and came within a few feet of a Honda Odyssey minivan. There had been plenty of people out today enjoying the nice weather, so of course, the police set up a checkpoint. It was probably part of their 'Drive Sober' campaign I'd been hearing about. Brad and I gawked ahead at a flurry of police cars and officers.

"They've got nothing better to do on a Sunday afternoon?" Brad asked, shaking his head.

I shrugged. "They're just doing their jobs."

"I know. Still, I hate these checkpoints. Glad I'm not driving."

I turned to him and wondered what was putting him on edge about the traffic stop. Was he bothered by the inconvenience of the checkpoint, or was he worried about something else regarding the law?

I added nothing to our one-sided conversation and began a slow crawl behind the minivan. The traffic started and stopped as some cars were waved on to bypass the checkpoint. Hopefully, I wouldn't be stopped. Police officers made me nervous.

"I don't understand why they are doing this during the day," Brad said. "Why not a Saturday night?"

"Yeah," I muttered, biting back my thoughts. Brad was the kind of man who loved to criticize anyone and everyone, as if he were perfect. Fortunately, I wasn't on the receiving end of it most of the time. But it made me wonder if he held back on me to spare my feelings. Did he think I couldn't handle any judgment, that I was too fragile?

I gripped the steering wheel tightly, enough to make my knuckles turn white. My nostrils flared as a sudden fury flowed through my chest. I couldn't explain. I let go of the wheel and shook out my hands. What was happening?

"Good thing Abby's asleep," Brad said, twisting to look at the backseat.

"Uh-huh," I replied, my voice flat. I exhaled and made the rising anger leave my body. It took a few moments, but it worked.

Brad wasn't wrong about it being good that Abby was asleep. The few times she had seen this many police officers were when we had passed car accidents. If she saw the checkpoint, she'd be concerned that something bad had occurred. She was a gentle soul who didn't like to see people hurt. We did our best to explain such circumstances.

I stared at the flashing lights and shuddered. I wasn't the most confident driver on a good day. That wasn't my problem, though. The lights were pulling at the depths of my mind, drowning me in a pressure I didn't want to face. I wished Brad could take over, but the idea was impossible given the eagle eye the officers had on each car.

It was our turn to approach the checkpoint. I wasn't religious or anything, but I found myself praying to God to be let by without needing to stop. The nearest officer in the line shifted her gaze to mine and sent a flutter to my heart. She waved me on.

Without thinking, I slowed down as if I'd been told to stop. The officer looked annoyed and made a big gesture to wave me through. We reduced the flow of traffic as a result, adding to the chaos. I mouthed *sorry* and sped up again.

We bypassed the line of cars that had been instructed to stop. The path ahead was still crawling, but we were progressing along and would soon be clear of the delay. The lights from the police cars danced in my mirrors and pulled my attention. I stared at the red and blue beacons and felt their tug. They drew me in. They took me back to that day, back to that park, back to that shadow that—

"No," I muttered, shaking off the memories before they could form. My grip on the steering wheel went slack as dizziness overtook me.

"What is it? Are you okay?" Brad asked.

"Uh, yeah," I said, recovering. "I'm fine. Just wish this traffic would clear up."

He leaned forward in his seat with a narrowed gaze. "Shouldn't be long from the look of things."

"That's good," I replied, gripping the wheel again. My sudden dizzy spell evaporated as quickly as it came. This happened when I let things build up in my mind. As long as I didn't think about the past, I could keep it under control.

We were almost through. In a few minutes, we'd be on our way back home, and I'd have a chance to read the article. I'd probably find nothing and realize I was overreacting to what I thought I saw on Brad's face last night. Then everything would get back to normal.

With a sigh, I focused my attention on the road. The traffic should have been clearing up, but ahead, a car had broken down just past the checkpoint, of all places.

"You've got to be kidding me," Brad said.

"It's okay," I muttered. "We'll be home soon." But I wasn't speaking to him. I was giving myself a pep talk. The stress of the drive would be over soon enough. I just had to hold on.

I glanced back to check on Abby, but something caught my eye far behind. It made no sense. It couldn't be real.

It was him.

The man from the park. The one from five years ago. I couldn't make out his face, but I *knew* it was him. He was standing in the distance with a hoodie on over his head and had that same domineering stance I saw that day.

"You—"

We slammed into the back of the minivan. Ripples of thunder pulsated through the car, leaving the windshield cracked and splintered. The jolt of the crash was like a meaty slap to the chest.

"Jesus," Brad yelled.

With the car stopped, I immediately spun to check on Abby and saw her brows screw in tight as her eyes darted left and right.

"Mommy?" her voice squeaked as she clutched her rabbit tight. Before I could reassure her that everything was fine, she burst into tears.

"Oh, baby, you're okay. You're okay. We just had a little accident."

"What the hell?" Brad roared.

I shook my head and ignored him as I took my seatbelt off. I exited the car and opened Abby's door. She tried to leap from her booster seat toward me, but was still strapped in.

"Mommy!" she cried. I unbuckled her, then pulled her in tight. I patted her back and hushed her as best I could.

Brad stared at me with both his palms raised from the front seat. "What was that?"

I continued to ignore him and struggled to locate the man I'd seen, the one who'd distracted me. He was gone.

"He was here," I whispered.

"Who was here?" Brad asked.

"Nothing," I said quickly, glancing past him as the driver of the minivan stepped out of his car. He rubbed the back of his neck and glared straight at us.

"Brad," I begged, directing him with my eyes. He faced the front of the car and sighed when he saw the upset driver I had just rear-ended. "Great. Just great. Exactly what I need today." Brad shook his head, then climbed out. He approached the minivan driver and did his best to calm the man down. Abby continued to bawl in my hands.

"It's okay, baby. Mommy's here. Nothing's going to happen to you. Okay? Ever. I'll keep you safe."

Abby nodded and sniffed as I held her as tightly as I could. Brad and the man conversed as a police officer joined in. Their exchange soon turned into an argument. Hands were waved, and some choice words were thrown around. The driver behind us stomped on their horn, adding to the confusion.

This was supposed to be an enjoyable afternoon at a park. What had I done?

CHAPTER TWENTY-ONE

After the police officer cleared a few traffic cones for us, Brad moved my car over to the side of the road. We then exchanged insurance information with the fuming minivan driver and realized my SUV wasn't safe to drive.

"Can we go home?" Abby asked.

"Soon, baby. I promise." I pulled her in tight as cars full of curious faces continued to pass us by. Had I seen him? Had I really seen the man from the park from five years ago? It didn't seem possible.

I pushed the ridiculous thought from my mind as best I could.

As we waited for a tow truck to arrive, Brad gave Fletcher a call. We needed someone to take us home, and Brad didn't want to spring for an Uber — or so he'd said. I suspected he was just using the expense as an excuse to see his friend.

"Fletcher," Brad shouted over the noise of the traffic. "Thank God you answered."

Fletcher always picked up when Brad called him. So instead of a peaceful trip home in a rideshare, I'd have to endure the Brad and Fletcher hour. I suppose it could be worse.

Brad and Fletcher went way back. They had been roommates in college and had kept in contact over the years. To this day, they catch up every two to three weeks.

Fletcher was around a lot more after we lost Imy. And as painful as it was to admit, he was instrumental in helping Brad get through the harder days. I should feel a deeper sense of appreciation for Fletcher. He'd been a stable friend for Brad and an unofficial uncle to Abby. I wanted to be on board Team Fletcher, but that ship had sailed after what happened at one of his parties.

"Thank you, thank you. You're a lifesaver," Brad said on his call to Fletcher. "I'll see you soon." He hung up and walked back to Abby and me. "Fletcher's on his way. Should be here in twenty minutes. Just depends on how long he gets stuck in this traffic."

"I thought he was working today?" I asked.

"He finished an hour ago."

"That's great," I said, flashing a grin.

"What's wrong?" Brad asked, arms outstretched. "Fletcher's helping us out of a jam. You could show a little gratitude."

Again, I knew I should have been more grateful, but I couldn't help it. Brad only partially understood how I felt about his friend. "I'm sorry," I said, "I'm just tired."

Brad's eyes narrowed as if he were trying to analyze me. He seemed to settle on not pushing the topic and asked, "Is that why you had this accident? Or is there something else going on?" He pointed to the front end of my car. The damage had rippled its way around the sides to one door.

I didn't want to let Brad in on the truth. He was already trying to send me to see Dr. Corbyn. If I told him I had crashed my car because I swore I saw that man from five years ago, then he'd have enough ammunition to force me into more than just an extra session. Brad had accused me of having paranoid thoughts in the past. I didn't need to make it easier for him to justify having me placed in psychiatric care. Not again.

"I was tired," I replied.

Brad homed in on my lie with a piercing gaze, but he didn't press me any further. Instead, he dropped to Abby's level and checked if she was okay. The two of them chatted away, leaving me to my own thoughts.

I took a small walk to be by myself, if only for a minute. I hadn't seen that man. Not him. Not that monster. He wasn't here. Abby was safe. I told myself whatever it took to calm down.

The police lights around me didn't let up, forcing my mind to drift back to that day in the park. In moments like these, it was unavoidable and came for me like a runaway train. Sometimes I just needed to let the memories come. When they did, I prayed they would pass me by without causing too much damage.

They'd sat me down in a chair at the hospital after everything unfolded. It had been so quick. One minute, I was enjoying a pleasant time at our local park with my daughter. The next, she was gone. Her four years of life ended faster than it took for the ambulance to arrive.

The police asked me question after question at the hospital. Then they repeated those same questions and made me answer them all again. It wasn't enough to know what had happened. They needed to understand the how and the why. I didn't know what to tell them. All I could say was the truth that no one wanted to hear. It was no accident. She hadn't drowned on her own. Imogen and I weren't the only ones by the lake in the park. A man had been watching us, and when the moment was right, he drowned my daughter while I was powerless to stop him.

The police didn't believe me.

"How much longer, Mommy?" Abby asked as she walked up to me.

I blinked several times, pulling myself back to reality. "I'm not sure, baby."

"Not long," Brad said, strolling over to us. "Uncle Fletcher will be here soon."

"Yay!" Abby said. She loved Fletcher. It wasn't her fault; he often bribed her with expensive toys and chocolate. We told him not to, of course, but he never listened. Fletcher could afford to throw his money around, given how much of it he had. I never understood what he did for work, but it had something to do with the stock market. With a hint of jealousy, Brad explained it to me once. It sounded like one of those high-risk, high-reward jobs that aren't for the faint of heart or for people with families.

Since college, Brad and Fletcher had been stuck in an endless pissing contest to see who was more successful. From the way I saw things, defining success was a relative term. For some, it was all about money and status. For others, it was about family and happiness. But for Brad and Fletcher, it was the former.

They bragged about promotions, returns on investments, what car they drove, and how much they spent on haircuts. It was exhausting, and frankly, a waste of time. The two men were on different planes of existence in terms of lifestyle. You couldn't compare a family man with a single playboy.

A few minutes later, Fletcher arrived in one of his many impractical two-door sports cars. He didn't have any children, so he'd never had to worry about owning anything as boring as a minivan or a Toyota Highlander.

"Brad," Fletcher called as he exited his Porsche. I stared at the exorbitant vehicle and wondered how Abby and I were going to cram into the back seat for the ride home. We all knew Brad would be up front with Fletcher.

"Thanks for doing this," Brad said, as the two men approached each other. They met in the middle and slapped hands together in a rugged handshake.

"Anything for you, Brad," Fletcher said, squeezing Brad's elbow with his spare hand. Then he spotted me and released his grip. "Maia, how are you?"

I summoned the smile I'd used at our anniversary dinner and returned his greeting. "Hi, Fletcher." He marched over to me, arms out wide, and drew me into a firm hug. He knew I wasn't a hugger, but it didn't stop him. I swore he did it on purpose. Just another excuse to touch me.

"Apologies for not making the dinner last night. Had an early start on a Sunday of all things."

"It's fine," I said.

"What happened, Maia?" he asked after pulling away. He still had two hands on my shoulders.

"I'm not sure. I think—"

"Wait, let me guess. You were daydreaming about yours truly."

Fletcher laughed louder than the traffic at his own joke. I responded with some fake laughter to keep him happy. It didn't take long for him to home in on Abby and step away from me. I moved back from the group and lost my smile. Fletcher turned on the charm with my daughter, as always, much to Abby's delight.

Brad and Fletcher exchanged pleasantries with their arms crossed over their puffed-out chests. I overheard them talking about the accident I'd had and the damage done to the car. Each of them gave their unwanted expert opinion.

"Can we go home, Mommy?" Abby asked.

I faced her and looked down into her glossy eyes. "Yes. Uncle Fletcher's here now. We'll be home soon enough. And then I think it's time we watched a little TV to rest."

Abby jumped up and down at the prospect of more TV. I had to stop plonking her down in front of the box when I got overwhelmed, but that's what happened most days. I often needed time to myself, but to keep her close by. It was the only way to get my head straight. And when we got home, I was going to tend to something important: the news article.

I quickly realized Fletcher would be the perfect distraction.

CHAPTER TWENTY-TWO

Brad and Fletcher didn't disappoint. They talked nonstop the entire way home. I swear the journey took three times longer than normal. I'd read somewhere that our brains process the passing of time depending on the situation we find ourselves in. Since I couldn't zone out from the conversation Brad and Fletcher were having, I was stuck taking in every second of it. I usually had the opposite problem when it came to my concentration, but after seeing that man on the side of the road and crashing my car, I was on full alert. It was like I was trapped in survival mode.

I scrunched my legs tightly in the tiny back seat of Fletcher's Porsche with Abby. The smell of the leather upholstery was getting to me. Abby seemed okay, humming away to herself. We'd taken her booster seat from my car and installed it safely into Fletcher's sports car. Everyone was fine and comfortable except for me.

We eventually got back home after hitting multiple swells of traffic. The delay at the police checkpoint ensured we got caught up with everyone else who thought it was a nice day to head out of town. That part didn't surprise me. What I didn't expect was Fletcher's reaction. He stayed calm and level the whole time. He was usually a bit of a reckless driver, from what Brad had told me. Maybe having Abby in the car made him think twice about speeding.

We finally arrived home. As soon as Fletcher pulled into our driveway and stopped, I rushed to get Abby and myself out of the car. I didn't know how much longer I could have existed in that cramped space. I helped Abby climb down and felt grateful for some fresh air.

"Mommy?" Abby asked, her tone sweet. "Are you okay?"

"Yeah, sweetheart. I'm good. I just need a second to stretch my legs. It was a bit squishy in there."

Abby giggled. "Not for me."

"Sorry about that," Fletcher said. "I can honestly say that's the first time anyone's used the backseat. For driving, that is." He burst out laughing again as he gave Brad a friendly elbow to the stomach.

I ignored the inappropriate joke that went straight over Abby's head and took her inside. "Thank you for the ride," I muttered to Fletcher as we passed.

"Any time, Maia. The four of us should catch up next weekend. Maybe head out for lunch. My treat."

"Sounds good," I said over my shoulder with a strained smile. And when I saw Fletcher's eyes, I found that glint of animosity that was always there. It faded in an instant as Fletcher went back into charming mode for Brad. I had thought many times about telling Brad who Fletcher really was, but I didn't want to come between them. Brad seemed to need Fletcher. I also had my doubts if Brad would believe me if I said something bad about his best friend. Fletcher could do no wrong in Brad's mind.

I took Abby inside and set her down with a late afternoon snack and some TV. It would give me a chance to start dinner and find time to read that article. I couldn't believe how long it had taken me to do so. The thought of it had been rattling around in my head since I'd read the headline. I'd contemplated looking it up while in Fletcher's car, but I didn't want to deal with any potential consequences that might come from reading the article in a confined space with nowhere to go. I still had no idea what awaited me, but I had a sinking feeling it wouldn't be positive.

With Abby sorted and dinner started, I finished doing some quick tidying up and finally had time to myself. Brad was still out front, still chatting away to Fletcher. They wouldn't be done for a while. It was funny — my husband could talk to his friend for hours on end, but if I wanted to discuss something important with him, it was an absolute chore.

With Brad distracted, I opened my cell phone's browser and reloaded the article from four years ago. The story filled my screen again, waiting to be read. There was no going back now. I had to read this. With a sharp breath in, I started.

LOCAL BROOKFIELD TERRACE MAN MISSING

A local man from Brookfield Terrace has been reported missing since Tuesday evening, sparking concerns among residents.

Oswald Taylor, 42, was last seen leaving his home on Elm Street at approximately 7.30 p.m. on Tuesday. According to family members, Taylor, a known hiking enthusiast, was believed to be heading toward the nearby Cliff Woods, a popular local spot for evening walks and nature activities.

"We are deeply concerned for Oswald's well-being," said Julia Taylor, Oswald's wife. "It's not like him to be gone this long without contacting anyone. We are desperate for his safe return and beg anyone who might have seen him to come forward."

The Brookfield Terrace Police Department has launched a full-scale search operation, employing drones and search dogs in the Cliff Woods area. Local volunteers have also organized search parties, combing the surrounding areas for any signs of Taylor.

Taylor is described as 6 feet tall, with short brown hair and green eyes. He was last seen wearing a blue jacket, black hiking pants, and a red backpack.

"We are doing everything we can to locate Mr. Taylor," said Police Chief Noah Stone. "We ask residents to remain vigilant and report any information that could aid in the search."

The local community has rallied on social media, sharing Taylor's photo and information, hoping for clues to his whereabouts. The Taylor family has expressed gratitude for the support and the efforts of the Brookfield Terrace Police Department.

Anyone with information regarding Oswald Taylor's whereabouts is encouraged to contact the Brookfield Terrace Police Department immediately.

Brookfield Terrace News, reporting for our community

I scrolled down to the photo of Oswald Taylor. My cell phone slipped from my fingers. It bounced on the kitchen bench with a hideous thud. I snatched up my phone again and didn't see much damage, but a cracked screen was the least of my worries.

I took another look. Memories came to me. Ones I wished I could erase. His face had been a blur, but now I could see it as clear as day. There was no longer a shadow.

Oswald Taylor looked identical to the man I'd seen that day in the park. The man who'd drowned my daughter. He was smiling in the picture, gripping the straps of a backpack with both arms, dressed as if he were someone who enjoyed hiking.

"You," I seethed through clenched teeth. Painful memories played in my head on repeat. Then a fire filled my insides and threatened to spill from my very being. This monster had dragged my little girl into the lake at the park and filled her lungs with water. All while I screamed at him to stop. By the time he'd let go, it was too late. He'd killed her and rushed to leave while I tried in vain to save her.

The man I'd seen on the side of the road and in the mirror wasn't real. That much I understood. My mind had conjured him up to remind me of that day. As devastating as it was to remember the worst moment of my entire existence, I only had one question on my mind: how did Brad find him?

My head throbbed.

No one had believed me that day. Brad included. I'd told the police and Brad about the man who had drowned Imogen, but the possibility was dismissed. No one else had witnessed what he'd done to my baby, so the incident was ruled an accident. But if Brad hadn't believed me back then, along with everyone else, why had he been looking at an old news article with a photo of Imogen's killer?

There was only one possibility, and it was sending a jolt of fear through my core. Maybe Brad *had* believed me that day. Maybe he'd even tracked this Oswald Taylor down.

Maybe my husband had killed this man.

I heard the front door open as Fletcher took off in his Porsche. Brad chuckled as he came inside. With jittering hands, I lifted my phone and placed my back against the kitchen door. I deleted my browsing history three times in a row and double-checked that the site was gone. I could easily find it again later, but I couldn't risk Brad seeing it on my phone now. Not when I didn't fully understand what I had found.

I turned to the dinner I'd started on the stove and prayed Brad didn't want to talk to me. There was no telling what I would say if he saw my face.

CHAPTER TWENTY-THREE

Brad

It had been a long day, made even worse by Maia's little accident earlier. Her rear-ending that Honda minivan had me questioning just how much she knew. If she had found that article on my cell phone and visited the site, maybe what she read had distracted her to the point she couldn't concentrate. Or maybe she was exhausted from the social pressures of last night's party. Whatever it was, I had no way of knowing without being direct, and it was driving me up the wall.

I was thankful when Fletcher took my call. Even if it was only to have someone to talk to, he has always had my back, no matter the problem. "What's going on with Maia?" Fletcher had asked me as we talked outside my house. "I mean, I'm used to a cold shoulder, but not that damn icy."

"Sorry about that," I'd said.

"Don't sweat it. I've had worse. So what's up with her?"

"It's nothing."

"Come on," Fletcher said, moving closer to me. "We both know it's not nothing."

"I shouldn't say."

"Is it about . . . you know?"

"Maybe."

"Maybe? That doesn't sound promising."

A thought crossed my mind before I spoke again. Maybe telling Fletcher a few things could benefit me. My suggestion to Maia of seeking extra therapy hadn't gone down well. I knew it wouldn't. I was just trying to plant the idea in her mind that her behavior had pushed me to contact Dr. Corbyn. With enough pressure, maybe she'd think twice about reacting to that article and forget what she'd read. Fletcher could help me with my problem.

He flicked me on the arm with the back of his hand. "Come on, Brad. It's me. We've been through it all."

I sighed, glancing around to make sure Maia or Abby weren't nearby, and then I said, "Okay, I'll tell you, but you have to promise me you won't say a word to anyone."

"Of course," he nodded, but I wanted him to say something. I wanted Fletcher to share what I had to say with everyone he knew. History told me he wouldn't be able to help himself. He was only good at keeping big secrets. The kinds you took to your grave.

The more people who heard about Maia's declining mental health, the easier it would be for me to discredit anything crazy she might share with anyone foolish enough to listen. It was a cruel and poorly thought-out plan, but the alternative was a step I didn't want to take.

I filled Fletcher in on Maia's current condition. I told him how she had been struggling emotionally after the anniversary dinner, and how she had been confusing her memories. I told him I was concerned about her mental health. To be honest, it wasn't much of an exaggeration.

"I suggested she see her therapist sooner than planned," I said.

"How'd she take it?" Fletcher asked.

"Not well. She freaked out and started accusing me of all kinds of things that weren't true. She got so angry that I'm pretty sure it's what led to her rear-ending that minivan." I shook my head and turned away from Fletcher, feeling like a character in a soap opera. "I should have been driving, but it was a long day after a long night. I just wanted a break."

"Hey, don't beat yourself up," Fletcher said in a hushed voice. "You're doing what you can to help. Just like always. Sounds to me like she needs to see someone, and fast. Maybe she wasn't ready for the dinner party."

"I've been wondering the same thing myself," I admitted.

A moment of silent understanding passed between us before Fletcher spoke again. "I'm sorry to hear it. Is there anything I can do to help?"

"No. You've done enough for me for one lifetime. This isn't your problem. It's mine. I'm going to contact Maia's therapist tonight and book her in for a session tomorrow. I don't know how I'll get her there, but I will. I can't just stand by and wait for her to do the right thing."

"That sounds like a smart plan. If you need my help with anything, you call me. Day or night. Got it?"

"Thank you. I just might."

"Okay," Fletcher said, sounding like I had unloaded too much on him at once. And I had, which would compel him to tell a certain someone and spread the gossip. No one could hold on to that kind of information for long.

After pacing a bit, Fletcher changed the subject to something more cheerful. We chatted for a few more minutes, shifting from serious talk to golf.

"Well, I better head off," Fletcher said. "Got to meet you know who."

"That's still going on, huh?" I asked.

It was Fletcher's turn to glance around and make sure no one was listening. "I can't say much, but she's a firecracker."

We shared a laugh and shook hands. "You should probably go before she hunts you down. Thanks for the help today."

"Anytime. You know I'd do anything for you, Brad."

And he would. A long time ago, I helped Fletcher with a major tax problem he was having — one that came close to bankrupting him. I made it all go away with some crafty accounting work using my experience as an internal auditor. It's safe to say that I helped him avoid prison time. But I cashed in that favor four years ago and then some.

I headed inside. Leaving Maia alone for too long wasn't a good idea. Not until I knew where her head was with this article business.

"Hey," Fletcher called out just before reaching his car. "I've been meaning to ask. Have you told Maia yet about . . . ?"

The bridge of my nose wrinkled as I feigned trying to figure out what Fletcher was hinting at. "*That*. No, not yet. And with everything going on, it might be a challenge, you know?"

Fletcher gave me a crooked grin. "Yeah, I get it. Maybe once this has all blown over."

"Exactly."

Fletcher got in his car and left without another word. I continued to the front door.

Before my fatigue took over, I called Dr. Corbyn's office. Being a Sunday meant it was after hours, so I left a concerned message about Maia's mental health. With any luck, Dr. Corbyn's administrative assistant would hear a certain level of desperation in my voice. It was all part of the show.

As I opened the front door, there was a bit of optimism in my step. Fletcher would spread the word about Maia's struggles. Her doctor would call in the morning. And within a few days, everyone we knew would have heard all about it. Each person who caught wind of the situation would embellish the story of Maia's problems. If she accused me of anything from that news article, I would have a defense to fall back on. Now I just needed to get her to see Dr. Corbyn to seal the deal.

I wasn't enjoying what I was doing. Despite everything, I loved my wife. But I was trying to save her from something far worse than a bit of public humiliation. She didn't know how awful this problem could get if she let it.

I walked into the living room and said hello to Abby. She barely registered my presence. I couldn't compete with a flashy cartoon, so I moved to the kitchen. When I opened the door, I found Maia cooking dinner. She was stirring a pan of sizzling stir-fry vegetables that Abby wasn't a huge fan of. I couldn't see her eyes, but her focus was on the pan like there was nothing else in the world. I needed to see if anyone was home.

"Fletcher was thinking we could play a round of golf next weekend. Would that be okay?"

Maia kept stirring the pan with a wooden spoon in slow circles, like I wasn't in the room. She was daydreaming again. It was getting worse. I stepped around to her side and leaned in. She gasped when I came into her peripheral vision. "Whoa," I said. "It's just me."

"Sorry," she said, short of breath, her eyes darting about the kitchen like prey searching for its predator.

"Is everything okay?"

"Uh, yeah. Just a little rattled from the accident, I think."

"Okay," I said, staring through her lie. She glanced away from me like sustained eye contact wasn't possible, and I knew why. Without a doubt, I knew exactly what had her so on edge. It was practically written on her face.

She had read the article.

CHAPTER TWENTY-FOUR

Maia

After dinner, I gave Abby a bath and got her off to bed. Brad stayed in the living room, watching some comedy series on TV that I didn't really care about. When I came down to sit with him, he hardly said a word to me. I took a cautious seat next to him. After all, I was ninety-nine percent certain he was a killer.

Within a few minutes, I pulled out my cell phone and started scrolling through Facebook, making sure Brad could see my screen. Our roles had been reversed from earlier in the day. I had no way of knowing for certain, but I believed he knew I had read the article. There was an energy about him that told me so. When he came inside and found me making dinner, I'm sure I gave everything away the moment our eyes met.

Now, he was watching me. He wasn't directly staring, but I could feel his sideways glances.

After I read about Oswald Taylor, I couldn't help my visceral reaction. I knew Brad was coming into the kitchen while I was making dinner, but I froze up the second he got close. When he leaned around to get my attention, I reacted without meaning to. It was about the dumbest thing I could have done. It made me wonder if it was safe for me to be alone with him. I've never been

126

afraid of my husband, but if what I suspected about Brad was true, then everything had changed.

My brain barely registered the images as I scrolled through my Instagram feed. All I could think about was Oswald Taylor. It was surreal to put a name to the face that had been in and out of my mind for five years. But it was even harder to think Brad may have killed him. It wasn't like I hadn't wished death upon Imogen's killer or that I hadn't imagined myself drowning the man with my bare hands. It was all just too much to process.

"Where are you going?" Brad asked as I stood to leave the living room.

"Uh, to bed," I said in a timid voice. "It's been a long day. You can keep watching your show." I offered him the warmest smile I could manage, but I doubted it would be enough to keep him at bay.

He stared at me for a while longer with a face I knew all too well. He was weighing up his options, trying to decide whether to come to bed or stay up. On one hand, he needed to keep tabs on what I was up to, but on the other, if he followed me, it would be obvious what he was doing. I left before he could make up his mind.

Brad didn't follow. I glanced back a few times to make sure, feeling like there was a lion stalking me. How long was I supposed to keep this up? The rest of my life? Or until he decided he needed to do something about me. I could run to the nearest police station, but there was no point. I had no evidence other than an old article about a missing man who I alone believed had killed our daughter. Plus, Brad was treating me like I'd gone off the deep end. That's why he was talking about an unscheduled session with Corbyn. No, I needed to find out more about Oswald Taylor before making such a rash decision as going to the police.

Before I went to bed, I checked in on Abby. She was already sound asleep, sprawled out in an awkward position. Imogen used to sleep the same way. It killed me how much they were alike. But that wouldn't last long. Abby would grow older and would change. All the while, Imogen would stay four years old for eternity. I could never picture her any other way.

I kneeled down and brushed a strand of Abby's hair out of her face, but it fell back into place, defiant of what I wanted. I tried to move it again, but the strand felt somehow thicker and wet.

"What?" I whispered, twisting the hair between my fingers. Water flowed from the thin lock and down the palm of my hand. I stood and took a step back, seeing that Abby's hair was saturated. But I had dried it after her bath. I'd used a towel and a hair dryer. I didn't understand.

As I stumbled farther away from Abby, my feet landed in what could only be a deep puddle. My socks soaked right through to my skin. When I looked down, the entire floor in Abby's room was underwater. This was impossible.

I charged back to my daughter and found her drenched from head to toe. Her wet hair had covered her face. The water level rose as I moved, splashing the cold liquid in all directions.

"Abby," I called out as I dropped to pick her up, but something pulled me away. I fell into the ice-cold water up to my chest. As I struggled to stand again, a crashing wave engulfed Abby's bed. She didn't move as the bubbling torrent in her room washed up and over her entire body. I tried to yell her name again, but I choked on a mouthful of water. It stung my nostrils and burned my lungs as the levels rose past my chin. When the water filled the room, I could no longer see Abby. I went under.

I heaved in a lungful of air and gasped awake. Patting around in the dark, my eyes came into focus and found a soft, dull glow of light leaking in from the hallway. I was in my room, in my bed. But how? I had been checking on Abby, then . . .

Sweat coated my forehead as I struggled to catch my breath. Brad was snoring beside me. I reached for my cell phone and picked it up with clammy hands. I checked the time and saw that it was two in the morning. When did I come to bed? I had left Brad downstairs and was stopping by Abby's room to see if she was okay. Then all hell broke loose, and the room filled with water.

It felt so real.

I pushed the tangle of covers away and swung my legs over the edge of the bed. Brad was sound asleep, facing away from me on his side of the bed. My heart was still galloping in my chest, and there was only one way to calm it down. I had to see her, just to be sure. I needed to see Abby.

With my cell phone in hand, I slipped out of the room and padded down the hallway. Cool air wrapped around me like a shroud. Remnants of the dream clung to my every step.

When I got to Abby's room, I hesitated at the door. My hand trembled as I reached for the knob. I still couldn't understand how that was just a dream. It was all so terrifyingly real. Maybe more of a hallucination than anything. Either way, I apparently went straight to bed last night and had no memory of doing so. That section of time was gone. I took a deep breath and tried to steady my thoughts.

When I opened Abby's door, I found her room bathed in the soft ambiance of the nightlight we always left on for her. Abby was there, peaceful and undisturbed, in her bed. Her chest rose and fell the way it was supposed to, and her hair was splayed out on the pillow, dry.

Relief drowned out the thoughts in my head as I stepped into the room. I shouldn't have disturbed her like this, but I just wanted to make sure she was real and brush the softness of her cheek with the back of my hand. I dropped by her side and did so. Abby reacted to my touch but didn't wake.

I stood and stayed in her room for a moment longer. Then I planted a gentle kiss on her forehead and left.

I had to keep her safe. No matter what it took.

CHAPTER TWENTY-FIVE

After I closed Abby's door, I contemplated going back to bed. But I knew I wouldn't be able to sleep. Not until my mind could slow down its racing thoughts. The thought of lying down beside a potential killer was too much.

With some time to myself, I headed downstairs with my cell phone and sat at the breakfast bar. One glass of water and two aspirins later, a sense of calm washed over me. The hallucination was still fresh in my brain, but I felt like I was back in control of myself again.

By habit, I stood to leave the kitchen and head to our second living room to read. But as much as I'd have loved to get lost in a story, I didn't have the time. I needed to do some digging.

I decided to use my midnight wake-up as an opportunity to investigate who this Oswald Taylor was. Or is. He could have still been alive. All I knew for certain was that the man I'd seen in the news article was the one who had drowned Imogen. I had blocked out his face for some time, but I could never forget this monster.

"Oswald Taylor," I said out loud. Was he alive, or had my husband dispensed justice on this piece of dirt and killed him four years ago?

I was still in shock. Things had progressed at a stagger-ing rate since the dinner party. And there seemed to be a silent acknowledgment between Brad and me. The way I saw it, we were each aware of the article. But what that meant, I had no idea. All I could do was make wild guesses.

Brad joked that he'd once killed a man. But I was positive it was no joke. He'd killed Oswald Taylor. That was what this was all about. Of course, it wouldn't be hard to argue that these thoughts were far-reaching and were all in my head, but they were there and were refusing to be ignored.

I settled on the small sofa in the second living room, using the light from the passageway to the kitchen to see. I unlocked my cell phone and searched for the article online a second time. I should have saved it when I had the chance, but I didn't want to risk Brad finding proof I'd read the story.

Part of me wondered if I should just come out and ask Brad about Oswald Taylor. Would that be smart? Or would I be risking more than an awkward conversation? Not that I thought Brad would ever harm me. I'd never seen him be violent in his life, especially not toward me. And yet, here we were.

I found the article and reread it. Then two more times for good measure. What did it all mean? Brad had looked at that website at two in the morning and lied to me about it. He said he'd been asleep all night. But his phone had told me otherwise. He was on that specific website, reading that exact article, when I was out of the room.

I bookmarked the story and searched for the name Oswald Taylor. Not much came up — just a few clones of the article. I checked them all. None had any updates. It was like this man went missing one year after he'd murdered our daughter, and that was the end of it. But there had to be more to the story.

Further down, I found a different article that wasn't as old as the first one. It also contained a video. With a sharp breath in, I hit the play button. After watching an annoying advertisement, the video played. There wasn't much to it. Just a follow-up story interviewing the last person to have seen Oswald alive. It was just like the original article had said. He was out at night walking somewhere he frequented a lot, and was never seen again. Was that when Brad had done it? At night?

The camera panned to the edge of Cliff Woods. Brad and I had walked there a few times in the past with Imogen. The area had been relaxing to me, but now there was a sinister energy about it I couldn't shake. What had gone on in those woods four years ago?

A creak groaned in the kitchen. It must have been Brad. On occasion, he would wake up when I had left our room and would come down to check on me. I rushed to grab a novel from the bookshelf and opened it to a random page. I shoved my cell phone down the side of the sofa, hiding it in the cushions.

I was breathing too fast for the book I'd grabbed: *The History of the Decline and Fall of the Roman Empire* by Edward Gibbon. Crap. It was one of Brad's books. I fumbled with the tome and struggled to jam it back in the bookshelf as Brad left the kitchen and walked straight into the room I was in. Our eyes met in the half-light.

"I thought I'd find you here," Brad said. "Couldn't sleep?"

"Yeah. Sorry if I woke you."

He waved me off, pursing his lips. "I'm not sleeping well myself, so don't stress. Did you have a bad dream again?"

I stared at him, wondering how that question had come to him. He had been fast asleep when I'd shot awake.

"It's okay if you don't want to talk about it," he said.

"No, it's fine. I was having another nightmare. A bad one."

Brad walked farther into the room and sat beside me. He leaned back on the sofa and placed an arm around me. His touch sent a rod up my spine. It took everything in me not to overreact.

"Let's hear it," he said.

"You want me to tell you about my dream?"

"Yeah. Maybe it'll do you good to talk about it."

I hesitated for a moment, unsure if I should indulge him. Brad's concern seemed genuine, but I didn't want to talk about what had happened. Not with what I thought he was capable of. Plus, he was pushing for me to see Corbyn. I didn't need to give Brad more ammunition to make that happen. "It was nothing," I said.

"I'm sure it wasn't nothing."

I sighed. "It's not important. It was a stupid dream that freaked me out. There's no cause for concern."

Brad nodded. "Okay, sure. But maybe this one is worth talking about."

My skin bristled at his words as I pulled away from him. "I don't feel like it, okay?"

"Whoa. I'm just trying to talk to you."

"Are you? Or did you come down here to check on your crazy wife?" I could hear myself overreacting, but at the same time, I couldn't help it. There was a sudden rage inside me, itching to come out. I needed to reel myself in. Or maybe this was an opportunity to deflect a little.

"Maia, please. I didn't mean to—"

"I know what this is about," I said, cutting him off. I removed his arm from my shoulders. "You're trying to convince me to see Dr. Corbyn sooner than planned, aren't you?"

Brad's expression hardened. "No, I just want to help you."

"By checking on me with that look? By thinking every bad dream I have is a sign I'm falling apart?"

"Don't be stupid," he said, swiping a hand through the air.

"So I'm stupid now?"

"You know what I mean. God, this is so typical. I'm going out of my way to make sure you're okay, and this is the thanks I get."

"No, Brad. There's more to it than that. You think you can fix me after what happened to Imy? Well, I've got news for you: nothing's ever going to fix that. She's gone. She's dead. And it's all my fault." The words hung heavy between us. There was a moment of silence as I grappled with what had just slipped out of my mouth. Where had that come from?

"It wasn't your fault," he said with a certainty that wasn't simple pandering. "And I'm not trying to fix you, Maia. Nothing can ever change the past — for either of us. I just miss my wife. I miss us."

His words hit me like a gut punch. Forget the dark looks he'd been giving me. Forget the article. Forget the man he may have killed. And forget that damn game last night. This was the real Brad. He was still in there. "I know," I whispered. "I miss us too."

The conversation lingered as we sat in silence. I didn't know what else to say. I moved closer to him and allowed Brad to wrap his arms around me. His honesty made me forget everything. I pressed in tight against his chest and closed my eyes.

CHAPTER TWENTY-SIX

Brad and I chatted for another two hours. We spoke about our anniversary dinner, our friends, Abby, and, occasionally, Imogen. We rarely talked about Imy in such a way. It was always a hard conversation to have without one or both of us breaking down into sobs — usually me.

That day in the park will haunt me forever. But if I'm being honest, I can't remember everything that happened. One second, Imy was safe and playing. The next thing I knew, Oswald Taylor was dragging her under the water, and I didn't know why.

After that coward had fled, I pulled her lifeless body from the water. The lake had soaked through her clothing and hair. I'll never forget the sound of the dripping water as it flowed from her back into the lake. I tried everything I could to save her, to make her tiny lungs work again, but it was too late. Her eyes were glassy. Her body was cold. My baby was gone.

I didn't stop trying to revive her, even when the EMTs arrived. Imy just needed a few more seconds to live. They had to pull me away and restrain me in the end. All the while, I screamed for them to let me go. Imogen needed me. She needed her mommy.

At the hospital, I refused to believe that she was gone. Imogen was not dead. How could she be? Not after I'd spent four exhausting years raising her from a helpless speck to the thriving child she had become. How many nights had I sat up with her, rocking her to sleep? How many tantrums had I guided her through? How many hours of my spare time had I spent researching better ways to care for her every need? The entire point of my existence was her life.

And then, this evil beast came along and took her from me.

The police told me otherwise. They called it nothing but a tragic accident. They didn't believe me.

Our local park had a playground. And beyond that was an alluring lake with a wide body of water that was deep enough to reach over my head. They kept repeating the fact to me as if I hadn't been aware of it. They treated me like I was too hysterical to understand what had happened. According to them, no one else had been there. Nobody had witnessed a man rushing to leave the area, especially not the one I'd described.

I told them the number of times we'd visited the lake before. It wasn't unfamiliar territory for us. Brad and I had taken Imy there just two days prior without a problem. I'd never once been worried about her playing near that lake. Plus, she'd been taking swimming lessons since she was a year old. She knew how to swim, certainly enough to save her own life.

It was no accident, but I had no way of proving foul play. And the more I spoke about it, the less seriously the police took me. Oswald Taylor had gotten away with murder. Or so I'd thought.

For the longest time, I wished they'd arrested me. That they had thrown me into the darkest cell in the world and had never let me out again. I deserved it for failing to protect her, for failing to stop him. That feeling would never leave me. Still, something had changed.

I hadn't confirmed anything yet, but there was a chance Brad had brought our daughter's killer to justice. It was possible he'd given that bastard exactly what he deserved. Was I supposed to be happy about it? And if I were, if the thought of my baby's killer dying at the hands of my husband brought me joy, what kind of sick person did that make me?

I was overthinking everything.

Brad hadn't believed me back when I first told him about the man who'd murdered our baby girl. He gave me that same face the police officers did — a mix of pity and disgust. I never wanted to see that look from him again.

The following year was a blur. All I remembered from that time was a constant flow of emotions. One second, I was seething with rage. The next, I'd fall into a dark depression. But I know what I saw that day. And after seeing Oswald's photo, there was no mistaking it. He had been there. His hands had gripped Imogen's body like a vice.

Brad got me through the aftermath. When I wasn't at home hiding under my covers in the dark, I could be found at therapy. He drove me to every session. He had to manage my grief and his own. I don't know how he survived.

Then, after a year of this suffering, I discovered I was pregnant with Abby. Everything changed again. In an instant, I regained a sense of hope and purpose. The future was looking bright. But when Abby was born and I held her in my arms for the first time, panic filled my heart. Someone was going to come along and take her from me, just like Oswald had. I was going to lose my child again. I couldn't shake the thought. And to this day, I haven't. No matter what I tell myself, I will always be afraid.

"We should go to bed," Brad said.

"I know. I'm supposed to meet with London in the morning for coffee."

"You should cancel."

"No, I can't. I haven't been out with her in the longest time. You know what she's like if she gets ignored for too long. She'll do something reckless."

Brad chuckled and stared into the distance for a moment. "I honestly don't understand how the two of you are even friends. You're nothing alike."

I shrugged. "People don't have to be carbon copies of each other to be friends."

"True. I guess I've just always wondered what you talk about. I don't mean this in a bad way, but you're married with a kid. She's still out there living the party lifestyle. Someday, that's got to change."

"Maybe. But I could say the same about Fletcher, couldn't I?"

Brad's eyebrows raised. "Damn, you're right."

I shoved his shoulder. "I'm always right, honey."

He chuckled again.

I stood from the sofa and tugged on Brad's hand to follow. He resisted for a moment. "Maia?" he asked.

I glanced down and saw the question coming. I knew what he was going to say.

"Will you consider seeing Dr. Corbyn? I can make the appointment."

I stared at my husband and wondered what this man had sacrificed for me. What part of his soul had he given up to protect our family? I had no other choice but to say, "You can make the call."

CHAPTER TWENTY-SEVEN

Brad

The morning light filtered through the curtains as I sat at the breakfast bar, nursing my second cup of coffee of the day. The steam rose lazily from my mug as I held it in one hand while my other hand massaged my temple. No amount of caffeine could shake my exhaustion.

When Maia gets going on a late-night chat, it's hard to bring the conversation to an end. We used to have talks like this before we were married, back when I had the energy to sacrifice hours of sleep. But even though it had drained me, it was worth it. I could tell Maia was trusting me again. Maybe trust wasn't the right word, but she seemed to accept that I had her best interests in mind. She may have read the article, but I still had time to keep her from the rest of it.

My phone vibrated, snapping me out of my thoughts. It was a call from Dr. Corbyn's office. Perfect.

"Hello, Brad speaking."

"Good morning, Mr. Fairbanks. This is Lisa from Dr. Corbyn's office. I'm just responding to the voicemail you left us yesterday. You mentioned some concerns regarding your wife, Maia."

I took a quick breath. "Hello, Lisa. Thank you for returning my call." I explained everything to Mason's administrative assistant, recounting the events of the dinner party and the aftermath. I exaggerated Maia's behavior where I could, but I was careful not to go too far. I didn't want Lisa to think I was lying. Normally, my opinion wouldn't go far given Maia's private medical information was being discussed. But I'd had her sign a release form when she first came to Dr. Corbyn. It allowed me to speak about such matters openly with Dr. Corbyn's staff.

We went through a few more standard questions until Lisa asked if I had any other concerns Dr. Corbyn should know about before booking Maia's session.

I thought about the car accident. It had been minor, but it was worth mentioning. There could be consequences, though. Maia could lose her license. Then again, if her license was suspended, it would keep her at home and make it harder for her to dive deeper into what she had read in the article.

"There was a minor car accident," I finally said. "Maia was driving and zoned out. We were all okay, but it could have been a lot worse."

"I see. Thank you for letting me know, Mr. Fairbank. I'll pass these notes along to Dr. Corbyn. Would Maia be available for a session this afternoon?"

I glanced at the clock. I'd have to move some things around at work to take care of Abby, but I could make it happen. "Yes, thank you. That would be great."

After ending the call, I found Maia in the living room, brushing Abby's hair. "Maia," I began, "I got in touch with Dr. Corbyn's office this morning. They have an opening this afternoon. Do you think you could manage it?"

She glanced up from her brushing and seemed all too aware of Abby's presence. I made sure not to say what it was Maia was doing. Abby didn't need to learn about her mother's therapy sessions. On a typical day, we booked Maia in for an evening session, so I could be at home with Abby. We didn't want our three-year-old attending. There was a hint of resignation in Maia's eyes as she looked at me. "This afternoon?"

"I can come home early for Abby and drive you there."

Maia chewed on her lip for a moment, then nodded. "Okay. If you think it's for the best."

"It is, honey," I said, stepping into the room. "Just one extra session to get us back on track."

Maia's gaze flicked to Abby, who showed zero understanding of the conversation as she played with her bunny. I swore Abby knew more than she let on sometimes. She's had to deal with a lot since she was born. If I could get us through this, maybe Abby would avoid a therapist's chair in the future.

Maia finally looked back at me. "All right. One extra session."

I nodded, trying to keep my expression neutral. If I had read the situation correctly, it meant I'd guided Maia to therapy earlier than planned without raising suspicion. It was a fine line to walk, but a necessary one. And it was for her own good, even if she couldn't see that yet.

As Maia turned her attention back to Abby, gently detangling her hair, I stepped out of the room. I had a plan in place, at least for now. I knew it was a risky game I was playing, but if things got any worse . . .

"It won't come to that," I muttered to myself. I retreated to the kitchen to finish my coffee.

As I took a gulp of the potent brew, I felt a surge of energy. I was going to fight through this mess. I'd carry this burden — for Maia, for Abby, for all of us. The ends would justify the means, or so I hoped.

CHAPTER TWENTY-EIGHT

Maia

Brad had arranged for a rental car to be delivered to our home this morning.

The insurance company said the repairs on my car could take up to a month. With Abby loaded up in her booster seat in the back of the white rental, I ran late to meet London for coffee. I could already picture her sitting at the café, huffing and puffing as she waited for me. It was easy to enjoy such an existence when you never had to ferry a child anywhere. London has only ever had to worry about herself.

As we hit the road, the thought of caffeine was the only thing keeping my eyes open. After a slow drive through town, we reached the café and found a parking spot out front. It was a Monday morning, just after nine, so the coffee shop wasn't as busy as the roads had been, with commuters scrambling to get to work on time.

Some days, I miss having a job. I used to be an executive assistant at a mid-sized marketing and advertising agency in Syracuse. It was a fast-paced, stressful environment, and my boss was a bit of an ass most of the time, but it had been nice to have the routine and to come home with Brad after a long day. I left that job right before Imy was born.

I slid into a booth across from London and guided Abby into her spot. She'd brought along some coloring sheets to fill in to the best of her ability. Just like Imy, she loved to color. That, a few toys, and the promise of a hot chocolate would keep her entertained for the next hour. I'd already given her toast and juice for breakfast.

London's eyes flicked to Abby. "Hello, dear," she said with a forced smile. "Didn't expect to see you here."

I scanned my surroundings, then focused on London. "She goes everywhere with me. You know that."

"Yes, I know. But I figured after the dinner party, she might be ready for some playdates or whatever it is kids her age get up to."

My brow furrowed. This was not a good start. Maybe I should have canceled today like Brad suggested. I had thought about it, but his suggestion made me feel guilty. "I'm sorry. It's difficult for me to arrange a sitter. Next time, okay?"

London waved a hand dismissively. "It's fine. More the merrier and all that, right?"

I forced a smile of my own, ignoring the hint of venom in her voice. Something was going on.

We ordered our coffees, and I couldn't help but notice London seemed a touch unsettled. Her gaze kept darting around the café, and her expensive nails tapped on the table. She had always been a little restless, but this wasn't like her.

Before I could ask what was wrong, her phone rang. She glanced at the caller ID and beamed before answering. "Hey, you," she said in the affectionate voice I'd only ever heard her use around men. "No, I can't talk right now, sorry. I'll call you later, okay?"

I raised an eyebrow at her as she hung up. "New guy?"

London hesitated for a moment. "Uh, not exactly."

"One of your exes?"

"Nope."

"Wait, not the guy who stood you up the other night?"

She sighed, deflating against the table. "Yes, that one."

I frowned, ready to scold. "London! Come on, you deserve better than this."

"No, I don't," she muttered, avoiding my gaze.

"Yes, you do. Please don't give this jackass another chance. He had his shot, and he blew it."

"This is different. You don't know him like I do."

Oh, God. She was already convincing herself that this guy would be different from the rest of the pathetic men she'd dated. I could have sat back and said nothing, but frankly, I was sick of seeing this happen again and again. "I know him well enough to see that he's happy to bail on you."

"You don't understand."

I shook my head. Why did she do this to herself and allow these awful men into her life? I bit my lip, debating whether to ask who he was. It didn't matter. With any luck, he'd be gone before long.

Our coffees arrived, along with Abby's hot chocolate. Her neck straightened at the smell of her small cup. It had whipped cream and marshmallows on top. I rarely let her have this much sugar, but this was a special occasion. At least, it was supposed to be.

"That looks yummy," Abby said, her eyes wide with anticipation.

I helped Abby push her coloring to one side so she could concentrate on drinking her hot chocolate without making a gigantic mess. As I finished helping her, curiosity about London's new man got the better of me. If she was going to keep seeing him, I figured I should at least pretend to be interested in who he was. Or at the very least, know his name.

I opened my mouth to speak, but London beat me to it. "So, how have you been?"

"Fine," I lied.

London gave me a telling stare. "Come on, Maia. You can be honest with me. How have you really been? I'm sure the party would have been a lot to handle."

"Like I said, I'm fine. What's brought this on?"

"Nothing," she said, waving me off. "You just look like you could use an extra therapy session."

I blinked rapidly. "What do you mean?" London knew I saw Corbyn once a month. But she looked almost guilty, like she knew something she shouldn't. She couldn't possibly have known I had an extra session booked in for today.

London shifted in her seat. "I . . . I shouldn't say."

"Yes, you should. Did Brad tell you?" I asked, but the thought sounded insane. They didn't talk to each other. I doubted they even had each other's contact information.

"No, not Brad." She hesitated. "I heard it from Fletcher. He's the guy I've been seeing."

I almost knocked my coffee over. "Fletcher? As in Brad's Fletcher? Are you kidding me?"

She nodded, avoiding my gaze. "He mentioned Brad was worried about you. And I guess they spoke about you needing to see Dr. Corbyn sooner than later."

My heart sank. Fletcher. Of course, he'd tell her. He's a loudmouth gossip on a good day.

"It's not a big deal," London said. "Extra therapy's a good thing, trust me. I know. There's no shame in it. When I'm struggling, the first person I call is my therapist. I have her on speed dial."

London had her share of problems. And she was open about it as well. She'd told me about her childhood and how her mother would physically attack her father. On more times than she could count, London's mother had thrown an empty wine bottle at her father's head during an argument. He never once raised a hand at her in return and had spent years taking her violence.

London had even told me that her childhood was the reason she couldn't stay in a relationship for long. She always drove the men in her life away, fearing she would one day hurt them the way her mother had harmed her father. It was incredibly sad. I'd told Brad all about it once. He found it hard to believe.

I glanced at Abby, who was thankfully busy diving headfirst into her hot chocolate. I didn't like her hearing about these things.

London's hand landed on mine and gave it a tap. I pulled away without meaning to.

"Whoa, sorry," she said.

I shook my head, unable to focus. I didn't know who to be madder at — Fletcher or Brad. I tried to hide my face from the world. This felt like a violation of my privacy. Of all the people Brad could share my personal struggles with, Fletcher was not the one. I didn't mind so much that London knew, but not through a network of whispers.

"Are you okay?" London asked.

"I'm fine. No, wait. Does this mean Brad knows the two of you are dating?"

London pursed her lips, then gave me a weak smile. "I'm sorry, Maia. We weren't sure how to bring it up with you. It's no secret how you feel about Fletcher."

My mouth hung open as I pulled away from the conversation. Unbelievable. Brad was going to hear all about this the second he got home. If he thought he could break my trust and tell his loose-lipped friend about my mental health, then he had another thing coming. I realized our chat last night was just a way to get me back on his good side. What the hell kind of game was he playing?

I took a deep breath, trying to steady the whirlwind of thoughts in my mind. Abby happily colored beside me, doing her best to make her unicorn pretty. She loved the damn things. My angel was enjoying her drink, blissfully unaware of the problems clouding the world around her. If she weren't here, I would have stormed off by now.

"Are you okay?" London asked again.

I waved her off, crossing my arms over my chest. "I'll live."

"I'm sorry I brought up therapy, but this is a good thing." She inched closer to me and lowered her voice. "I can see how much you're struggling post-party."

"I'm doing fine. I just need the people I thought I could trust to not speak about me behind my back. Understand?"

"Yes," she said, retreating.

An uncomfortable silence built between us. The moment Abby finished her drink, I planned to get out of there.

"It won't be easy," London said, "but things are going to improve. God knows you've lived a sheltered existence for the last five years."

"Are you trying to piss me off today?" I snapped. After a second, I expected London to storm out on our coffee meet-up, but she held her ground.

"Maia, I love you. We've known each other forever. You've seen me at my absolute worst and have helped me more times than I can remember. Let me do the same for you."

"How?" I asked as I stared at my coffee.

"By taking you out more. Doing things like today. Hell, we could go on a double date. Fletcher and I with you and Brad. You don't have to hide at home thinking bad things are going to happen."

"You don't get it," I said, holding a palm to my face. "You never will." I leaned down and kept my voice as quiet as I could. "My daughter was killed in front of me. I was supposed to be the one to protect her. Do you honestly think going out for coffee and dinner will ever fix that?"

London retreated and didn't reply. I pulled back as well and glanced at Abby. She still had some hot chocolate left, but it was time to go.

CHAPTER TWENTY-NINE

I took Abby home after cleaning the chocolate from her face. I had planned on taking her to a few shops while we were out as part of my get-out-of-the-house-more plan, but London's confession had left a sour taste in my mouth. All I wanted was to go home and crawl under a thick blanket. Unfortunately, that wasn't an option with a three-year-old around.

As we arrived at the house, Brad texted me a time for my therapy session, the one that he and apparently the entire world knew about. It wasn't until three that afternoon. How delightful. He claimed to have called Dr. Corbyn's office in the morning, but I suspected he had left them a voicemail overnight. He was desperate to get me in there.

With time on my hands, I set Abby up with some fun activities and grabbed my cleaning supplies. Just because I'd rather hide under a rock didn't mean I could skip my schedule. Besides, I needed some distracting monotonous labor. Today, I was supposed to clean the bedrooms.

I liked to start in our bedroom first, since it was the biggest and often the messiest. Brad, while being a hard worker, could be an untidy person to live with. He was odd. He liked to keep his home office neat and perfect, but was forever leaving his clothes lying around the floor for me to pick up. I'd lost count of how many times I'd told him about it. He probably figured it was my job to handle. I'd give anything to see him run the household for a week.

I started by dusting every surface from top to bottom. The motion became almost meditative after a short time. There was something about wiping dirt and grime away that brought me peace. My thoughts drifted off with the dust particles. Cleaning was the only therapy I needed.

I made the bed, smoothing out the wrinkles in the sheets with slow, deliberate hands. Then I fluffed our pillows and gave the room a silent nod of approval.

Next, I tackled Abby's room. Her colorful toys and plush stuffed animals were strewn about the floor as per usual. I picked them up one by one, placing them back in their designated spots with precision. I knew where everything was supposed to go. The room would be chaos again before nightfall, but I reordered it all the same. I changed her sheets and took out a set of bedding with logos of her favorite cartoon characters. I couldn't help but smile at the love she had for such things. I wish I could make myself that innocent again.

With Abby's room sorted, I moved on to the last bedroom that needed my attention. I stood before the door with closed eyes. This happened every time I went into Imogen's room. My hand hovered over the doorknob the way it always did. A familiar pang tugged at my heart as I opened my eyes and focused.

Taking a deep breath, I opened the door and saw her room. The space was a snapshot in time, preserved as it had been on Imogen's last day. Her little bed was neatly made, and I had arranged her favorite stuffed animals on the pillows and had pinned the drawings she'd made for Brad and me to the bulletin board.

What I would give to see her in this room again, drawing a picture for us.

I dusted her dresser, careful not to disturb the small collection of trinkets and toys she had once cherished as if they were the most important things in the world. Kids are experts at loving everyday objects like they're more precious than some hundred-dollar toy they received for Christmas.

I ran a cloth over the picture frames on the walls and stared at Imogen's beautiful face. Each photo held a moment of her too-short life and kept those memories alive. But each day, they faded a little more from my mind. One day, I wouldn't be able to see her as clearly.

I vacuumed the carpet, sliding around her toys. I knew she was gone, but her presence was so powerful in this space. This was Imogen's room. Now and forever.

With my cleaning supplies in hand, I move to the door, ready to leave. When I took one last glance around Imogen's room, I blinked with confusion. My hand fumbled for the light switch, even though daylight spilled in from the windows. I couldn't understand what I was seeing.

The walls were bare. There were no framed photos, no bulletin board, and no bed.

Her closet was empty, and there was nothing in the room but the worn carpet and the lingering imprint where her dresser used to stand.

My knees buckled. I dropped my cleaning supplies and grabbed the doorframe to steady myself as it hit me. All of it. Imogen's room wasn't intact. It hadn't been for a long time. I'd cleared it out after her death, insisting we purge the house of her belongings. I practically boarded the room up and hadn't allowed Brad to use it for anything. It was like the room had never existed.

I stumbled into the middle of the empty space and stood there with my hands over my mouth. I turned slowly in a circle, as if Imogen's old room might reappear. But there was nothing. Just stripped walls and silence.

CHAPTER THIRTY

I rushed to leave Imy's empty room and headed to the nearest bathroom to splash water on my face. The icy liquid did what it could to distract me from the hallucination I'd just had. Once I had pulled myself together, I headed downstairs to make Abby some lunch. I knew I shouldn't have left her alone for such a long time, but despite my fear of taking her out of the home, I was trying harder and harder to give her the opportunity of some independent play.

I found Abby where I'd left her, sitting at the living room table, working on some crafts. She'd added stickers to her coloring, and had attempted to glue pipe cleaners and buttons to the pages. Both containers had spilled over the table. It was a mess and a half, and her hands were sticky, but I could see she'd enjoyed herself. As soon as we cleaned up and had a bite to eat, I planned to sit down with her and do something a little more educational, like read her a story or work on some counting.

I helped Abby sort out the glue and took her to the kitchen for some lunch. She helped me make the sandwiches by buttering the bread as best she could. When I was feeling up to it, I tried to get her involved in as many tasks around the home as I could. She would normally have followed me about while I cleaned, happily running a cloth over the walls, thinking she was helping, but I needed some time alone to decompress after meeting with London.

I still couldn't believe London had the audacity to bring up my extra therapy session. Not everyone was as laid back about seeing a psychiatrist as she was. Why couldn't she have kept what she'd heard to herself? My God, Brad was going to get an earful tonight once Abby was tucked in bed.

"Mommy?" Abby asked.

"Yeah, baby?" I replied, trying to keep my tone light.

"Why is Aunt London sad?"

My eyes widened at the question. Abby was more perceptive than I had realized. She gazed at me, eager to know why London and I had been upset with each other. How could I explain the complexities of adult friendships to a three-year-old?

I hated the idea of lying to my daughter, but maybe it was better than anything the truth offered. "She wasn't sad, honey. We were just having a little disagreement."

"What's that?"

I sighed. Why are children always so eager to learn about the world around them? Don't they realize how much easier it is to stay in their innocent bubble? I'd live there forever if I could.

"Sometimes one grown-up thinks they are right, and the other grown-up is wrong, and they like to tell each other about it. Does that make sense?"

Abby stared at me with a wrinkled brow. She shook her head, clearly not understanding. I considered trying to explain it better, but kept it simple. "Don't worry about it, honey. Let's have some lunch."

"Okay," she said, easily distracted by the promise of food.

Deciding we both could use a break, I took our sandwiches to the living room and told Abby we could watch a few episodes of her favorite show while we ate. With my help, she carried her plate and drink to her special tray, which was set up right in front of the TV. I used to let Imy do the same thing on days when I needed thirty minutes of downtime.

As we ate our lunch, Abby was engrossed in watching cartoon dogs rescue people from ridiculous situations. I wasted time scrolling through my phone, hoping it would distract me from my looming therapy session. I know it seemed like I was making a big deal out of it, but I was dreading seeing Dr. Corbyn. And with good reason. I didn't like the man.

I had tried to communicate this to Brad back when I first started seeing Corbyn, but he dismissed it. "Dr. Corbyn has come highly recommended," Brad had said. I wasn't sure why. He didn't seem like a good therapist to me. For one, we rarely spoke about Imogen's death or that day in the park. If anything, he seemed to want me to forget that traumatic time in my life, like it was easier to treat me than to address the problem. I had wanted to talk about the incident and the man I had seen drag Imogen into the water, but he always said that I wasn't ready to discuss it.

A shudder ran down my spine at the thought of going to therapy, causing me to drop my cell phone. It landed on the floor with a thud and bounced into the hard leg of our coffee table. "Dammit," I cursed in front of Abby. I bent down to pick it up and found a nasty crack on the front of my phone.

"Great," I said, standing. I took my cell phone into the kitchen to wipe off the scratch so it wouldn't cut me or Abby the next time she reached for it.

When I went into the kitchen, a shadow passed over the sunlight pouring in through the sheer curtains by the sink that overlooked our backyard. It was only for a second, but it was enough to block out the light. Someone had just walked by the back of the house.

Someone was outside.

I rushed over to the window and pulled the sheer curtain aside to get a clear look outside. But there was no one there. Why would there be? This was our backyard. For someone to be in it, they would have to have come through our locked gate.

I stared out of the window for a few seconds more, but didn't see anyone. Maybe it was a bird or a cloud blocking out the sun. Maybe I was on edge thinking about therapy. I didn't know what I was going to tell Dr. Corbyn about my latest discoveries. I was about to turn around and go back to Abby when I spotted the door to our garden shed swaying in the breeze. It made a bang as it thumped closed before opening again.

"What the hell?" I let out. Without a word to Abby, I placed my phone on the bench and hurried to the back door. I scrambled to unlock it and rushed out into our backyard.

I scanned the area, half expecting to see a person skulking around. There was no one there. I took cautious steps farther out into the yard toward the shed, scanning the fence line as I went. Again, I found nothing. There was no one creeping about where they shouldn't have been. But the door of the garden shed was banging in the breeze. There was typically a great big padlock on the door at all times, but I could see the lock was missing, and there were fresh shoe prints on the ground. Had someone been going through our shed?

I opened the door and found the usual things inside. Rakes, shovels, a lawn mower, and a leaf blower. We even had a machete that had never been used. I didn't even know why we had one.

We paid a gardener to take care of the lawns and plants. Brad had the shed neatly arranged for the man who came once every two weeks. I ran a hand over some items and stopped when my hand found a gap in the row of shovels and rakes. Something was missing. I wasn't into gardening and rarely ventured into the back-yard other than to play with Abby, but I knew there was supposed to be a shovel here. It was one that had a long handle and a strong steel blade. I remembered Brad using it before to dig up a section of the backyard when we discovered there was a drainage issue. As far as I knew, he hadn't thrown it out. So why was it missing?

As I ran my eyes over the empty spot for the tenth time, Abby came outside.

"Mommy?"

Snapping out of my daze, I realized I had left her alone with the back door wide open. Abby started walking outside toward me.

"Imy," I shouted. Abby froze on the spot. I moved away from the shed and rushed to her. I scooped her up into a tight hug.

"I've got you," I whispered into her ear.

"Mommy?" she asked. "I'm not Imy. I'm Abby." She giggled at me like we'd been playing a game.

"Why did you say that just now?" I blurted.

"My name is Abby. Silly Mommy."

It took me a second to realize, but she was right. I had called out for Imy and not Abby. I shook my head and brought Abby back inside.

CHAPTER THIRTY-ONE

"Can we go back outside?" Abby asked when I'd put her back in the living room.

"Not right now," I replied, glancing away.

"Please," she begged.

"No, sweetheart. Just watch some TV, okay?"

"All right," she said, defeat lining her answer. Fortunately, it didn't take long for the cartoon dogs to brighten her up again and pull her focus. I used the opportunity to slip away from my daughter and sat down on the sofa.

What was I doing? I had left Abby all alone with the back door wide open so I could chase shadows. What if someone had been outside and was waiting for her to follow me outside? Someone like Oswald Taylor?

"It can't happen again," I muttered under my breath. As fast as I could, I hurried to the kitchen and retrieved my cell phone. I wanted it on hand in case I spotted any more shadows creeping around our backyard.

I had to solve the mystery of the missing shovel.

I'd only seen Brad use it back when we had the drainage issue. Despite being an accountant who spent his days behind a desk, he was in good shape. The problem we'd had in our backyard had required him to dig a trench that was deeper than he was tall. He could have hired someone to do the work, but he wanted to find the source of the problem before he got the professionals in. The more I thought about it, the more I realized what else that shovel could have been used for.

Had he once used that same shovel to bury Oswald Taylor? If that was the case, then why the hell would he have kept it?

I gave my phone's screen a wipe with a thick sponge to remove any fragments of glass from the crack. Once I'd cleared the debris as best I could, I looked up the article and Oswald's photo online again.

He was smiling in the picture. He looked cheerful. He was gripping the straps of his backpack like he was about to go on a long hike and didn't look like a person who spent his time drowning four-year-old kids.

Had Brad buried him somewhere in Cliff Woods with the missing shovel?

"Stop it," I let out. I was making a wild assumption. Brad's behavior coupled with the article and a missing shovel were hardly proof he was a killer. I needed more if I was going to accept that reality.

I was reaching for quick answers. My thoughts could easily be dismissed as pure nonsense. All I had was a feeling in the pit of my stomach. One that was now threatening to bubble up from the depths and overwhelm me. I still needed to find out more about Oswald Taylor. He was the key to everything. With my cell phone out, I glared at his photo again. The longer I gazed into his eyes, the more I saw.

"Why did you do it?" I asked the picture. No one replied, and no answers came to me. My eyes fell to Oswald's hands that were gripping his backpack in the photo. On his left wrist sat a watch. One I'd seen many times before. One that looked exactly like the watch Brad had in the desk drawer of his study.

I stumbled to my feet and rushed for the stairs. I stopped at the base of them and quickly moved back to the living room to check on Abby. She was happily engrossed in her show, so I dashed for the stairs again. I clipped the door frame on my way into Brad's office. I ignored the pain in my elbow and charged to Brad's desk, practically falling into his chair once I'd reached it. I yanked hard on the drawer that I'd seen the cracked watch in. The watch was gone.

"What?" I spat out. This wasn't happening. I clambered to open the other drawer and found nothing again. I haphazardly lifted the few items that were inside each drawer, making a mess of Brad's neat organization. I didn't care. I knew that damn watch had been there and now it was gone. With my cell phone still in my grip, I looked at Oswald's photo again and zoomed in as far as I could on his watch. I knew it was the same, but I had no way of confirming it. I closed my eyes, picturing the one I had found in this very room. Despite the crack, it was a match. It had to be. And now it was gone.

If Brad did indeed have the watch of a missing man, what did that mean? And why did it have a large crack in the middle of it? There was also the damn shovel to consider.

I opened my eyes and didn't know what I was supposed to do next. I thought about going to the police, but I wasn't sure what to tell them. I had no evidence to back up my thoughts. Plus, I wasn't sure if I wanted to go to them in the first place.

I needed a clearer picture of the situation before I did anything crazy. Brad had arranged for me to see Dr. Corbyn. If my psychiatrist got wind of what was going through my head right now, it wouldn't go down well.

As I dismissed the decision to speak to the police about Brad, an idea overtook my every thought. One I knew would fail if I was stupid enough to follow through with it.

I knew in that second that I would ignore any rational argument I might come up with to forget the moronic idea. I had to speak to Oswald's wife, Julia Taylor.

She would be able to tell me what her husband was like and might clue me in as to why he had murdered my child. Maybe she would have an update on Oswald's missing person case that wasn't public, something that could suggest that Oswald was no longer missing, but dead.

Even if she knew nothing, surely there would be something she could tell me I didn't have access to. The only problem I had was my appointment with Dr. Corbyn today. I had to attend a damn therapy session while Brad looked after Abby. But maybe my scheduled visit could benefit me.

A smile tugged at the corners of my mouth as I thought of a plan to go see Oswald's wife. I didn't know where she lived in Brookfield Terrace. I didn't even know if she had stayed in town after her husband went missing, but while Brad was busy with Abby, I was going to try my hardest to find her.

CHAPTER THIRTY-TWO

Brad

It was the second time today I'd left the office, but leaving early felt strange. It was something I hadn't done in a long while. I didn't like to admit it to myself, but I often found excuses to stay at the office for longer than I needed to. Things were just easier there. And with Maia acting the way she was, my urge to hide from my problems at work was even greater.

As I was halfway home from Syracuse, I thought about the conversation I'd had earlier in the day with Dr. Corbyn. It was always hard getting Maia to agree to any extra sessions with him. Especially when she was going off the rails like this. Mason had been the only therapist Maia had seen since Imogen's death, and she wasn't a fan of him. But I was glad that I had persevered and compelled her to go today. Maia needed to hear certain things from the mouth of a professional. Things I couldn't tell her. It was in her best interest.

Mason was able to fit in a three o'clock session today. I wasn't surprised. He prioritized my calls over anyone else's and for good reason.

Finding Mason at the start of this ordeal was the greatest challenge. I needed someone I could trust. Someone who would do whatever I asked of them. I went through more than a dozen therapists, offering them extra cash payments to allow me to tailor Maia's sessions to what I needed. None were willing to risk their license for the amount I was prepared to pay them. Some even threatened to call the police, making claims of abuse. But they didn't understand what was at stake.

Not only did I want access to session notes, but I wanted to have complete control over Maia's therapy. When it became obvious that no one was willing to take my money, I chose an alternative route.

As an internal auditor, I had access to some extremely sensitive information. One of my firm's major clients happened to be a private healthcare network. They themselves had a near-endless list of clients whom they worked with. Among them were several hundred mental healthcare professionals. I had to break all the rules, but I dug through the data I had access to until I found some unusual claims activity from a local man named Dr. Mason Corbyn.

"I really need you to work your magic with her again today," I had said to Mason over the phone.

He sighed down the line. "Brad, how long are we going to keep this up for? I've had a few close calls with the State Board lately and need to tread lightly. I can't keep doing this. You'll have to find another therapist."

"Not a chance," I said. "Maia needs to see you. You have a solid history with her. She trusts you. If I go to someone else, we'll have to start over. I can't have that."

Another sigh filled my ear from Mason. "I'm sorry, Brad, but I have to insist. If I get caught, I'll lose everything."

It was obvious that Mason needed a reminder of what I knew, so I shifted tactics. "You'll lose everything if I leak to the insurers that you've been fleecing them for years. I'm sure they'd love to hear about all your upcoding and phantom billing. I don't think you can practice if you're in jail for fraud."

The line went silent. I could practically hear Dr. Corbyn's mind ticking over with thought. We both knew he wouldn't say no to me. "I really shouldn't be doing this," he started.

"And you probably shouldn't have rounded up your check-ins to sixty-minute sessions or billed insurance providers for sessions that occurred during times when your office was closed, but here we are."

A lengthy sigh came down the line.

"You know me," I said. "If you play ball, I won't tell anyone about your 'extras'." I almost felt bad, working over a shrink like this, but it had to be done.

In Mason's sessions with Maia, the focus was not on processing the past or coming to terms with what had happened that day at the park. It was the complete opposite. Dr. Corbyn's job was to make Maia forget everything. I was fortunate enough that Maia's memory had already suffered after Imy's death. She had suppressed parts of that day and what came next all on her own. This was just maintenance to keep those memories secure.

Maia once told me that, in the time between Imy's death and Abby's conception, she could barely remember feeling alive. I needed things to stay that way. I needed the truth to stay in the shadows where it belonged. It was bad enough that she'd seen the article. If she ever remembered what had happened all that time ago, I'd have to intervene in a way I didn't want to. I wouldn't have any other options left. I prayed we never reached such a point.

"Okay," Mason said. "But only for a few sessions more. Then you will need to sort something else out, got it?"

"Got it," I said as a smile etched itself across my features. Dr. Corbyn had no idea how many conversations like this I had recorded over the years as extra insurance. The way I saw things, he would need to keep doing what I wanted for as long as I asked. If he ever said no to me, I'd send off a few files on my home computer anonymously to the right people and destroy his business overnight. He would have no way to prove it was me.

"All right. What did you want me to say to Maia today?" Mason asked.

Relieved, I told him how I wanted the session to go. Mason wasn't happy about it, but he agreed. I just had to get home to pick up my wife and daughter so I could take Maia to her session.

Before I did that, though, I needed to sneak into our backyard and put the padlock I'd accidentally taken with me back on the garden shed. I had held onto that shovel for too long. The damn watch as well. I don't know why I had been so stupid and kept them. Maybe it was just my guilt forcing me to cling to what I had done. Or maybe I wanted a reminder of how bad things could get if I let them. Whatever it was, I knew there would come a day when my luck would run out.

Either way, I had at least removed them from our home and placed them somewhere safe. I tried to destroy them, but apparently, I still wasn't ready to get rid of them. It made me wonder if I needed a therapy session.

CHAPTER THIRTY-THREE

Maia

Julia Taylor wasn't hard to find. In her campaign to locate her missing husband, she had made multiple public posts on social media telling people what street she lived on in Brookfield Terrace. A quick search on Google's Street View showed me a residence that had the surname Taylor written on a mailbox halfway down her road. All I needed was to show up unannounced at her home and hope she was there and in the mood to talk. And all while Brad was busy watching Abby for me when I was supposed to be attending a stupid therapy session.

What could go wrong?

I believed Brad meant well when he pushed me to attend these extra sessions. He was trying to help in his own special way. What I didn't appreciate was how far he was willing to go. One time, when I refused to see Dr. Corbyn, Brad threatened to have me committed to a psychiatric center again if I didn't see Corbyn. At first, I thought he wasn't serious. But he made the call in front of me and gave me a look that told me not to test him. I had no choice but to do what he'd asked. I couldn't go back to that place. The sounds that echoed through the hallways still haunted me.

I'd been put into one of those facilities before Abby was even conceived but it hadn't happened since. It was a dark time in our history, one I thought would never be a possibility again. Not with me seeing Dr. Corbyn each month. If I became too much of a problem now, would Brad try to send me away again? If he truly was a killer, it would benefit him to have me locked up and doped out of my mind on sedatives.

A heightened level of apprehension was charging through me as I waited for Brad to arrive to pick us up. My theory was that Oswald's watch had been damaged in a scuffle with Brad and that he had kept it as some kind of sick memento. Maybe even a reminder of what he had done. It seemed risky as hell. As for the missing shovel, I wasn't sure what to make of that discovery.

The one person in the world I wanted to talk to about all this was Brad. But I couldn't. The conversation would end in one of two ways: I'd either come across as unstable, or I'd be right and Brad would have no choice but to deal with me. How far would he go to keep such a dark secret?

I was spinning in circles, gripped with indecision. Why did this have to happen to me? I knew it was best to keep everything to myself until I had something concrete I could show to the world. That meant I had to act normal around Brad and everyone else.

Just as I was about to let the next wave of anxious thoughts flood my mind, a small voice broke through the noise.

"Mommy, Bunny's arm came off," Abby said, her lower lip quivering as she held up the stuffed toy she'd had since birth. Its right arm was dangling by a few threads. Imy had done something similar to the fox comforter she had as a baby. I blinked myself back to the present and reacted as I was supposed to.

"Oh, honey, come here," I said, trying to keep any worry out of my voice as I kneeled down to her level. I took the bunny from Abby's small hands and examined the damage.

"How did you do that?" I asked.

"I don't know," Abby said, sniffing with watering eyes.

"Hey, it's okay. We'll fix her."

"Promise?"

I nodded with the best smile I could muster. On closer inspection, I found the necessary repair was within my skill set. It was a minor problem in the grand scheme of things, but with everything that was going on, it felt like too much. Still, I had to persevere. To a three-year-old, this might as well have been the end of the world.

"Mommy will fix it," I said, trying to sound reassuring, though my mind was still occupied with thoughts of Brad, Oswald Taylor, and Julia Taylor.

Abby's big eyes looked up at me, wide with concern despite my words. "Will she be okay, Mommy?"

"Of course, sweetie. Mommy can fix anything, right?" I forced another smile, hoping it would calm her down. If I didn't, Abby would be upset, and the last thing I needed was a meltdown when Brad arrived.

We moved from the second living room to the kitchen. In there, I rummaged through our junk drawer to find a small sewing kit I kept for stuffed-toy emergencies. I sat down at the table with Abby in my lap. She was eager to supervise the operation as I threaded the needle. She watched me closely, her little fingers gripping the edge of the table as if she could somehow will her bunny back together. I knew the feeling well.

"Hold her still for me, okay?" I said, handing the bunny back to Abby as I carefully started stitching the arm back on. All the while, a ticking clock echoed in my mind. Brad could have arrived at any minute and would be impatient to get underway. I still wasn't sure if I was going to go to Julia Taylor's house or not.

The logistics of it all were simple enough. I could take a rideshare to Julia's home and be there in under ten minutes. I had an account set up with enough credit on it that I wouldn't need to use any of our cards. That way, Brad couldn't see a transaction. I'd had the account topped up and in place for emergencies. Ever since we lost Imy, I needed to feel prepared for any situation.

As I worked on Bunny, I tried to keep my thoughts from spiraling. If Brad had been at the center of Oswald's disappearance, what would that mean for us? If Brad confessed the truth to me, was I supposed to accept it and continue with our marriage as if it were not a big deal?

"Ouch," I let out as I accidentally stabbed myself with the sewing needle.

"Are you okay, Mommy?" Abby asked, dread filling her already fragile voice.

"I'm fine, sweetheart. Just a little prick." I wiped my finger down my jeans to clear away the blood. There wasn't much, even so, I didn't want Abby to panic.

"There we go," I said, tying off the thread and cutting it with a pair of scissors. "All fixed."

"Thank you, Mommy!" Abby beamed, hugging her bunny tight.

I kissed the top of her head and felt a pang of guilt for being so preoccupied that I allowed her to damage her favorite toy. "You're welcome, baby. Now, how about we clean up before Daddy gets here? Can you go wash your hands and brush your teeth? I'll help you in a second."

Abby nodded. Her smile hadn't faded at all. She ran off and out of the room, heading up to her bathroom. I stood and sighed. The moment of calm had passed, and the reality of what I wanted to do came crashing back.

I didn't have much time. Brad would arrive shortly, and I still had to find enough courage to sneak out on my therapy session. Typically, during these extra sessions, I would find my way there while Brad stayed at home with Abby. But this was different. He was driving us. Most likely, he would wait in the car and give Abby the iPad to watch while he stared at his cell phone for an hour. If I were lucky, it would be enough of a distraction.

I had to get to Julia's house on my own, with no one else knowing about it. I thought about taking Abby with me, but she might have said something to Brad after the fact. Plus, I didn't want to take her anywhere near a potentially dangerous situation. I had no idea what Julia Taylor was like. And I had no clue how much she understood about her husband's disappearance. It wasn't worth the risk.

As I followed Abby upstairs to help her get ready, I heard Brad pull into our driveway. It was time for me to put on a show and act like I was going to do what I was told and see my therapist.

CHAPTER THIRTY-FOUR

In the upstairs bathroom, I tidied up Abby's hair and made sure her face was clean as she attempted to brush her teeth. It always amazed me how much food a three-year-old could get on themselves. Imy had been the same way. No matter what she was eating, you could guarantee half of it would be smeared on her face.

"Done," I said to Abby before I let memories of Imy take over.

"Thank you," she said in her squeaky, polite voice. I worried how long her positive attitude would last. Inevitably, Abby would one day turn into a moody teenager who would communicate solely through grunts and sighs. The thought always led me to ask the same question: would we ever have another child?

"Honey," Brad called from downstairs. "Are you ready?"

"Just a minute," I yelled back, shaking my head. I hated having to scream across the house. It was a bad habit Brad had; I had asked him multiple times to stop doing it, but he never listened.

"Go grab your iPad," I told Abby.

"Okay," she said with a bounce in her step.

We let Abby keep the tablet in her room, but she wasn't allowed to use it without our permission. Plus, she didn't know how to unlock it. One day, she would see me entering the six digits that kept it locked and would memorize them. Would she realize those numbers were her dead sister's birthday?

As I left the bathroom, Brad reached the top of the stairs. He was wearing what he typically wore to work: gray slacks, a white button-up shirt, and a navy tie. It was simple and professional, nothing flashy. That was Brad, in a nutshell. He never liked to stand out. Even when he bought his BMW, I could sense it was not a vehicle he wanted to drive around. It almost felt like he was playing a role to keep up with his coworkers or Fletcher. I wondered who the real Brad Fairbanks was.

"Ready?" he asked when his eyes found mine.

"Yes," I nodded. "Abby is grabbing her iPad. I figured it would make things easier for you while I'm . . . you know."

"Thank you," he said. "That's very considerate of you."

I gave him a half smile that faded with the sudden awkwardness. This was the way it always was before an extra session. He knew I didn't want to go, and I knew he wouldn't let me get out of going. We'd had many arguments in the past that had gotten quite heated about my mental health. I'd been to see Corbyn countless times over the years and felt like it had never achieved a single thing. We never delved into anything deeper than what I liked to call surface-level therapy. I'd told Brad several times I didn't think Dr. Corbyn was good at his job, that he just ticked off the boxes when I saw him, and seemed more concerned with letting me off the hook when it came to my guilt. I had even asked Brad on more than one occasion to see someone else, but he would insist that I stick it out with Dr. Corbyn. Brad seemed convinced that Dr. Corbyn was the best therapist in the area.

A past session came to me — a sliver of a memory about that day at the park. Despite not wanting to, I'd asked Dr. Corbyn to help me dig deeper. Corbyn had said, "You're making such great progress. You don't want to go backward by obsessing over this, do you? The next time you start to remember, just breathe and let go." I'd told Brad all about it, but he didn't want to hear it and rattled off the same rehearsed speech each time I complained. He'd simply say that therapy took time and didn't happen overnight.

In a way, I was kind of glad Dr. Corbyn wasn't very good at his job. Even when I was feeling brave enough to face what might have been buried in my psyche, I didn't like to discuss Imogen's death. He never made me relive it. As a result, parts of that day and the year that followed were still a blur of misery and pain. I could hardly remember a thing from that time.

Only that someone had murdered my child.

"How was your day?" I asked Brad as Abby returned.

"You know. Same old. How about you? How was your coffee date with London?" he asked as we all headed for the stairs.

"Fine," I said, not mentioning anything about my friend grilling me about therapy. I should have been on Brad's case about what he had told Fletcher. I also should have asked him about this thing between Fletcher and London, but I didn't want to start an argument in front of Abby. She had seen enough of them in her brief existence.

The awkwardness continued as we left the house. Brad locked up and guided Abby toward his BMW while I followed.

As we drove the short distance to Corbyn's office, I realized that if I were to sneak away to visit Julia, I'd be leaving Abby all alone with Brad. I couldn't do that, could I? Would Brad hurt his little girl? No. Not in a million years. Despite everything, I only saw love in his eyes when he looked at Abby.

She would be safe. It wasn't ideal, but if Brad was guilty of killing Oswald, he had probably done so for the right reasons. Sure, murder was morally wrong and against the law, but what that son of a bitch had done to Imogen was beyond forgiveness. I would have happily watched Oswald suffer a slow and painful death for his crimes. If Brad had indeed killed that man, he'd done the world a favor.

Running around playing detective was not the best thing for my mental health, but I had to learn the truth. I had to speak to Julia Taylor and see what she knew.

"Is everything okay?" Brad asked, giving me another sideways glance.

"Yeah," I said, facing him with a smile. "I'm just a little nervous, is all."

"It's only been three weeks."

"I know. This happens every time." I hoped what I'd said would be sufficient to get him off my case. It was going to be hard enough to get out of the session without him finding out about me leaving after two minutes.

My plan was simple. I was going to fake getting a text during my session with Corbyn. I would say it was from Brad, and that something was wrong with Abby. I would tell him to bill me for the hour, so it still looked like I had attended the session. I could even ask him to reconfirm my monthly visit a week from now. I'd then exit the office via the back door into the alley and rush to catch a rideshare out to the Taylor residence.

It would be tight, but if I pulled it off, I could attempt to speak to Julia while simultaneously avoiding therapy. A win-win if ever there was one.

We reached the parking lot of Dr. Corbyn's office. It was quite busy. There weren't many spots left. Brad got a space out front as another vehicle left and reversed in the way he always did. That meant he'd be facing away from the office with his head buried in his phone while Abby played on the iPad. No one would see me leave my session.

"Where are we?" Abby asked, glancing around the parking lot with curious eyes.

"Mommy just needs to go see a doctor," Brad answered.

"Is she hurt?"

"No sweetie."

I took off my seatbelt and turned to face her. "Mommy is okay, baby. I just need to talk to the doctor for a little while."

"Can I come?" she begged with wide eyes.

"No, honey. You're going to stay here with Daddy and watch the iPad."

"But I wanna come with you," she said, clawing her hands toward me. The pleading in her eyes stabbed at my heart. And in that moment, I considered going to the appointment and staying. Maybe seeing Dr. Corbyn was exactly what I needed.

I stared at the floor and thought about the past few days. As hard as it was to disappoint Abby, I knew I had to find Julia Taylor and speak to her about her husband.

"I'll be back before you know it," I said to Abby, giving her the biggest smile I could find.

"Okay," she muttered in defeat. I pulled out her iPad and unlocked the screen. A fresh wave of guilt washed over me with the thought that my three-year-old would be staring at another screen for a full hour. I'd read enough articles to say how bad screen time was for children, but what was I supposed to do? Brad wouldn't play with Abby for more than fifteen minutes before he'd either get bored or frustrated. He didn't have the same knack for playtime that I did. I didn't hold it against him. He worked hard for a living and was most likely too exhausted to go the extra mile. Plus, if he was busy staring at his own device, he wouldn't notice me trying to escape.

"Okay," I sighed, ready to do what I came to achieve. And as I opened my door and was halfway out of the car, Brad had something to say.

"Maia," he said.

"Yes?" I paused, one leg planted in the parking lot.

"I know you don't enjoy coming here, but please, do your best to listen to Dr. Corbyn. Like me, like all of us, he just wants to help you."

I stared into Brad's eyes and saw genuine care. He meant what he was saying. Focusing on the mission at hand, I said, "I'll do my best. I promise."

"Thank you. We'll be waiting for you."

"Bye," I said as I left. When I approached Dr. Corbyn's office, I put on my game face. As I glanced back at Brad, he already had his cell phone out and was busy staring at his screen. This was going to be easier than I thought.

CHAPTER THIRTY-FIVE

Dr. Corbyn shared an office with two other mental health care professionals. The waiting room was small and sleek, with pale gray walls that held a few abstract paintings. I'd spent hours trying and failing to decipher them over the years. A smeared coffee table covered with out-of-date magazines sat at the end of three dark blue chairs I knew were uncomfortably firm.

The administrative assistant barely glanced up from her computer screen when I entered. She was too busy typing on her keyboard while taking a call on her hands-free headset. I waited patiently for her attention, ever aware that the clock was ticking.

"Can I help you?" the administrative assistant asked when her call had ended. I'd never met this person before. She must have been new.

"Maia Fairbanks for Dr. Corbyn. Three o'clock."

The woman checked something on her screen, clicked a few times on her mouse, and smiled with thin lips. "He's running a little behind, sorry. Please take a seat."

"Sure," I let out under my breath. Corbyn had a habit of going overtime with patients throughout the day. So if you had a three o'clock appointment, you could be certain he'd be running late. I found an empty chair by a man with a thick mustache who looked to be in his late fifties. He wasn't the sort of person I often saw in a place like this, but more and more people were needing therapy these days. Despite things like advanced technology and social media, our lives were becoming more complicated.

Once I was seated, I took out my cell phone and loaded up the Uber app. I could see at least a dozen drivers in the area, all buzzing around, ready to pick me up the second I made a request. But I couldn't order a ride just yet. Not until I'd gone into my session and faked an emergency.

Every minute that ticked by added to the tension that was clenching up in my shoulders. From what I looked up online, Julia Taylor was twelve minutes from my current location. With the time it would take for a driver to arrive and for me to sneak out, I would need at least fifteen minutes to attempt a conversation with her. Then I'd need the same time to make it back. Brad was expecting me out by four o'clock. Maybe five minutes longer. It didn't give me a lot of space in the middle.

The session was supposed to start at three, and last around fifty minutes, but as I was currently experiencing, Dr. Corbyn wasn't sticking to the plan and would run over time.

Placing my unlocked cell phone at my side, I attempted to pick up a magazine and read. I spent a few minutes flicking through pages like a child looking at the pictures in a book that was beyond their comprehension. I had hoped the distraction would help me pass the time without feeling more and more anxious, but I couldn't concentrate.

What was taking Corbyn so long? Did he have any idea how bad it was for him to keep patients waiting like this? I couldn't have been the only one who felt this way.

"Maia?" Corbyn called from around the corner which led into his office.

I placed the magazine down and knocked my cell phone to the floor like an idiot. "Sorry," I blurted. Panic rippled through me as soon as I heard Corbyn's voice. It made little sense, as he was supposed to be an easy person to talk to. Yet it had never felt this way.

"It's okay," Dr. Corbyn said as I scooped up my phone and locked the screen. "Take your time."

"Sorry," I repeated, hoping he didn't see that I had the Uber app open. Not that it would be important. I doubted he cared how his patients got themselves to and from his office, as long as they paid their bill or had the right insurance.

I followed Dr. Corbyn down the narrow hallway into his office. Although it shouldn't have been, my heartbeat was drumming too fast for a simple therapy session. He gestured toward the chair across from his desk, the same uncomfortable one I always sat in. The room smelled of old books and something artificial, like lavender air freshener.

"How are you, Maia?" He asked in his practiced tone.

I forced a tight smile. "I've been better." There was no point trying to present myself as being fine. Otherwise, I wouldn't have been there.

He nodded as if he understood, but I wasn't convinced he did. He leaned back in his chair, adjusting his watch before folding his hands on the desk. "You seem tense."

I crossed my arms. "Long day, I guess."

"Mm." He scribbled something on his notepad, barely looking at me. I hated that the most. It made me feel like I had already been reduced to bullet points.

Dr. Corbyn clicked his pen and set it down. "I get the sense you're preoccupied." His eyes met mine. "Why are we here today? What has concerned Brad enough to call my office and book in a session a full week before you're due to see me?"

I hesitated, weighing up my words as carefully as I could. "Well, I—" I paused, doing my best to act like I'd received a text.

"Excuse me a moment." I fished out my cell phone from my bag and made a show of navigating to a text. "Oh," I uttered.

"Is something wrong?"

"Yes. There's an emergency at home with Abby. I'm afraid I have to go." I shifted my gaze to Dr. Corbyn. "You can still bill me for the hour."

Corbyn studied me with a worried gaze. "Uh, that won't be necessary."

"I insist," I said as I rushed to leave, needing the session charge on record. There wasn't much time to argue, so I hurried out the door. If Dr. Corbyn didn't charge our account for the full session, I would deal with that problem later. I had to go.

I opened the Uber app and hovered a thumb over the order button. Brad was standing out in front of the office, leaning against his BMW. He was staring straight at me. I hesitated. I had no other choice. I turned around and dashed into the restroom.

He was making sure I attended my session.

CHAPTER THIRTY-SIX

Brad

I leaned against the side of my car, arms crossed, as I watched the entrance of the building. I could see straight into the building, down the narrow hallway that led to Dr. Corbyn's office. Maia had seemed skittish before she went inside. Enough that I thought it would be best to monitor the room she had gone into. It was the right call to make. She had been in there for barely a few minutes when I saw her slip out into the hallway.

She had her phone out and was staring at it with an intense concentration until she saw me. She paused when our eyes met through the glass. For a second, neither of us moved. We were locked in a state of distrust, as if we had both caught each other doing something wrong. I recognized her look of guilt right away. Her shoulders looked tense and matched the fear in her eyes. She pushed open a door to the nearby restroom and disappeared inside.

Where the hell was she sneaking off to?

I pulled out my cell phone and sent Mason a text asking him what was going on. A moment later, he replied, telling me that Maia had possibly faked an emergency to escape the session. Not only that, she had insisted that Mason still bill us for the hour.

A minute passed. Then another. When she finally stepped out again, she hesitated in the hallway with her fingers flexing at her sides. I could see an internal battle playing out in the way she hovered near the door.

I stayed where I was and didn't shift my gaze. Maia avoided looking at me and retreated back to her session.

My suspicions were correct. She hadn't left the session to get some air or use the bathroom. She had planned on disappearing somewhere on her own while I was busy watching Abby. But where? And why?

Hopefully, Mason would do his job and dig deeper to find out.

A knock on the backseat passenger window caught my attention. Abby needed something. I opened her door and took a knee by her side. "What is it, sweetheart?"

"I miss Mommy."

"I know, honey. I do, too. She won't be much longer, though. I promise."

"Okay, Daddy. Will you play with me?"

"I'd love to, but Daddy has some work to do on his phone. You just play your games, all right?"

Her head drooped as a frown etched across her face. I hated to disappoint my little girl, but there was far too much at stake. I couldn't be distracted. I needed to find out what game Maia was playing. I knew she'd read the article, and that she was becoming confused by the smallest thing. But there was something else that I wasn't seeing. If I wasn't careful, her memories would come crashing through the haze and threaten to destroy everything. I had to figure out what it was she had planned on doing during her session, and there was only one person who could help me.

With my cell phone in hand, I closed Abby's door and made a call.

CHAPTER THIRTY-SEVEN

Maia

Coming back into my session was an enormous embarrassment, but I powered through it as best I could. Fortunately, Dr. Corbyn didn't ask me about it.

"Where were we?" Corbyn asked. "Ah, yes. We were about to get into your reason for being here today. You were about to answer my question. Then you had your . . . interruption."

"I was," I said. "I can't remember what I was going to say, sorry."

"That's fine. We'll start over. What has been upsetting you lately?"

With a heavy sigh, I used the session time the way I was supposed to and gave an honest answer. "I guess I've been thinking about the past a lot. I've been remembering things."

His lips pressed into a line. "Memories can be tricky."

I let out a scoff, not meaning to. "That's one way to put it."

He studied me a moment longer before leaning forward. "Maia, I've said this before, but sometimes, looking backward does more harm than good. The mind is selective. It warps things and distorts them, especially when emotions are involved."

My shoulders stiffened. "You think I'm misremembering what happened?"

"I think," he said, emphasizing the word, "that you're holding on to things that might not be as they seem. Have you considered that dwelling on the past is keeping you from moving forward?"

My jaw clenched. "I don't think I'm dwelling, considering the subject of those memories." I hated to say Imogen's name in front of him.

"No?" He tilted his head. "Tell me, what does remembering these things do for you? Does it help you feel safe? Does it give you clarity? Or does it just make you anxious and suspicious?"

I opened my mouth, then shut it.

He let the silence I gave stretch. "Sometimes, we have to choose which memories serve us and which ones don't."

A chill crawled up my spine. I wanted to argue and push back, but something about his measured voice made it hard to untangle my own thoughts.

I blinked and shook my head. "You think I should forget?"

"If a memory does nothing but cause you distress, ask yourself: is it worth keeping?"

I fought not to react. How could he say such a thing? Was I supposed to pretend that my little girl wasn't murdered by some freak while I was twenty feet away and helpless to stop it?

He leaned back in his expensive chair again, not letting his eyes wander from mine. "Maia, you've made progress, yes. But reopening old wounds can undo that." His voice softened. "Is that what you want?"

I stared at him, my breath uneven. The logical part of me knew what he was doing. He was planting doubt and making me second-guess myself. But another part of me, the part that had been unsteady for a long time, wavered. I didn't know what to say.

Dr. Corbyn smiled like he could sense the shift in dynamics. "Good," he murmured. "Now, let's talk about something else."

I stabbed my nails into my palms and welcomed the sharp pain. I wanted to get the hell out of this room, but I couldn't just up and leave. Not with Brad watching the door. Instead, I forced myself to stay still and listen.

Dr. Corbyn tapped his pen against the edge of his notepad as he read through something he'd jotted down. His quiet rhythm seemed to add to my stress levels. "Before we move on," he said. "I'd like to ask you a question, Maia."

I exhaled, bracing myself. "What is it?"

His eyes flicked toward the door before settling back on me. "Why did you try to leave earlier?"

My stomach clenched. I should have known he'd ask this question. I'd been hoping we were going to slide past it, but no such luck. "I told you. It was a false alarm," I said, keeping my voice as even as I could. Lying to a therapist was about as easy as it sounded.

Dr. Corbyn tilted his head again. It felt like he was studying me under a microscope. "And yet, when you walked back in, you looked . . . embarrassed."

"I wasn't."

His lips twitched like he wanted to smile. "Then what was it?"

I swallowed hard, gripping the arms of my chair. He wasn't going to drop this. God. "I just—" I hesitated, choosing my words meticulously. "I wanted to leave. I got overwhelmed."

His fingers drummed against his notepad. "I was right here. We could have discussed what was going through your head before you took such a step."

I forced a shrug. "I came back, didn't I?"

He studied me a beat longer before nodding. "You did. But the question is why?"

"What do you mean, *why*?" I asked, my jaw clenched.

"Why come back? If you wanted to leave, why push yourself to return?"

I glanced toward the door. Brad was out front. I couldn't see him, but I could almost feel his presence through the walls between us. "I don't know," I muttered, looking down at my hands.

Dr. Corbyn exhaled as if he had already figured out the answer himself. "Perhaps," he started, "you're afraid of what running away means."

A sharp pang went through my chest, and I stiffened. "I wasn't running away."

His brow lifted. "No? So where were you going?"

I hated how he could pick apart my thoughts. He was always one step ahead of me before I could even form my own conclusions. It didn't seem possible. He continued to stare, waiting for a response, but I wouldn't give him one.

Finally, he gave a small, knowing nod. "All right, Maia," he said, setting his notepad aside. "Let's move on."

For the rest of the session, we went over the usual things. We rehashed old techniques I'd been taught to help calm me down when I felt like I was spiraling. He double-checked I was taking my meds and reemphasized the need to take extra tablets whenever I thought I needed them. I complained about the fog they put me into, but once again, he dismissed it.

The session ended after what seemed like a longer time than normal. As I stood and smoothed out my clothing, I could feel Dr. Corbyn's eyes on me, still pulling at the threads of my thoughts.

"Maia," he said as I was about to leave. My hand was on the doorknob, ready to twist.

He smiled. "Try not to dwell so much on what's behind you. Some things are better left where they belong."

I forced a tight smile and nodded. He didn't say another word, so I stepped out of the room.

The hallway felt too bright after the dim office. My pulse quickened as I made my way to the front desk. The administrative assistant said something to me, but with the stress of the session, I could barely register what it was. I simply smiled and nodded until she told me I could leave. I exited the building and walked to the car, reminding myself to breathe.

Brad was still standing by his car, watching me. I came to a stop and looked at him. We just stood there, separated by a few yards of pavement, locked in a silent stare.

Finally, Brad walked around to the front passenger door and opened it for me. He made a gesture for me to get in and said, "Let's go home."

CHAPTER THIRTY-EIGHT

I couldn't stop thinking about my session with Dr. Corbyn. This was one of the most confronting meetings we've ever had. It was as if someone was egging him on to push me to my limit.

"How did it go?" Brad asked me as he drove us home.

"Fine," I lied. There's no way in hell I would let him in on the details of my disastrous chat with Corbyn. Brad would only see it as another reason to send me back there. I twisted in my seat to look at Abby. She gave me one of her beautiful smiles in return. She was so excited when I climbed into the car. You'd swear I had been gone for days. It felt like it. I should have sat in the back with her and made sure she was okay, but I was so flustered from speaking to Dr. Corbyn that I couldn't think straight.

When I faced forward, a dizziness overcame me. I held a hand to my forehead and groaned.

"What's wrong?" Brad asked.

"It's these damn tablets," I said. "They make me so dizzy sometimes."

"That's frustrating," he said, not truly understanding beyond a base level, "but you need to keep taking them."

"I know. I wasn't saying that."

"It's okay," he said, quick to jump on the defensive. "I was just reminding you that—"

"Please don't," I snapped. "I've been taking these things long enough to—" I cut myself short. Brad gave me a sideways glance. I looked away as a terrifying thought came to me. One that shouldn't have taken this much time to form.

What if these tablets weren't good for me?

I thought back over my history of taking them. All they ever managed to do was make me dizzy and drowsy. It was like I had permanent brain fog. And when I took an extra dose, it knocked me about. I was able to push through and function, but they made things worse. They made me want to sleep. They made it hard to remember.

"Oh, God," I whispered to myself. Fortunately, Brad didn't notice. Otherwise, he may have seen the look of shock on my features. I felt trapped in his car with what was swirling around inside me. These tablets messed with my memories. Did they make it harder for me to recall the past? Oswald Taylor's face had been a blur until I'd seen his photo.

I was due to take one when we had dinner tonight. Whatever happened when we got home, I had to make sure that didn't happen. I needed to get off these damn things. I didn't even know what they were called. I'd forgotten the name. Dr. Corbyn had prescribed them to me years ago and had continued to do so. I'd always assumed that he had my best interests at heart. But he'd been giving me tablets that made me forget.

I thought about our chat today. He kept saying that the past wasn't worth remembering, especially if it was full of bad memories. He'd said, "If a memory does nothing but cause you distress, you have to ask yourself: is it worth keeping?" I remembered the line, word for word, because I couldn't believe it came out of his mouth. Why had he said this? Why was he trying to make me forget the past?

"Are you excited about going home?" Brad asked Abby as I grappled with all kinds of possibilities.

"Yeah," she said with an abundance of energy. She had done well to sit in the car this long, given her age. I would need to give her some time to run around when we got home. But how was I supposed to do such a thing when I could feel myself losing control?

I had always had my doubts about Dr. Corbyn, but this revelation was too much to ignore. He wasn't there to help me. His visits were designed to make me forget. And the man who had arranged for me to see this particular psychiatrist was sitting next to me in his BMW. Brad was always so insistent that I keep seeing Dr. Corbyn. Was he influencing my therapy sessions? Was I really about to walk down this path? It wasn't such a stretch, given what I already thought of him.

When we arrived home, I didn't have time to contemplate what Brad may or may not have done. If he had been conspiring with Corbyn to manipulate my therapy, I would have to work out what to do with that knowledge later. Parked in my driveway behind my rental was London in her Mercedes-Benz E-Class Coupe. She climbed out of her car the moment Brad came to a stop.

"Aunt London again?" Abby said with a giggle.

"Yes, Aunt London," Brad said through a clenched jaw. He faced me and asked, "Why is she here?"

I shook my head. "I honestly don't know. I was about to ask you the same question."

"Unbelievable," Brad muttered. "I suppose we should find out."

I got out of the car and helped Abby. She seemed happy to see London despite getting a somewhat cold shoulder from her at the café. We strolled up to London and said hello.

"Sick of the sight of me?" London asked, beaming.

"No," I said, doing my best to hide any anxiety about her sudden appearance. I didn't want her thinking she wasn't a welcome guest in our home, but she knew I wasn't the biggest fan of an unplanned visit. "What are you doing here?" I asked, forcing a grin.

"I'm here to take you out for dinner."

"Dinner? No, I can't. I need to organize our own food and get Abby off to bed."

"I'm sure Bradley can handle it," London said, facing him with a sting in her eyes.

His focus shifted between us. "I don't know, London. Maia just got back from a therapy session. It might not be the best idea."

"Or it might be the best idea," she said with too much irritation. More than when she usually spoke to Brad.

Brad shrugged. "I don't know. It's not up to me."

Why did he have to say that? I didn't want to go anywhere with anyone. I'd had enough for one day and now needed to work out if my possibly murderous husband had been drugging me for years. I also needed to find a way to visit Julia Taylor on my own.

"What do you say, Maia?" London asked.

"Aunt London," Abby said before I could answer.

"Yes, darling?" London replied, bending over.

"Can I come, too?"

"Oh, I don't think so, sweetie. This is just something for your mother and I. Besides, this way you get to have a fun night in with your dad. How does that sound?"

"Lots of fun," she said with glee. I wasn't sure if she understood what was being planned without my input. I was confident London was tricking her with her charm. I hadn't even agreed to anything either.

London looked up to me. "I know it's been a while since we had a nice girls' night out," London said, "but it could be good for both of us. What would you prefer? A night out with me? Or another boring night in with Brad?" When she said Brad's name, it was like the word had been dipped in malevolence. Something was off about her. I tried to speak, but only a garbled noise came out.

My eyes darted between London and Brad, then settled on Abby. I didn't want to be away from my baby like this. Especially after the day I'd had.

I exhaled. A night out might be exactly what I needed. Given the conclusion I had come to regarding Brad and my therapist, maybe getting away from the house for a few hours would help to ground me. God knows I wasn't feeling right about anything. I had no evidence to prove that Brad and Corbyn were working together to help me forget or that Brad had killed and buried Oswald. There could have been valid explanations for everything.

I turned to Brad. "Are you sure you can handle Abby for the night?"

Brad looked like he was about to give me an excuse why he wasn't up to the task, but London chimed in first. "Please don't insult the man. A big, tough man like Bradley can handle anything, can't you?"

He scratched the back of his head and said, "Uh, yeah. I've got it. You two have a nice night. Just don't be too late."

"We won't, *dad*," London drawled, already yanking me away from him. "Come with me, Maia," she said before I could change my mind. "Let's find you something to wear."

CHAPTER THIRTY-NINE

My day had gone from bad to worse. And not because London was now in my bedroom, going through my clothes. It was because I had twice as many problems as I did when I woke up.

Dr. Corbyn wanted me to forget the past. Brad may have killed Oswald Taylor, and now London was dragging me for a girls' night out, taking me away from Abby. I shouldn't have agreed to this impromptu idea. It was the last thing I needed, but unfortunately, London can be very persuasive when she sets her mind on something.

Needing a distraction, I asked an obvious question. "How are things going with Fletcher?"

"Oh, fine, darling," she said, waving me off as she pulled out a black dress that I hadn't worn in years. I didn't know if it would still fit.

"That's not what this is about, is it?" I lowered my voice. "You two haven't broken up or anything?" I know I only saw London this morning, but her relationships moved fast.

"No, no, no. Not since I saw you this morning," she said, laughing. "Actually, things are going well between us. For the most part. Call me crazy, but I think we might be perfect for each other. Neither of us wants kids. We both have money, and we each respect each other's independence. I'm not saying that we're getting married, but it's working for the moment."

"That's good to hear," I said, hoping it sounded as if I meant it. London and Fletcher breaking up would have made complete sense of why she had sprung this night on me. My only other theory was because of the way we left things at the café this morning. Maybe London wanted to make it up to me. Not that she had done much wrong. I had probably overreacted.

"Oh, this is perfect," she said, taking out a dark green, short-sleeved, polo knit midi dress. One I knew was rather snug around the waist.

"Anything but that," I argued. I'd worn the outfit once and hated it.

"Nonsense," London countered. "This is the one. Go put it on while I look up which cocktail bars we are going to visit."

"Cocktail bars?" I asked as I left my walk-in wardrobe to get changed in the ensuite. "I can't get drunk on a Monday night," I called out.

"Says who?"

"My three-year-old, for one."

London made another comment, but I couldn't make it out. I held up the dress to the mirror in the ensuite and shook my head. I had to find a way out of this night, and fast. London was going to buy me drink after drink until I passed out drunk. I couldn't afford the hangover such an evening would give me. Not when I had what felt like a thousand problems attacking me all at once. I still needed to see Julia Taylor on top of working out why Brad and Dr. Corbyn were actively trying to suppress my memory. This was a distraction and nothing more.

"How are you going in there?" London asked.

"Okay," I lied as I prepared myself to put on the dress. It was uncomfortable and snug, but wearable. Still, I'd rather she'd picked anything else.

"I'm coming in," London said.

"Not yet. I just need a minute."

"Okay. But don't be much longer," she called back. I couldn't compete with her energy. Not today.

As I stood in the ensuite, ready to get changed, I thought about the tablets I took three times a day and tried to remember what their name was. But I drew a blank.

I kept the bottle on my bedside table, so it wouldn't be hard for me to find the name. I leaned out of the ensuite and saw that London was distracted with her back to me, so I tiptoed out to take a photo of the bottle as silently as I could. I wanted to search for the name before London dragged me around Syracuse on a Monday night of all nights.

I got back to the ensuite with a new photo in my library and would look up the name online as soon as I could. I should've researched the drug name years ago. But back then, I was too numb to even think about such a thing.

With my cell phone on the vanity, I quickly got into my dress. I shuddered once it was on and tugged at it as much as the material would allow. It made little to no difference.

"I'm coming in," London declared. She didn't wait for an answer this time and barged into the room. "Oh, look at you, darling. That is perfect."

"I doubt that," I said, retreating into myself. It was no shock that I didn't ooze confidence. I was much more comfortable covering myself with something that wasn't so tightly fitting.

"Oh, shush," London said. "You look amazing. Trust me. Brad had better watch out. He doesn't know how lucky he is." She stared into the distance with a hint of indignation in her gaze. I couldn't understand what was going on with her.

London continued. "This will get you a few numbers tonight."

A smile tugged at the corners of my mouth as I chuckled. "I doubt that." London stared at me with a crooked smile. "Not that I'm looking," I quickly added. She was buttering me up so I wouldn't change my mind. I didn't know why, but she was determined to make this night happen. There was no way I was getting out of it. Not without crushing my friend. It wasn't like I had dozens of them all lining up to see me, either.

"All right," London said. "I just need to pop down to my car to fetch my dress, then it's time for hair and makeup."

"Okay, but nothing too fancy, please."

"I'll try, but no promises."

London left me alone for a few minutes to retrieve her outfit. I had thought that what she was wearing was flashy enough for a night out, but I was wrong. While I was alone, I looked at the photo of my medication and read the name of the drug I'd been taking for several years now. It was called propranolol. I was taking a dose of three 40mg tablets, three times per day. According to multiple websites I skimmed through, this was considered to be a high dosage for anxiety. Not necessarily overprescribing, but close to it.

I continued my search online and read what I could. Apparently, propranolol was a beta-blocker. I had no idea what that meant, but a quick search told me in simple terms that beta-blockers basically stopped adrenaline. Their job was to keep my body from reacting to stress. They were supposed to stop me from having a racing heart, shaking hands, or a rushed sense of panic in my system. It was supposed to put me into a state of forced calm.

I stared at my screen as I scrolled through several articles on the use of propranolol as a treatment for PTSD. I never liked to consider myself as someone living with post-traumatic stress disorder, but it was an accurate diagnosis. I read through more information online and did my best to understand what I was skimming through.

Stress hormones made memories stronger. That's why the bad ones stuck. It was why they never faded like they should. My brain had apparently been pumping out norepinephrine, locking them in and making them harder to forget. But this propranolol had been blocking the process. The idea was to keep my bad memories from hitting so hard, but what if it had been dulling them to the point where I could hardly recall them?

I flicked through the rest of the article. It claimed that studies had shown it could work. Some people who took it right after their trauma didn't develop PTSD at all. Others used it later, paired with therapy, to make their memories less painful. Their memories weren't gone but were weakened. The question that rattled around in my brain was what happened if you were taking propranolol while seeing a therapist who was actively encouraging you to forget the past?

I chewed my lower lip and continued scrolling, finding much of the same with varying opinions. Pacing the limited space of the ensuite, a wave of confusion washed over my mind. Had the drug been helping me all these years? Or had I just been numbing myself to erase the past?

London came bursting back into the room full of energy with a black dress on a hanger inside a dry-cleaning slip.

"What do you think?" she asked, showing it to me.

I gave her an artificial smile and did my best to feign interest. I still wasn't sure if Brad and Dr. Corbyn had been attempting to suppress my memories or if they had been trying to protect me from a horrific past. There was only one way to find out. I had to stop taking my meds. It wasn't a decision to be made lightly, either.

London left the room to get changed while I did what I could to keep it together. It was going to be a long night.

CHAPTER FORTY

Brad

I sat on the floor with Abby in her room. A wide grin stretched across her face as she played with her ponies while I watched and occasionally joined in. Though every time I did, it was the wrong action to perform. She was quick to tell me what to say or do.

Almost in a trance while we were playing, I thought about the phone call I had made earlier to Fletcher. I had asked him to do me a huge favor and beg London to show up at our house to take Maia out for the night. I'd told him I wanted it to come across as a spur-of-the-moment thing that I'd had nothing to do with. I'd told Fletcher that Maia needed a night out with her friend. He was happy to pass along the message to London, but there was a level of apprehension in his voice I couldn't quite understand. I thought about asking him if something was wrong, but thought better of the idea. Whatever problem Fletcher was having, mine was bigger. I could have called London myself, but she probably wouldn't have taken my call. She couldn't stand me. It hadn't always been the case. But after Imogen died, Maia became a shut-in. I was confident that London blamed me for that.

Fletcher dating London was working in my favor. That was something I never expected. When he first told me about it, I practically laughed in his face. London was a disaster of a woman. I tried to warn him she was too wild, even for him, but it only motivated him to continue seeing her. That was a few weeks ago, and they were still together.

With Abby's door open, I could hear Maia and London chatting in our bedroom as they got ready. It was impossible to make out the words, but I could tell London was leading the conversation, of course.

Abby made a dramatic gasp, yanking my attention back to her little plastic ponies. "Daddy, no!" she scolded me. Her tiny hands landed on her hips. "Sparkle doesn't walk — she flies."

I held up the toy in mock surrender. "Right, right. Flying. Got it." I lifted Sparkle into the air, giving it a slow, exaggerated swoop toward a plastic castle.

Abby's expression remained skeptical. "She goes faster."

I grinned and complied, making the pony zoom through the air with a sound effect that hopefully passed Abby's strict standards. She nodded approvingly and went back to arranging the other figures. My mind drifted back to Maia.

I wasn't stupid. I knew she was struggling, even if she wouldn't say it outright. The therapy session hadn't gone well. Mason texted me when I got home and told me everything. The aim had been to lay it on thicker than normal and do whatever it took to keep her memories where they belonged, but something had changed. It was almost as if Maia was onto the whole thing. That's why I was glad I'd set up this night with London. I needed her out of the house. I needed to know what she was up to.

I wasn't staying home. The moment the girls left, I'd wait fifteen minutes, then take Abby to my sister's. Claire and Richard had agreed to watch Abby for a few hours. I'd made up some emergency that both Maia and I had to attend. One we couldn't talk about. They didn't question it and were happy to help.

Once I'd dropped Abby off, I was going to head to West Fayette Street in Syracuse. Fletcher told me that's where London would most likely take Maia for the night. I wanted to see what Maia got up to when she thought I wasn't watching.

I heard footsteps in the hallway a second before Maia appeared in the doorway, arms crossed. Her hair was done, and her makeup was light but noticeable. She looked good. I missed seeing her in such a way. It was like staring at another person. But there was something behind her eyes. Something guarded.

"Are you sure you're okay to watch Abby tonight?" she asked me.

I resisted scoffing. This notion that I was too useless to look after my own daughter grated on me, but I let it slip for the sake of my plan. I met her gaze. "I'll be fine. Besides, I think you need a night out. These past few days haven't been easy on you."

She studied me like she was trying to decide whether to believe what I was saying. Finally, she sighed and pushed off the door frame. "I won't be too late."

"It's fine. Be as late as you want. Go have fun, honey."

She nodded and stepped into the room. She bent down to Abby. "You be good for your daddy, okay?" She gave Abby a big squeeze and a kiss on the cheek that left a lipstick mark. Abby giggled at the sensation.

"Bye," Maia said to me as she left, not giving me the same affection.

"Where's Mommy going?" Abby asked. I knew she hadn't understood what was happening.

"With Aunt London for some fun. She'll be back soon."

Abby's eyes grew large with concern. She was so used to having her mother around that she could barely cope when Maia had to be away from her for too long a time. That needed to change.

I listened for the sound of the front door opening and closing, then stood. I moved to the window and brushed the curtain aside a few inches. London's headlights flashed as she reversed out into the street.

Then I returned to Abby and asked her to stand. "We need to get you ready, sweetheart."

"For bed?"

"No, honey. You haven't even had dinner yet. We need to get you ready for a little adventure. How would you like to go see Thea for a playdate?"

Her eyes lit up. The novelty of something she'd been denied her entire life was enough to keep her happy.

"Can we go now?" she asked.

"Soon, honey. But I need you to promise me something first."

"What?" she asked, her brows knitted.

"We need to keep your visit to Aunty Claire and Uncle Richard's a secret. We can't tell Mommy about it. Do you think you can do that for me?"

Abby nodded with an open mouth. I doubted she understood or that she would keep the secret. Still, I had to try. And if Abby did say anything to Maia about her night with Thea, I would lay it on thick that she was talking about our dinner party. It wasn't perfect, but it would do.

I smiled to myself. Once a suitable amount of time had passed, I'd have Abby with my sister to be fed and looked after. Then I would be free to head to Syracuse and see what Maia was up to.

I knew my wife. She wouldn't last long with London. She'd call it a night at around nine and tell London she was getting an Uber home. It was what she was going to do on her way home that concerned me. I only prayed she didn't go where I thought she was planning on sneaking off to. It all depended on how much she was starting to remember.

This wasn't about trust. This was about keeping the past where it belonged.

CHAPTER FORTY-ONE

Maia

London drove us into Syracuse in her silver Benz. It was a nice car. Even I could admit that. But with every mile that grew between me and Abby, my heart rate increased. By instinct alone, I reached for my handbag to take a dose of my meds, but I froze at the zip. I still wasn't sure if the pills Dr. Corbyn had been giving me all these years were for my benefit or not.

"Are you in there?" London asked, grabbing my attention.

"Uh, yeah. I'm here, sorry."

"Excellent, because tonight is a good excuse to forget your troubles and enjoy yourself. God knows you don't do that enough, Maia."

I glanced sideways at London and wondered why she was being so protective of me. More so than usual. The mention of troubles also set me on edge. Had Brad been telling Fletcher all about my problems again? I should have said something about it the first time. I know Brad needed someone to vent to, but if that were the case, then why didn't he book himself in to see Dr. Corbyn?

"Where are we headed?" I asked, hoping to distract myself.

"West Fayette Street to some of the cocktail bars. I thought we'd start at Salt City Lounge and work our way down the street from there."

"Sounds fun," I said, forcing the words out. One cocktail bar was going to be enough for me, but London had plans to go to multiple locations. It was too much, especially with what I was dealing with at home. I shouldn't have agreed to this. Frankly, I was surprised Brad had let me. I'd just gotten back from an extra therapy session. None of us was thinking clearly.

Pushing my ranting thoughts aside, I attempted to look on the bright side and ignore the pit in my stomach that was trying its hardest to drag me back home. Who knows? Maybe I would enjoy myself for a change and forget about everything for a few hours. I needed to stop dwelling on the negative at every turn and start living again. That was supposed to be the plan, but the last few days had been a mess.

We reached West Fayette Street and found somewhere to park. It was dark, and the temperature had dropped. A chill ran down my spine. I didn't want to sound paranoid, but I was a big believer in listening to my body when it was trying to warn me. After the incident with the garden shed, I felt like I was being watched. It was enough to make me want to swallow my meds and let the chemicals do what they did best. But I couldn't. As painful as it would be to go without them, I couldn't continue living my life in a state of oblivion. I needed to remember again.

As I stepped inside Salt City Lounge with London, the warmth of the space wrapped around me. A dim glow of candlelight flickered off the room's dark wood and exposed brick. The air in the bar was thick with the scent of citrus and spiced liquor. A low hum of conversation ran like a tap and filled the building with energy.

I was entirely out of my element.

London prodded me inside. We walked by a large, circular mirror that hung on the wall, reflecting a golden glow from the chandeliers above. The setup made the intimate space feel a lot bigger than it was. I shifted my stiff posture while London strode ahead. She was already scanning the menu like she belonged here. I had never visited the establishment before. Apparently, it had only been around for three years. There had once been a restaurant here instead, but the business went under after the owner ran it into the ground.

Salt City Lounge was the kind of place London loved and thrived in. It was stylish, cozy, and effortlessly sophisticated. No matter where my eyes landed, something reminded me of her. It felt like a place people ventured to so they could sip expensive drinks and show their status to whoever was watching.

Spending time here was going to drain me.

"Right this way," a waitress said, pointing us along. We followed her to a reserved table down at the end of the room. "I'll be back shortly to take your order," she said as she left.

I settled into place and realized that almost every table was full. I had to check again, seeing as it was a Monday night. "How did you get this reservation at the last minute?" I asked.

London leaned forward. "I might know the owner," she said with a sly grin.

"How?"

London kept her voice down. "You could say we slept together."

I couldn't tell if she was telling the truth or not, but we both shared a laugh. Maybe I would enjoy myself and wouldn't attempt to flee home the first chance I got.

We ordered some Espresso Martinis. I added a slider to my order against London's wishes. There was no way I was going to drink on an empty stomach. As we sipped our drinks, it occurred to me that London had driven us to the bar. "How are we getting home?" I asked.

She waved me off. "Don't worry. We'll work that out later."

I tried not to let her lack of planning get to me. This wasn't London's first time going out drinking. She knew what she was doing. I would take off on my own at around nine or ten. I just had to survive until then.

"What's Fletcher up to tonight?" I asked to make conversation.

"Waiting at his place for me."

"Wow, you've got him trained well."

"Don't stress. He thinks he's getting lucky tonight." London cackled, and I joined in. It was nice to see her in a relationship that meant something. I truly hoped for her sake it lasted, even if the man she was infatuated with was Fletcher of all people. I wasn't sure if I was supposed to tell her what he had done all those years ago. It was a problem for another day.

My food came, and London ordered more cocktails. We chatted and drank. With every sip, I felt safer and at ease. After we'd been in the place for two hours, she was ready to leave and move on to the next one.

"Do we have to?" I asked. I hated shifting around like this. When we used to go out, it always bothered me when London would do this.

"Yes, we do. It's been so long since we've done this. I have to show you what you've been missing out on."

I didn't know if it was the alcohol in my system or my fatigue, but her comment caught me off guard. "It's not a joke," I said.

"What's not a joke?"

"My condition. I don't enjoy being this way. It's not a choice, you know?"

"I never said it was. We can stay here if you want," London said. Her tone made it clear that my needs were overshadowing anyone else's. Maybe I was being a touch ungrateful. London had gone to a lot of effort to give me her version of help, especially after we'd had an argument. Still, I didn't appreciate the notion that I was burdening her by wanting to stay in one place for the evening.

"It's fine," I said. "Show me to the next place. But I'm warning you now that I will have to head home after that. I've had a long day."

"Oh, come on. You can't go home that early. It's not like Bradley will be waiting up for you. Besides, things don't heat up in these places until people have gotten a few drinks into them. I'd hate for you to miss out."

There she went again, saying I'd missed out. I let her comment slide as we worked our way through the bar to leave. The volume of chatter had doubled. The noise was closing in on all sides, adding to my increased heart rate. I focused on my breathing as I reached down to my handbag again. It was taking everything I had in me not to pull out a fistful of tablets and swallow them dry.

When we left the cocktail bar, I stumbled out into the open air and allowed a cool breeze to wash over me. An instant calm simmered my brain to the point where dizziness took over. I made my way toward the nearest wall and had to lean against it.

"Are you okay?" London asked. No doubt she could see the sweat coating my brow.

"I think so," I said, but I knew I wasn't. I needed to go home. I needed to lay eyes on Abby, all tucked up and asleep in her bed. It was the only thing that would calm me down.

London continued to stare at me. At first, I thought she was annoyed. But her expression was filled with pity.

"Maybe you should head home," London offered.

"No, it's fine. I just need a minute, sorry," I said as I closed my eyes.

"Seriously, it's fine. This whole thing was a bad idea. I don't know what he was thinking."

My eyes popped open. "What who was thinking?"

"Uh, no one," London said. "Let me order you an Uber. I'll pay."

"Forget the Uber," I said, pushing off the wall. "You said that you didn't know what *he* was thinking. Who are you talking about? Brad?"

London laughed. "No, not Brad. I was talking about Fletcher."

I watched as she held her forced grin. She was lying to me. This had been Brad's idea. But he had acted so annoyed when we found London in our driveway. Had his reaction been a performance?

London was staring straight at me, so I did what I could to hide my thoughts. I didn't want to call her a liar and give her a reason to storm off with feigned offense. I needed to play along and find out why she had taken me out of the house tonight. What was Brad up to?

"Okay," I said. "You know what? I'm feeling a lot better. Let's go to the next cocktail bar."

"Are you sure? I'm happy to order you—"

"I'm fine, London. Like you said, I need to see what I've been missing out on."

She gave me a weak smile. "All right, then. Let's keep moving."

CHAPTER FORTY-TWO

The next cocktail bar was just as crowded as the last. London couldn't get us a table at this one, so we had to sit at the bar and wait for something to open up. We were warned that it could take at least an hour. I didn't care. I just wanted to find out why Brad had set this night up.

It could have been as innocent as him thinking I needed an evening away from the house. Or maybe he thought it would do me some good to leave Abby with him, but was too afraid to ask. Those were the nicer possibilities. Given everything that had been going through my head in the past few days, it was hard to accept anything so positive.

My brain, being my brain, came up with a whole host of crazy ideas. They ranged from infidelity to the downright absurd. I couldn't help it. The stress of being away from Abby with this discovery and everything else was overwhelming me. I needed to stop wasting time and ask London why Brad had set this night up. We were drinking in silence, as it was. She clearly was feeling guilty about something.

"I'm sorry to do this to you," I started, "but I have to ask."

London inhaled sharply, but didn't speak. She waited for me to continue.

"Why did Brad ask you to take me out tonight?"

"He didn't. Well, technically, Fletcher did. But, yeah, it was Brad's idea."

"Why the big ruse, though? Why did he act all surprised to see you at our house, like he had no idea about any of it?"

She shrugged. "I don't know what goes through your husband's brain, sometimes. Fletcher called me and asked if I could do him a favor. He explained that Brad thought it would be nice for the two of us to go out tonight, but he said it had to come across as my idea and not Brad's. That's as much as I know."

I shook my head, unsure what I was supposed to do with what London had admitted to me.

"I know it sounds weird, but please don't say anything to Brad," London said.

"Why?"

"Because he'll say something to Fletcher, then Fletcher will be pissed at me." Her voice was getting more frantic with each word.

"Okay, I get it. I won't say anything." I paused, taking in London's body language. "Wow, you've really got it bad for him, don't you?"

London smiled on one side of her mouth. "Don't tell anyone. I'm sorry for lying to you. I just thought it sounded like a nice idea. You and I haven't done anything like this in so long. Not since . . ." She trailed off, but I knew what she was going to say.

"It's okay," I said, lightly gripping her forearm. "I know I haven't been a good friend since Imogen died. Something inside me changed that day."

London nodded as her eyes watered. "Don't blame yourself. Everything that happened to you back then wasn't your fault."

"Everything? What do you mean?" I asked.

Wiping her eyes, she stared around the cocktail bar, as if she was trying to avoid my eyes. "I just mean with Imogen. That's all."

"Is there something else?" I asked, leaning close to her.

"Nothing."

I narrowed my gaze. "Are you talking about when I got pregnant with Abby?"

London shook her head. "Not that. I shouldn't say anything. I promised Fletcher I wouldn't, but Brad. He—" She cut herself off. "I can't do this. I have to go. I've said too much." And just like that, she took off, charging for the exit, leaving her cocktail behind.

"London," I called after her across the rowdy crowd. She kept going and picked up her pace. I scrambled my things up from the bar and followed. Where the hell was she going, and why had she mentioned Brad's name just now?

I struggled to push through the crowd of people. By the time I made it outside, London was halfway down the street, heading toward her car. She wasn't seriously thinking about driving it home, was she?

"London," I called out, but she ignored me again. I just wanted to talk. I just wanted to know what she was trying to tell me and to stop her from doing anything stupid. She'd had more to drink than me. Surely, she wouldn't get behind the wheel?

I dismissed the thought. She knew better. And she also knew something about my husband. I had to find out what that was.

I tried calling her cell phone, but she wasn't answering. I watched as she made it to her Mercedes and rushed to climb inside it. She fired up the engine and tore out into the street in a hurry, flying straight past me like I didn't exist.

"Oh, my God," I uttered. She was going to lose her license or have a crash. I didn't know if I should call Fletcher or the police. What if she hurt someone?

I stood on the sidewalk with a slack jaw as she vanished down the street. I didn't know where she was going. I only hoped it was close by.

My hands shook as I gripped my handbag and cell phone like they were too heavy for me to handle. I had to get away from the area.

Wandering down the street, I came to a small parking lot that was close to a waterway. I took a seat on an empty park bench. I held up my cell phone and saw that it was just after nine, right around the time I had wanted to head home. But not like this. Not with London leaving me with more questions than when we left the house.

I opened the Uber app and was about to find myself a ride home, but I stared at the screen and thought hard about what London had said — about what happened after Imogen had died. The only thing that stood out in my mind was me falling pregnant with Abby. I could never forget that moment when Brad and I had sex for the first time since we lost our child. I wasn't sure what spurred it on, but whatever it was, it had filled me with hope for the future. And it had happened exactly a year after Imy's death. But my having sex with my husband couldn't have been the thing that'd stuck in London's mind.

Then what was it?

I closed my eyes and concentrated as hard as I could. There was something in there, but it was like trying to decipher what was casting a blurry shadow without being able to see the object in question. "I don't know," I said out loud. A sigh escaped me. I was sitting alone on a park bench, talking to myself. I needed to go home and forget this night and write off London's behavior as nothing but one too many drinks. I just hoped she got to wherever she was going safely.

I stared down at my cell phone again to order that rideshare when it hit me. I was coming at this problem from the wrong angle. London was telling me about *something* that had happened after Imogen passed — something with Brad. Again, all I could think about was Abby's conception, and that was one year after we lost Imogen, but it was also four years ago. Four years ago, a certain someone went missing.

I rushed to find the article about Oswald Taylor again. "Holy crap." How had I not realized when I'd first read the article? Oswald Taylor went missing exactly one year after Imogen died. The same night, Brad and I conceived Abby. Is that what London was talking about? Did she know something about Brad possibly killing Oswald Taylor? But how could she have known a thing like that?

I needed to speak to London. I cleared my address from the app and entered Fletcher's instead. London had said she was going to end up at his home tonight. I didn't care how drunk she was.

We were going to talk.

CHAPTER FORTY-THREE

I only knew where Fletcher lived because of Brad. Over the years, Fletcher had hosted a lot of parties in his large home in Syracuse, and Brad had made me attend most of them. But that was before. After Imogen, I hadn't been back to Fletcher's home — not once.

Brad doesn't know, but Fletcher hit on me in the past. Actually, it was worse than that, and not some inappropriate comment or a bit of flirting. He came to me when I had been alone at one of his parties and baldly asked if I wanted to sleep with him. Initially, I had thought it was just one of his bad jokes or that he was drunk, but he was serious. When I said no, he dismissed my rejection and tried to kiss me. I could still feel his hands on me, gripping my shoulders tightly while I tried to twist away from him. It wasn't until I drove my knee into his balls that he gave up on the idea.

After that, it was like he had realized where we were and what he had done. He apologized ten times over and begged me not to tell Brad. "Please, Maia," he'd said. "I was drunk. It was just a stupid mistake."

I had thought about telling Brad at the time, but I decided not to, lying to myself that it was a case of too much alcohol and nothing more. But the real reason I never told my husband was for his sake. If I had told Brad, it would have meant the end of his friendship with Fletcher. I guess I didn't want that to happen. I let the moron off the hook, giving him a second chance. He'd never made the mistake again, but I couldn't look at him without remembering that leer in his eye when he tried to force himself upon me.

I asked the Uber driver to pull into Fletcher's long driveway. Despite my feelings toward the man, Fletcher had a stunning home. It was oversized, expensive, and had more bedrooms and bathrooms than he'd ever need — even if London moved in.

There weren't any lights on inside. There was only the dim glow of external lights casting long shadows across his perfectly manicured lawn.

The driver shifted in his seat, waiting for me to get out. I pulled out my cell phone and tried London again. She didn't answer. "Dammit," I muttered.

"Excuse me, ma'am. Are you getting out?"

"Just a second, sorry. I might need to go somewhere else. If you wait one more minute, I'll give you a good tip."

He sighed and turned away.

Wishing I didn't have to, I navigated to Fletcher's name in my list of contacts. I hated having him in my phone, but he'd made it on the list years and years ago. I had wanted to remove him after the incident, but I didn't want Brad to ever find out and ask why I had deleted his best friend's number.

I made the call. "Maia!" Fletcher answered with far too much enthusiasm.

"Sorry to be calling you so late," I said.

"Too late? You're kidding, right? This is early for me. Anyway, what can I do for you? Don't tell me London is hammered already." He chuckled down the line as if life were one big joke. And that's what it was to men like him. I shook my head and held back on chastising him for the comment about London.

"Nothing like that," I said. "Well, sort of. I'm trying to reach her."

"Reach her? I thought the two of you were going out tonight?"

"We were. We did, but, uh, we had a fight, and she kind of took off on me."

There was a long pause on the line before Fletcher spoke. "Oh, damn. That's no good. You know what she can be like, though." He chuckled.

"I do. That's why I was wondering if she was with you. She told me she was going to your place after."

"Not until later," he said.

"She said the two of you were going out and not to wait up for her. Her coming to my place after was a maybe at best."

"She's not with you or on her way to your place now?" I asked, looking directly at his house. It looked like no one was there, but the damn thing was so big Fletcher could have been in any of the rooms.

"No," he said. His voice wavered with what almost sounded like concern. "Anyway, if she hasn't made it to my place by now, I'd say she's gone home for the night."

"Okay," I said on autopilot.

I thanked Fletcher and hung up. Then I typed in London's address into my app and sent the order to my driver along with a decent-sized tip for the first trip. We got underway, resuming our silent journey.

Ten minutes later, we arrived outside of London's home. It was similar in a lot of ways to Fletcher's but had a more modern look and feel. London had shelled out for a pricey renovation five or six years ago, and now the place was nearly due for another major overhaul.

This time, I left the Uber and paced up her round driveway and was surprised not to see the silver Coupe parked where it usually sat. The lights weren't on inside either. Only her external ones. I climbed several steps and approached the front door. With a slow breath out, I rang the bell. No one answered, so I tried calling her again.

Voicemail. I left her a concerned message saying that I simply wanted to know if she was okay. It wasn't a lie. Her not being at Fletcher's or at her own home filled my insides with irrevocable dread. Had something bad happened to her? I wanted to know what she had been trying to tell me back at the cocktail bar, but more than that, I wanted to know she was safe. There was still a chance she had parked her car in one of her garages and had gone inside, but then again, she liked to have her car out and ready so she could take off at a moment's notice.

I didn't know what to do. I took a seat on the lowest step and thought back to our conversation at the cocktail bar. I wasn't sure how or why, but she knew something about Brad and possibly something else from four years ago. The way she had looked at Brad during our dinner party and had called him a killer was undeniable. What secret had Brad been forcing her to keep all these years? And more importantly, what had brought it up from the shadows?

With no idea where London was, I had to use this opportunity to go to the next best source. I opened the Uber app one more time.

CHAPTER FORTY-FOUR

Brad

What the hell was Maia up to? I'd followed her from West Fayette Street to Fletcher's house, but now she was sitting outside of London's home. Most likely, she was there looking for London after their little disagreement earlier, but my instincts told me that there was more to what I was seeing. Maia was a predictable person most days, but these two addresses were filling me with concern.

I'd thought that arranging for London to take Maia out for the night was a good idea. It was supposed to distract her for a few hours and lull her into a false sense of security. I'd wanted her to think when she'd left Syracuse and London for the night that she'd be entirely alone and free to go wherever she wanted. I wasn't expecting her to go to Fletcher's home and now London's, but I should have been grateful. There were worse places she could have taken herself to. Ones that could destroy everything.

As I continued to watch Maia, I wondered what her argument with London had been about. It couldn't have been anything significant. London was dramatic on a good day. No doubt she'd had too much to drink and had said something stupid — her specialty. After all, she didn't know a damn thing about what I was trying to keep Maia from remembering. I was certain of it. Only Fletcher could be trusted with such knowledge.

I hadn't thought about that night in several months, but these past few days were pulling up all sorts of memories. I wished I could have erased it from my mind. My life would be so much easier.

After it happened, I had been ready to go to the police. I even had my cell phone out to make the call, but then Maia uttered those words. The ones that changed everything. When I saw her face, I knew what I had to do.

The mind is capable of strange things when it's pushed too far. Especially when it can't handle the weight of certain realities. And that's what eventually happened. Maia's brain didn't like what it had seen and blocked it out.

Over the next few weeks, we talked less and less about what happened. It was like the night was fading from her mind. Then, when we found out she was pregnant, the subject was never spoken of again.

For four years, Maia hadn't remembered that night. But every day I woke could have been my last. It could have come back to her at any time and changed her mind. That's why I kept her dosed. That's why I made sure she spent time with her therapist. And if enough of her memories returned, or if something came along to threaten everything I had worked so hard to achieve, I had one last plan in place.

"One step at a time," I said, reassuring myself that we hadn't crossed that bridge. Not yet, but I feared it was just up ahead, inviting her in. And it was up to her to say no and walk in the opposite direction.

Maia stepped away from London's home with her cell phone out. Its bright screen illuminated her face with a sharp glow. I ducked down when she looked up in my direction. For a second,

I swore she had seen me, but I was just being paranoid. I wasn't driving around in my car — I was sitting in the dark in a rental she had no idea about.

In the mirror I was staring into, Maia didn't look flustered. There was no hint that she had just spotted her husband spying on her. But she wasn't relaxed either. Most likely, she was waiting for another Uber to arrive. I wasn't seeing any charges on our credit card each time she used the service. She must have set up her own account. I didn't know how she was funding her travel. That concern would have to wait.

A few minutes later, her driver arrived. I watched as she climbed in. The car took off and seemed to head back toward our home in Brookfield Terrace. Relief washed over me. She was going home. If she got home before me, she'd see my note saying how I took Abby around to my sister's place for a quick visit. If she called me, I would explain that the visit lasted longer than planned.

I started my rental and followed at a safe distance.

I shook my head and chuckled, wondering why I had panicked so much. Maia was still in the dark about that night. For whatever reason, I doubted that would ever change. Her mind never wanted to remember that moment. She was lucky, really. I would have given anything to enjoy the same luxury.

As the turnoff for our home came up, Maia's driver turned right instead of left. I sat up straight and checked the GPS in front of me. This wasn't some alternative route. This wasn't the long way home. I knew exactly where she was headed.

"Don't do it," I whispered, praying my wife could somehow hear my pleas and go back home where she belonged. But the driver kept going. He came to a stop at an address that could devastate everything in one fell swoop. It was Julia Taylor's home.

CHAPTER FORTY-FIVE

Maia

Julia Taylor's address was around twenty minutes away. I knew heading there so late at night was a crazy idea, but crazy was where the week had landed me. I had no clue if she was going to be home or if she even lived there anymore, but I had to try. I had to find out what I could about what happened four years ago before I lost my mind. With any luck, Oswald Taylor's wife would give me something.

London was holding onto a secret. Not just any secret, but one between her and Brad that involved me and possibly something from four years ago. Something about the night Oswald Taylor disappeared. It had to be significant for London to have run away from me in such a way and drive off in her car, half drunk.

Going to see Julia Taylor felt like a desperate move, one that was rooted in nothing but a gut feeling. I couldn't explain why, but something was drawing me to speak to her. It was like a memory on the edge of my mind I couldn't decipher. There had to be something she knew that could point me in the right direction. If not, I was out of ideas.

I sat in the back of the rideshare and tried calling London again. No matter how many times I attempted to get through or how many voicemails I left her, she wouldn't pick up or return my call. I wasn't just calling to avoid knocking on Julia Taylor's door, but also to ensure she'd made it home safe.

My driver arrived at the Taylor residence. It looked like it did online, but less kempt. The place had a quiet, almost forgotten feeling. Its pale blue paint was weathered, its white trim had dulled with time, and a wide porch stretched across the front with a railing that was intact but slightly warped. The house looked like it had endured one too many Syracuse winters without any maintenance.

I exhaled, pressing my palms against my thighs. This was it — Julia Taylor's house. The home of a woman whose husband had vanished four years ago, a man whom my own husband had been searching for in news articles.

The man who'd killed my baby.

I thanked the driver and stepped out onto an uneven pavement. I closed the passenger door and tugged at my dress. I looked ridiculous, overdressed for someone showing up on a stranger's doorstep at close to ten o'clock at night. The thought made me hesitate. What was I doing?

I should have called the driver back and gone home. That would have been the smart thing to do, but instead, I closed my eyes and found my breath again. I exhaled once more and opened my eyes. I forced my feet to move. It was time to get some answers.

The path to the porch was cracked and overrun with an uneven lawn that spilled over the edges. I reached the steps of the porch and took them one at a time, feeling each one groan under my weight. Prickles ran down my spine as I ascended the small steps toward the front door. Everything about this idea felt wrong, like there was someone breathing down my neck. But I knew it was just my mind trying its hardest to send me back home to where I felt safe.

I came to a stop at the front door and raised a fist to knock. There was a doorbell, but it had wires hanging out of it like it wouldn't function if I tried.

My hand stayed fixed in place. All I had to do was knock and see if Julia Taylor still lived here or if she was even home. That was the first step. I could take it from there one minute at a time.

"You can do this," I whispered.

Finally, I knocked.

The sound felt too loud in the night's stillness and seemed to carry. I stepped back, pulling my hand down as I swallowed hard. Nothing but a cool breeze found my ears as I strained for movement inside.

There was nothing.

I blew out my trembling breath and glanced back toward the street. My driver was long gone. If I left now, I'd have to wait on the side of the road for another ride, standing alone in the dark like some kind of lunatic who went around knocking on strangers' doors at ten at night. This was not the way I had envisioned my day going.

I turned back just as I heard the shuffle of movement on the other side of the door. Someone was home. The porch light flickered on above and buzzed. A curtain shifted as a face appeared in the narrow window beside the door.

A lock clicked, then the door cracked open a touch.

The woman's face was barely visible in the dim light, half concealed by a chain that was still in place. I had seen Julia's picture online from her social media campaigns to find her husband. This was *her*. I'd found Julia Taylor. Given everything that had been happening to me since the dinner party, it was a victory in itself.

Despite only being able to see Julia through a small gap, I could glimpse the toll the past four years had taken on her. According to what I knew about the woman, she was in her early forties, but looked older. Her dark hair was pulled back into a messy ponytail, with strands falling loose around a face that carried exhaustion in every line. She blinked at me with hesitation and a furrowed brow. She didn't look like she was going to open the door all the way for me. I didn't blame her.

"Mrs. Taylor?" I asked, keeping my voice low.

She said nothing as her eyes flicked past me and scanned the porch and her yard like she was expecting someone else to be with me. Then, finally, her gaze landed back on mine.

"Who are you?" she asked. Her voice was hoarse, as if she hadn't spoken much in a long while.

"My name is Maia," I said quickly. "I know it's late, and I'm sorry for showing up like this. But I need to talk to you about your husband. Do you have a minute?"

The door slammed.

The porch light was extinguished.

The lock clicked back into place.

I heard the sound of Julia walking away inside. "No," I let out like an exhale. I hadn't come all this way and risked humiliation to have a door slammed in my face. I knocked again, this time louder. "Julia, please. I just want to talk about Oswald." Painful silence followed as I waited. Almost thirty seconds went by before I heard her walk toward the front door again. The porch light came back on, and the door unlocked. Julia opened the door again, but this time she had removed the chain and faced me in full.

"What do you know about Oswald?" she asked with a tight grip on her door. She looked ready to slam it even harder than before.

With a measured breath in and out, I readied myself. "Is your husband missing?"

Julia's brow screwed up tighter than it did before. "Yes. That's why you're here, right?"

"Yes."

"Then why ask such a stupid question?"

"You don't understand. I—"

"I understand entirely. You thought it would be a good idea to harass the wife of a man who has been missing for four years. And at ten o'clock on a Monday night, of all things. What the hell is wrong with you?"

I waited a moment in case she had more to unleash. Her breath sounded labored as she stood there staring at me, her grip on the door tightening again.

"Mrs. Taylor, I am sorry for coming here like this. I never meant to upset you."

"It's a bit late for that."

The sound of a trash can falling over cut into our conversation. I glanced toward it for a beat but saw nothing. I waved off the distraction and faced Julia again. "I know. Trust me, I do. More than you can ever imagine."

Her shoulders stiffened. "What do you want, exactly? Because you've got about ten seconds before I slam this door again and call the police."

"I need to talk to you about your husband."

"Why?"

"I think I might know what happened to him," I blurted.

Julia's mouth hung open, and her eye twitched. "You what?"

What was I doing? If I thought Brad had killed the man who had taken Imogen away from me, I shouldn't have cared about his wife. But there was a pain in her eyes I couldn't cast aside. If she gave me something that could implicate Brad as guilty for Oswald's murder, I think I owed it to Julia to at least tell her the truth. But I needed to confirm it for myself first.

I took a breath in and out and closed my eyes for a second to level myself. When I opened them again, I looked right at Julia and said, "I think I know what happened to him four years ago."

CHAPTER FORTY-SIX

Julia Taylor took me to a dining room and told me to take a seat at the table. She disappeared into the next area of the house, into what I assumed was a kitchen. The dining room itself was small and worn, much like the rest of the home. A scuffed rectangular table sat in the center with four mismatched chairs surrounding it.

Julia returned and set a mug of coffee in front of me before taking a seat across the table. She didn't make one for herself and hadn't even asked if I wanted one. It was like she was running on autopilot. I knew the feeling.

"So, you think you know what happened to Oswald?" she asked.

I nodded, gripping my hands together in my lap. "I know this might sound crazy, but I have a theory."

"A theory? You can't be serious? Either you know or you don't," she bit out. "What are you, some kind of desperate reporter? Is that what this is?"

"No. I promise you I'm not here to cash in on your tragedy in any way. I'm just looking for the truth. Like you."

She stared at me for a while longer through eyes that looked to be clouded by four years of agony. My presence was only making things worse, but I had to do this. I'd come too far to walk away now.

She let out a tired breath. "I'm sorry if I seem angry. It's been a hard four years. Everyone was so interested in Oswald's case when he first went missing. Now, they don't care or come round looking for a quick interview so they can rehash what has already been said a hundred times before. They just see him as a missing person and nothing more."

I paused and chose my words carefully. "You don't believe that he went missing, do you?"

Julia's eyes flicked up to mine. "I know my husband," she said. "And I know the difference between when someone disappears because they want to and when they disappear because someone made them."

"So you think that something bad happened the night he was last seen?"

"I don't think that. I *know* it. Oswald would never just up and leave. Sure, he liked to go hiking whenever he got the chance. He went alone most times. But he also loved me and would never have done something like this."

I nodded, trying my hardest to show that I understood. Everything about this woman told me she believed her husband was dead, that he'd never come home.

"Tell me more about him," I said, knowing that I needed to build up trust with her. I didn't want to hear about the man who had dragged my little girl into a lake to drown her, but at the same time, it might help me understand why. There had always been an impersonal sense of randomness to Imogen's death.

"Oswald was a good man," she said, her voice calmer. "The kind who would pull over in the middle of a rainstorm just to help a stranger change a tire. He was patient and steady. He never raised his voice to me, not once in all our years together. Even when he was angry, he'd just—" She shook her head with a wistful smile. "He'd just go quiet for a minute, then say what needed to be said. No more, no less."

I nodded again, keeping eye contact. How was this possible? How could we have been talking about the same person? I did what I could to hide my contempt and swallowed my anger. Because what I had to say next was going to push the limits of my welcome. Again, I'd made it this far. I had to try. "I wanted to ask you something else about him."

"What is it?"

"This is going to sound strange, but did Oswald know a man named Brad?"

"Brad? It's not ringing any bells. Does this Brad have a last name?"

"Yes, Fairbanks. Bradley Fairbanks."

"Fairbanks," she said, repeating the word as her eyes drifted away. Then, as suddenly as she had disappeared to make me a coffee I didn't ask for, she stood from the table and left the room again. This time, she had a bounce in her step.

"Where are you going?" I called out.

"Just a minute," she replied without explaining further.

I stared around the space, noticing the cobwebs in the corner and the layers of dust on most surfaces. Mrs. Taylor had not been coping well since Oswald had gone missing. I understood her pain. After Imogen was gone, I didn't touch the cleaning schedule for months. Brad had to hire cleaners to come twice a week. I hated having them there, touching our things.

Julia returned to the room with some documents in her hand. She sat down and had glasses on now. With her index finger extended, she read some words in front of herself, going line by line until she stopped midway down the page.

"Fairbanks," she said.

"What is that?" I asked, wondering why she had a document with Brad's name on it.

"Maia Fairbanks," she said.

"*What?*" I spat. We both looked each other in the eye.

"That's you, isn't it?" she asked with a shaky hand. "You're her. Maia Fairbanks."

"What is that? Why do you have my name on a document?"

She shook her head and pulled the paperwork toward herself. "I don't."

"Yes, you do," I said, standing. "Show it to me."

She withdrew the papers and stood. "You need to leave."

"Not on your life. I want to know what this is all about. How do you know my name?"

"Get out," she roared.

"No," I fired back. "Not until you show me." I reached for the papers and attempted to snatch them from her hands. She held on tight. I could make out the top of the document. It was a police report. But not just any police report. The report was dated the same day Imogen was killed.

"Give that back," Julia yelled as she twisted away from me, taking the documents with her. "You don't understand." She stood with the crumpled papers in her hand.

We held each other's gazes and panted. My eyes darted to the report and back again. I could get the document with another try, but was I willing to resort to such a thing in the home of a woman who was about to call the police and have me arrested?

I took a step toward her right as the front door banged open. We both looked in that direction with narrowed brows. Had one of her neighbors heard the commotion and was coming to see if Julia was okay?

A figure appeared at the threshold of the dining room and stared straight at me. My jaw dropped when I realized who it was.

"Hi, honey," Brad said.

CHAPTER FORTY-SEVEN

Brad didn't look away. He didn't even bother to say who he was to Julia Taylor or why he was there. All he seemed to care about was me.

My nose wrinkled. "Did you follow me here?"

He didn't answer and finally gave some attention to Julia, who seemed more confused by the situation than I was. His focus homed in on the police report in her hand. The one that apparently had my name on it. "How much of that did she see?" he asked without introducing himself or apologizing for his intrusion.

"Are you Brad? Are you her husband?" she yelled at him, ignoring the question.

"Just tell me and we'll leave right now."

"*What?*" I seethed. Brad held up a finger to silence me without looking. He was treating me like a dog that was demanding to be fed before dinnertime.

"She didn't see any of it. Now get out."

"Fine," Brad said. "We're going. I'm sorry for the interruption." He walked toward me with a hand outstretched.

I swatted him away. "I'm not going anywhere with you," I yelled.

"Maia, come now. So help me God, I will call the police."

We held each other's stare for a beat as something came to me. "Okay then, call the police."

He chuckled with a sneer and shook his head. "Just come with me. Now." His hand clutched my arm and pulled. Julia looked on, shock and confusion lining her forehead while Brad dragged me out of her dining room. I tried to resist and stop him, but he was too strong for me. In all our years together, he'd never handled me in such a way. And it all clicked into place. He wouldn't be treating me like this, taking me away from Julia Taylor's home if he didn't have something to hide. I did the only thing I could.

"My husband is dangerous." The words escaped me and stopped Brad in his tracks. I continued while I still could. "You know my name. This is my husband, Bradley Fairb—"

A hand flew over my mouth and silenced me. Brad threw all his might into dragging me out of the room and was trying to get me out of Julia's home. I tried to resist and fight back, clutching his wrists, but Brad wouldn't let go. Where was he taking me? What was he going to do when we got there?

"I'm calling the police," Julia yelled. I didn't know what she would tell them, but it didn't matter. Just as long as they came and put a stop to Brad. All I had to do was avoid being dragged away to wherever it was Brad was planning on taking me.

I let go of his wrists and threw my arms out, finding purchase on the doorframe to Julia's home. I held on as tight as I could. Brad released his grip for a second. Long enough for me to rush back inside the house and away from him.

"Maia," he yelled. "You need to come with me. Right now."

"I'm not going anywhere with you," I yelled as I retreated into the dining room.

"Yes, you are," Brad called after me. He gave chase and cornered me in the room. The dining table sat between us as we stared each other down. Off in the kitchen, Julia was on the phone with the police.

"Why did you come here?" Brad asked.

"You tell me," I fired back. "What would make me come to this woman's home in the middle of the night?"

Brad exhaled and kept his voice down. "I know you read the article."

"Of course I did. What? Did you think I was going to ignore the way you've been behaving or the fact that you were looking up the disappearance of a man from Brookfield Terrace four years ago? Not to mention whatever secret you and London have been keeping about the whole thing."

"London?" he asked, seeming confused. He stared for a moment longer as something ticked over in his mind. "You don't understand." His eyes flicked between me and the kitchen where Julia was.

"What's there to understand? I know what you did, and I know why you did it."

Brad's brows narrowed. "What is it exactly you think you know, Maia? I want you to say it."

My mouth opened to speak, but I couldn't bring myself to utter the words. My hands were gripping the backrest of a chair in the room as tightly as possible. I wanted to call him a killer, but it wasn't as simple as uttering the word. There was so much power behind it.

"Screw you," I yelled as I picked up the chair. I threw it at him and watched as it collided with his face. Brad yelled out in pain, so I used the distraction to get the hell out of the house. I bolted past him and hoped he would follow. There was no sense in Julia Taylor being harmed just so I could get away. She hadn't done anything wrong. Our husbands were the psychotic ones.

I crashed into a wall. A sharp pain radiated up my side as a result. It slowed me for a second, but I ignored the sting in my flesh and kept going. Brad charged after me as I'd hoped he would.

If I could coax him outside, the police would soon arrive and handle him. I'd danced around it all for too long. Brad needed to go to prison for what I now knew he had done.

As I crossed through the front door, his hands found their way around me again and stopped me in my tracks. I tried to call out for him to let go, but a sharp prick pinched against the skin in my neck. It was gone before I could react. But then came a burn like ice and fire all at once. It spread out from my neck like a poison.

"What . . ." I tried to say as a familiar dizziness rushed through my system like I'd stood up too fast. The floor tilted beneath me as my limbs tingled. A second later, they were too heavy to move. Brad had sedated me. A flash of a memory from before Abby was born flooded my mind.

He used to do this to me. All the time.

The chemicals rolled through my body and sent me to the floor. Brad caught me and lowered my limp form the rest of the way. I tried to speak to him, but the words wouldn't come. Darkness crawled in at the edges of my vision as I watched him stand over me with Julia at his side. They were talking as if nothing extreme had just happened. Brad's eyebrow was bleeding from the chair I'd thrown at him, but there was calmness in the room. I reached out to them both as two police officers arrived.

Then everything went dark.

CHAPTER FORTY-EIGHT

Brad

That was a close one, to say the least. And not just with Maia, but with Julia Taylor and the police. Once I had Maia out cold, I calmly explained everything to Julia. All it took for her to buy my story was for me to talk up her husband and tell her that Maia was unstable and that she had an obsession with Oswald for all the wrong reasons. With the police report backing up what I was saying, she accepted my version of the truth and updated the cops before they arrived at her home. With the drastic nature of the call, they insisted on still attending for a welfare check.

I apologized to the officers over and over when they came through the door. By that point, we had Maia laid out on Julia's sofa, taking away some of the drama of the incident. They checked on her to make sure she was breathing and that she was unharmed. I told them about the situation.

A quick call to Dr. Corbyn sealed the deal, backing up what I had told Julia as well. I had anticipated a problem like this and had cautioned the good doctor in advance to be available to take a late-night call at a time of my choosing. I didn't expect to need to use the call so soon. Mason played his part well.

After a quick threat from me reminding him of his fraud, Dr. Corbyn told the police that Maia had admitted to him she was off her meds and had seemed disoriented and paranoid in their session earlier that day. He painted a picture that she was most likely suffering from a stress-induced psychosis. I followed up, saying that I had tried to keep her home for the evening, but she had gotten dressed up and taken off on her own, using her Uber account to travel all over town. I told them she'd met with a friend of hers at a cocktail bar who had grown concerned and called me, saying that Maia was talking about going specifically to Julia Taylor's address to confront her about her missing husband, Oswald. London wasn't going to tell the police otherwise if she was asked to back up what I was saying. Not once had I told Fletcher to keep her in line.

Dr. Corbyn texted me after the call and said he was going to doctor up some false session notes and start the paperwork on having Maia put into an emergency admission for forty-eight hours at Madison Ridge Psychiatric Center in Syracuse. He knew a doctor there who would help with the situation, provided I paid for it. It wasn't going to come cheap, but I had no other choice.

While inside, Maia was to undergo psychiatric observation and would be monitored by the doctor Mason knew could handle the job. The kind who was just as shady as Mason had been with his fraud. It wasn't the first time I had placed Maia in one of these facilities before.

The first time it happened, I didn't have control of the situation and had to rely on Maia's unstable behavior to keep her inside. It was too risky and didn't last. This time would be different, though.

The police officers assisted where they could and contacted an EMT to ensure Maia was medically sound for admission. I explained that she often got violent during these episodes and would need to be restrained. That was why I had to sedate her. It was a simple thing to sell with a bleeding face. Nothing was more convincing than blood.

From what they could see, Maia had attacked me with the chair. What they didn't know was that I'd made sure to *not* move out of its flight path when she threw it at me. I added to the chair's damage by slicing at my brow with a small pocket knife once I had injected Maia with the sedative. Julia was too focused on my wife to notice. It was an opportunity I couldn't pass up. Maia was lucky I caught her in Julia Taylor's home and not outside of it. That could have resulted in an entirely different outcome.

Julia even jumped in during the discussion with the police and said that Maia was asking strange questions when she appeared on her doorstep late in the evening. Maia claimed to know what had happened to her missing husband. That part of Julia's input had me on edge. I didn't know what Maia had told her. But Julia said that Maia didn't seem to offer anything concrete about Oswald's disappearance other than bad feelings.

I'd suspected as much.

Maia still hadn't discovered the truth yet. At least not all of it. She had been close, though — too close. That damn police report could have destroyed everything.

I sat in the back of the ambulance as it transported a semi-conscious Maia to Madison Ridge Psychiatric Center. She rolled her head toward me and forced her eyes open. The sedative was wearing off. She stared at me with a hatred I'd seen before. But soon, she would receive another dose along with some powerful drugs that would keep her in the dark. I just needed her to forget tonight and to forget the news article. We could get back to normal and start again. She would one day look at me with love in her eyes. She just had to let it all go and bury any thoughts of Oswald Taylor where they belonged.

Mason said I could keep Maia in the facility we were traveling to under the emergency admission for fifteen days. After that, if she didn't show any signs of improvement the way I wanted her to, I would have to find other means to keep her in the dark. And if I couldn't manage that, I would need to end this battle once and for all. And there was only one way to do such a thing.

We arrived at the facility. I took a breath and sighed. I hated places like this, but I had gotten to know them well. My cell phone rang just as we were about to exit the ambulance. I looked at the caller ID and saw that Fletcher was calling.

"Fletcher, hey. Can I call you back? I'm kind of in the middle of something."

"*Brad*," he insisted, panic tinging his voice.

"Slow down," I said. "What's wrong?"

CHAPTER FORTY-NINE

Maia

Three days passed by in a blur. All I could remember was a series of disconnected moments. Each one was laced with screams and a constant swirling of nausea. All I know for certain is that I've been placed inside a psychiatric center. I'd been somewhere like this before.

It was the kind of place that swallowed sound. The walls were white, and the floors were gray. The air was choked with antiseptic, and the windows all had bars. I had no phone and no contact with the outside world. But worst of all, I had no way to see Abby.

The thought alone made me sick. I pressed my hands against my stomach, as if I could stop the ache, but it was no use. The weight of everything was crushing me. I was trapped in here, and my daughter was out there in the care of a man I knew was a murderer. I knew he wouldn't harm her. He loved his little girl, but the thought of her being in his sole care sent a panic to my core. I wanted her to be with me and no one else.

My door unlocked. The weighty portal creaked open, kicking my pulse up higher than it already was. Before I even looked up. A staff member named Dr. Harland entered the room with his paperwork held under his arm. He flashed a smile at me. The man was always too calm and composed for someone who worked in a place like this. He was clean-shaven and sharp-eyed, wearing an expression that was just neutral enough to feel rehearsed. He didn't wear a white coat like the other doctors. Instead, he was wearing a navy-blue T-shirt under a tailored blazer, along with a pair of dark jeans. If anything, he looked like he was visiting the place.

"Maia," he said, greeting me as he stepped farther inside. He closed the door behind him. "How are you feeling today?"

I swallowed hard, compelling myself to sit up on the stiff mattress. I couldn't act scared or show any signs of paranoia. "I'm feeling much better," I said, keeping my voice steady.

Dr. Harland studied me, tilting his head. He was probing me for a lie, as always. I kept my expression as relaxed as I could, forcing myself to meet his gaze like I wasn't thinking of ten different ways to escape this place. Like I wasn't counting down the minutes until I could get back to Abby.

"That's good to hear," he said, taking a moment longer to stare. After an awkward silence, he pulled up a chair and sat across from me. He took out his notes and started flipping through them. "We had a bit of a rough start, didn't we?"

I nodded slowly. I didn't know what I had done when they first brought me in, but I had flashes of it all. I remembered rugged hands holding me down right before a needle was pricked in my neck. All the while, I was screaming Brad's name. The next flash I remembered was waking up restrained to my bed in the middle of the night. Faint yells could be heard down the halls, and I added to them. A nurse soon came in and asked me to calm down, but I couldn't. I had to tell them about my husband. It wasn't until they flooded my veins with more drugs that I stopped.

"I think I was just overwhelmed," I said, careful with my tone. It was another lie. Well, for the most part. I had been overwhelmed. A lot had happened. Brad had exposed his true nature to me and had manipulated this situation to the point where I had been locked up and was now being treated like a deranged individual. "I think I needed a rest, you know? Just some time to clear my head."

Dr. Harland smiled again. "That's a good realization, Maia," he said as he wrote more notes. I wondered what he was writing and how truthful he was being.

"I want to go home," I said in a gentle voice. "I miss my daughter." There was no lie there. I ached for Abby. The thought of her little face and her small hands reaching for me was unbearable. What had Brad told her? That I had gone away for a while? That I was sick? He was going to turn her against me. I knew it. I only prayed she didn't believe his lies.

I gripped the blanket on my lap, pressing my nails into the fabric to keep myself from shaking. I had to stay calm and in control.

Dr. Harland let out a breath, shifting in his chair. "We'll get there," he said. "But I think we need to talk a little more first."

Of course. He wouldn't let me walk out just like that, not after the incident at Julia Taylor's home. Brad had made me out to be a violent threat. I'd overheard Dr. Harland saying as much. I should never have thrown that chair at him.

I forced a smile. "Of course." This was going to take time. I had to be perfect and convincing. I had to show them all that I was sane and lie my way out of here. Because I knew the truth. I didn't know why, but Dr. Harland was just like Dr. Corbyn. He was a fraud under Brad's control. I couldn't explain how, but he was influencing them. The means didn't matter. Brad was in charge. And he wanted me to forget. He wanted to erase what I knew about the article and what he had done to Oswald Taylor. He wanted everything to go back to the way it was before our anniversary party.

Alex Sinclair

I could play that part. I could do what he craved and pretend to be the wife he needed. The kind who didn't know who he really was. And once I had them all convinced, once they let me out, Brad was going to pay for what he'd done to me and for every second he'd kept me away from my daughter.

CHAPTER FIFTY

I did what I could to keep track of the days. By my count, it had been almost a week, but I could have been wrong. The drugs they had me on made the task even more difficult and were a lot stronger than anything I was used to. Time had turned into something murky and slow. It stretched out like a thick fog I couldn't shake.

Every morning, the lights buzzed on at the same time, breakfast was handed out on identical trays, and the staff spoke to me in their trained, too-calm voices. Everything about the place was designed to make me compliant and to keep me from thinking or remembering too much. Dr. Harland came to see me every day. He always acted like we were making progress and that we were on the same side.

"You're improving, Maia," he told me one afternoon as he watched me the way someone watched a lab rat to see if their experiment was working. "Your mind has been under a great deal of stress. It makes sense certain memories might feel fickle."

I forced a small, neutral smile to play along. I had to be what he wanted me to be. It was the only way out back to Abby. "I guess I was just exhausted," I murmured, keeping my tone light.

He nodded, like I had just confirmed something important. "That's good of you to recognize. Exhaustion can warp perception.

It can make us believe things are worse than they really are. It can even make you believe in problems that aren't real."

This wasn't the first time he had used such a speech on me. And it wasn't the first time I had wanted to throw my chair at him, just like I had done to Brad. Whenever he spoke, I had an uncontrollable urge to claw my way out of this place to find Abby and run. But I had to be careful. Because he was watching. Brad was watching. He may not have been in the room with me, but everything Dr. Harland observed, Brad would find out about it. No other possibility made sense.

I nodded again and allowed Dr. Harland to believe I was falling for his manipulation.

Every day, the orderlies handed out little paper cups of pills like they were communion wafers. The same pastel-colored capsules stared back at me, waiting to be ingested. The orderlies watched with indifference as they waited for me to swallow the next dose of haze. Every day, I tried to avoid it.

I tucked the pills under my tongue or attempted to dissolve them in the corner of my cheek, so I could spit the chemicals out, but the staff had seen it all. They inspected my mouth like I was a dog at the vets. Someone was always watching.

One time, an orderly was too busy to complete an inspection, so I hid the tablets in the corner of my mouth and rushed to the bathroom to flush them down the toilet. It made a slight difference to the overall way I was feeling, but missing one dose wasn't enough. I had to stop them all. I tried harder to deceive the staff. I created a distraction when it was time to take my meds by setting off one of the more sensitive patients. I wasn't proud of it, but I didn't belong there the way the others did.

During the chaos, I hid my tablets again and snuck away. But when I went into the toilet bay to dispose of them, I got caught.

"Stop," a nurse from behind me said before I made it into a stall.

I hesitated, then did as I was told. She instructed me to open my mouth, so I did, sticking out my tongue, showing empty gums.

She narrowed her eyes.

"Have some water from the tap. A whole mouthful."

"Okay," I said, forcing myself to drink. The damn tablets dislodged from under my tongue and went down. She lingered in the doorway with disappointment etched across her face. She made a note and scolded me for hiding my meds. Then, she walked away. No doubt she was off to tell Dr. Harland all about it. I suppose she was only doing her job. She didn't know who that man really was.

And Dr. Harland must have found out because he started pushing harder, digging into my mind like a surgeon with a dull knife. "Let's talk about Oswald Taylor," he said one morning, flipping through my file. "You are convinced he is connected to your daughter's death, aren't you?"

My breath stalled. Had he really asked that question? I shrugged, giving him a semblance of an answer.

Dr. Harland leaned forward, lowering his voice like we were sharing a secret. "The mind protects itself, Maia. It creates false memories to help us cope. Wouldn't it be easier to just let go of the things causing you pain?"

I shrugged again, but then I saw the lake and the cold water. His hands gripped Imogen. There was a struggle. Then she was gone. He was there. It hadn't been a dream. And Brad knew I was right. That was why he killed Oswald. So why was he doing all this to me? Was it to hide what he'd done? Did he think I would tell the police the truth and have him sent to prison? He wanted me to live in the dark. But as painful as the truth was, I needed to know everything.

But acting like I wanted to know the truth wouldn't set me free from this nightmare.

Alex Sinclair

My jaw clenched. I knew what he was doing. He wasn't helping me to heal. He was trying to erase the things I wasn't supposed to remember. I forced my lips to speak. "Maybe you're right," I said. "Maybe I got it all wrong."

He smiled, seeming pleased with himself.

At night, I would lie awake. My body curled into itself on the too-firm mattress, counting the slow, steady ticks of the clock I could hear beyond my room. Only one thought consumed me: Abby.

Her laugh, the way her hair smelled after a bath, the way her fingers had coiled around mine when she was drifting off to sleep. I was away from my baby, and there was no greater pain.

My breath hitched.

I had to get out of there. But I couldn't do it yet. I had to wait. I had to be patient. And I had to let them think they were winning.

242

CHAPTER FIFTY-ONE

Brad hadn't come to see me once. I shouldn't have been surprised. The man was a coward. He thought he could keep the darkest secrets from me. I didn't care. I didn't want to see him. I was afraid of what I would do the moment we locked eyes. The only person I hoped to see apart from Abby was London.

I'd asked about visitors as soon as I'd been sound enough to have the thought. I wanted to see my daughter, but I was told the hospital wasn't a safe environment for her. I couldn't have agreed more if I tried, so I asked for a message to be passed along to Brad to keep her away. She'd endured enough in her brief life. She didn't need to see her mother in a psychiatric facility.

I was sitting out in the common area, alone, as always. Some of the other patients had tried to make my acquaintance, but I never gave them enough in return to allow any friendships to form. It wasn't that I couldn't use a friendly face to get me through the long days. I just didn't want Dr. Harland or the nurses to think I was getting used to Madison Ridge. This place wasn't my home and never would be.

It was after lunch, after my latest dose of fog had been administered, when a nurse came to me saying I had a visitor. My eyes perked at the prospect that London had heard all about my troubles and had taken the time to come and see me. But she wasn't my guest.

It was Brad.

"I don't want to see him," I said without thinking.

"But he's your husband," the nurse said.

"And?"

She stared at me for a beat, then gave me a smile. "I know it's hard having people on the outside see you in a place like this, but it will do you good. I promise."

It took me a long while to say something back as I realized I was not coming across as a team player. Not wanting to cause a scene and reverse the efforts I'd made with Dr. Harland, I accepted my fate and agreed.

During the walk to the visitation room, I tried to imagine what Brad wanted. Had he come to gloat? Or did he want to look me in the eye and remind me who was in charge? I paused at the entrance to the room and exhaled. Whatever reason Brad had for finally coming didn't matter. I just needed to put on a show and convince him to let me out. Getting home to Abby was more important than the truth or my ego.

The visitation room was as sterile as the rest of Madison Ridge. It had white walls, caged windows, and bolted-down chairs with cheap tables between each pair. If they wanted us to feel like inmates in a prison, then well done. Mission accomplished.

Brad was already seated at the far end of the room. His posture was relaxed, and his hands were clasped on the table in front of him. He looked like he always did — put together and in control. Normal. It made little sense, considering where we were.

When I got close enough to see his eyes, things changed. They flickered the moment he saw me. I tried not to react. I couldn't. I had to play my part and be the wife he wanted me to be.

I crossed the room, making him wait as I made my approach. I couldn't move too fast. If I did, if I let this moment come too soon, I wasn't sure I could keep my face from twisting into something dangerous.

When I sat down, he let out a slow breath. I folded my hands in my lap and stared at him. "Why did you take so long to come and see me?" The question left my body on its own.

His jaw tightened, but just for a second, right before he gave me that calm, patient-husband look he wanted the rest of the world to see. But I saw a flash of anger. "I thought it would be best to give you space," he said.

I held his gaze and resisted the urge to laugh. He hadn't come to see me sooner because he was avoiding me. Which meant he was only here because he needed something.

I let the silence stretch, watching how his fingers tensed against the table. Then, he sighed and leaned back.

"How are you?" he asked.

I tilted my head with a narrowed brow. "Do you actually care, or is that just what you think you should say?"

His lips pressed into a tight line. He took another breath and said, "I don't want to fight with you, Maia."

"Of course not," I muttered. My plan had gone out the window without me even trying. I couldn't help but feel like I'd squandered an opportunity. This was going to be harder than I had anticipated.

Neither of us spoke as we sat in silence. I stared at the scuff marks on the table and thought of the night at Julia Taylor's home and what had followed. I needed to forget what he had done to me and fake some appreciation. It was the only way out.

"How is Abby?" I asked. I had to know she was okay.

"She's doing her best. She asks about you a lot."

"What do you tell her?"

He sighed. "Just that you aren't feeling well and that you'll be home as soon as you get better."

I didn't respond to that and asked, "Where is she now?"

"With Claire and Richard. They've been helping out."

"And what have you told them and everyone else we know about your wife?"

He shook his head. "What do you want from me, Maia? I'm doing my best here."

"This is you doing your best, is it?" I asked, knowing my voice was getting louder than it should have. I exhaled and brought myself down a notch. I didn't want to be dragged away by a pair of orderlies.

"Yes, it is," Brad said. "I don't like this situation any more than you do. I mean, honestly, do you think I want you locked up in here?"

There he was, my husband, the liar. I had to give it to him. His performance was spot on. He almost looked like he cared. Almost.

And because I knew how to push him, because I wanted to push him, I let my voice soften just a little. "Have you heard from London? I'd thought my friend would have come to see me by now."

Brad's entire body stilled. It was so small and quick. Anyone else might not have noticed. But I did. Just like I'd seen his expression that night at the dinner party. I knew him. I saw the way his fingers tightened. The way his breath caught, like he hadn't been ready for the question. Something cold slid through my stomach.

"Maia," he started, then stopped.

I suddenly felt like I was standing on the edge of something. A drop-off into an unknown, much worse than what I had been preparing for. My pulse kicked up. "Brad. What?"

He let out a slow, steadying breath, then looked me in the eye. "London's dead."

The words crashed into me. My heart stopped, and my body stilled.

He kept talking with a gentle nod. "There was a car accident the night you were brought here. The police said she'd been drinking. She was driving too fast. Her car slammed into a utility pole. She didn't make it."

I felt the words before I could process them. They seeped into my bones before their meaning became real. I shook my head. "No."

His expression didn't change. "Maia—"

"No," I snapped. It couldn't be true. Because if I let what he was saying settle, if I let it be real, I wasn't sure what it would do to me. But he didn't argue. That was what scared me the most. Brad liked to push and poke me until I broke. But now he just sat there like he had all the time in the world.

I stared at him and tried to read the truth on his face. Was he lying to me? Had he killed her? He wanted me to believe it was a drunken accident, that the timing and circumstances were all a coincidence.

But I knew better.

Brad had shown me his true self. And I knew he had been following me that night. I'd thought it over in my head again and again. He must have seen us fighting and thought London had told me the truth. That pushed him to kill my friend.

London knew something important enough about Brad that she had risked driving her car while drunk to avoid telling me. And she hadn't gone home or to Fletcher's that night. At least not before I was shot full of sedative. She knew something dark about Brad, and now he was telling me she was gone. Just like that.

I swallowed against the rising bile in my throat. I had to keep it together and stay calm.

Brad watched me carefully, like my every movement might tell him something vital. I took a slow breath and forced my hands to stop shaking. And then I said exactly what he wanted to hear.

"It's all my fault," I said, lowering my gaze. "I'm sorry."

"It's not your fault, Maia," he said. "London made a terrible choice. Unfortunately, it cost her everything. I'm sorry she's gone. She was a good friend."

I glanced up at him as I sobbed. His shoulders had relaxed. Just a little. But I caught it. He thought he had me. He thought I was breaking. But I wasn't. Brad had just told me exactly what I needed to know. London was gone. But I was still here. And I wasn't done yet and wouldn't be until he paid for what he had done to my friend.

CHAPTER FIFTY-TWO

Brad

Maia and I spoke for another ten minutes, but she had little to say. I wasn't surprised after what I'd just told her. It was a gut blow, to say the least, but she needed to hear it. My visit hadn't gone exactly as planned, but I'd gotten across what was essential for Maia to know. And before I left, I emphasized the importance of her therapy and reminded her it was the only way she could come home to Abby.

I hated using our daughter as a bargaining chip, but it was an effective tool in this fight. And it was a fight. Despite Maia trying her hardest to show me she was adjusting, there was still a burning rage behind her eyes. One that I understood would take a long while to extinguish.

On my way out, I spoke to Dr. Harland, away from the rest of the staff. This wasn't the first time I had come by Madison Ridge since Maia had been placed in the facility under an emergency admission. I had to drop in every few days and pay him in cash to get updates on the situation and continue to sway his approach to how he treated my wife. Mason hadn't been wrong when he told me that Hartland was happy to be paid for "customized" treatments.

Dr. Harland wasn't able to watch Maia twenty-four seven, but he had enough influence to keep her under control. He'd told me he upped her medication overnight. Apparently, her behavior got worse during that time. Her nightmares were keeping her awake, pushing through the powerful meds, requiring her to be sedated more often than not. Any night she wasn't under such control, she would act out and accuse the staff of being involved in a large conspiracy. They weren't, of course, but Maia had developed a deep level of paranoia. To her, everyone was a potential enemy.

"What's the end game?" I asked. Day fifteen was fast approaching, and Maia wasn't showing enough signs of improvement to be released. She was also remembering things she shouldn't. Things I couldn't come back from. Dr. Harland had been working hard to decipher what it was she knew, but she had been lying to him in every session and was trying to convince him otherwise.

"I don't know if there is an end game, Brad. What you want to achieve could take months. You can't just click your fingers and erase what she knows. Sure, I can keep her in a constant state of confusion and make her seem less than credible, but she's not going to forget what brought her here. Not anytime soon."

"So, what do you recommend?" I asked.

He took a moment as he scratched his chin. "You'll need to take her home. If we reach day fifteen, I'm going to have to make an assessment. That can't be avoided. And once that happens, I have to either send her home or commit her to go deeper into the system. If she goes beyond emergency care, I can't control her therapy."

"Do you know anyone deeper in the system who would be open to my input?" I asked, doing my best not to insult Dr. Harland.

He shook his head and stepped closer. "I can only get away with this because of the emergency admission. There's a lot less scrutiny at this end of the game. But from here, things will only grow beyond your control."

My brow raised. I couldn't allow Maia to go deeper into therapy with a doctor I wasn't controlling. I was lucky enough to have found Corbyn and Harland. If Maia fell further into the system, she might uncover something I'd been trying to keep buried. What needed to happen was clear to me now.

"Okay," I said. "Send her home."

"At day fifteen?"

"A day before. Make it look legitimate. I'll take her back to Dr. Corbyn and we'll find a way."

He nodded. "I wish I could do more, but my hands are tied. Take her to Mason, like you said. With any hope, she'll forget and improve."

"Thank you, doctor," I said as I handed him an envelope with his payment. He placed it inside his jacket pocket like we were two mobsters making a deal. This extra care was costing far more than it should. There was only so much money I could take from our savings before it became a problem.

I left Madison Ridge and returned to my car in the parking lot. I unlocked the door and climbed in on the driver's side, exhaling once I'd settled in behind the wheel.

What I had told Maia about London was true. Her friend was dead. But there was far more Maia didn't know. I thought about the conversation I'd had with Fletcher after he found out about London. It hadn't been easy, but it was one we needed to have. I had to make sure we were on the same page.

I stared out the windshield of my car and was glad London was dead. She had come close to blowing the whole thing wide open. Fletcher was a mess with her gone, but he needed to get a grip on reality and move on. What was done was done. He was the only one who knew the whole truth, and this connection he'd had with London was filling me with concern.

I was beginning to wonder just how much I could trust him.

CHAPTER FIFTY-THREE

Maia

London was dead.

I couldn't believe it. I had lost the only person who could tell me the truth about everything. Brad had killed her because she knew too much. What did that mean for me if I didn't play along? I would find out soon enough.

I'd lost my oldest friend. I'd never felt more alone in my entire life. The only other time I'd felt this way was when Imy had died. Especially when I had been the one who failed to keep her safe. And just like Imy, I had failed my friend.

I couldn't stop thinking about London. There would be no more sarcastic comments or fun stories. No more late-night texts filled with gossip and a world outside my own. An existential dread washed over me.

I squeezed my eyes shut, pressing my fingers against my temples. How much loss was I supposed to endure in one lifetime? Apparently, witnessing my own child being murdered wasn't enough. There was room in my existence for more pain.

"This isn't fair," I sobbed in the corner of the common area. One of the patients had noticed my tears when I'd returned and was staring at me. I had to get it together. If I let myself dwell too long, I was going to unravel. I couldn't do that. Not here. Not with Brad watching. Not with Dr. Harland chiseling away at my mind, trying to strip me down into something easier to manage.

I had to come up with a new strategy and think about things clearly. Brad had killed London. I knew it in my gut. Maybe not directly, but he had done something to ensure she never made it past that night. She could handle her booze. She'd gotten behind the wheel with too much alcohol in her system before. She always made it home. Brad had done this. Which meant he was willing to kill to keep his secrets. And in doing so, he'd taken away the only person who could save me.

I was on my own.

The whole thing made me wonder if Fletcher was part of it. He was dating London. Did he care that she was dead? If so, Brad would have to take him out next. There didn't seem to be a limit to what Brad was willing to do.

It shouldn't have surprised me when I thought about it. He was happy to let me stew in this place and have me plied with drugs and more bad therapy to keep me quiet. What happened if I didn't play ball? What "accident" would I have once he got sick of the game we were playing?

I had been so focused on lying my way out of this place that I hadn't considered what came next. Escaping meant nothing if Brad saw me as a threat. I needed to be smarter than him and less threatening. For the sake of London's memory, I had to let him think I was broken. He had to believe that I was too afraid to fight. Then, when the time was right, I'd tear him apart. He would pay.

* * *

Later that afternoon, I was in the hallway walking by the nurses' station when I heard Dr. Harland speaking in the connecting office. His voice was low, but I could still make it out. He was chatting with someone just inside the door. I paused. There was no one else around, apart from a few patients.

I angled myself closer and kept my gaze forward, like I wasn't listening in as my pulse hammered in my ears.

"Maia's improving," Harland said. "The sessions have been very effective. She's far more cooperative now."

I clenched my teeth. Sure, I'd been doing my best not to reveal my true self in those sessions, but this seemed generous.

"Well, that's good news," a second voice replied. I didn't know who it belonged to. Another doctor or nurse, maybe.

Harland hummed in agreement. "Judging from her progress, I'd say that she'll be ready for release in a week. I'll make the final evaluation soon, but I see no reason to keep her here any longer than that."

My stomach dropped. One week. I was getting out. I almost felt dizzy with relief. Seven days, and I would see Abby again. Thank God. But as fast as any joy entered my heart, it soon left. The truth slithered through my mind, chilling me as it went. This was Brad's doing.

Dr. Harland had made no indication of my miraculous progress during our sessions. The overwhelming feeling I got from him was that it would take a long time to break me. So why the sudden rush?

I knew that once I'd been in Madison Ridge for fifteen days, things would change. I'd been told many times about the fifteen-day limit, but I didn't understand what that actually meant. Maybe once that amount of time passed, I'd be moved into another wing of the facility, away from Dr. Harland, to an area where Brad had no control over my care. The more I thought about it, the more it made sense.

None of the other patients seemed to stay in this area for long. Every day, I'd see patients being taken from our section and moved to a part of the facility I didn't have access to. The face in their bed would be replaced by a new one soon after. This was a temporary stay. I wasn't going to be moved to another section of the facility. Brad wanted me out. Whatever he thought he was going to achieve in here had failed. This meant I had exactly seven days to prepare myself for whatever he had planned for me once I was out. Because one thing was certain — Brad wasn't letting me come home because he believed I was better. The news about London's supposed accident was about as much warning as I was going to receive.

I didn't know how he was going to do it, but the second he got me home, he was going to kill me.

CHAPTER FIFTY-FOUR

The next seven days were a blur of anxiety and terror. On the one hand, I couldn't wait to get out of Madison Ridge, but on the other, I had no idea what I would face on the outside with Brad. Whatever he had planned for me, I had no choice but to face it.

I could have tried to throw myself further into the system for my own protection, but that would have meant being away from Abby for longer.

Instead, I'd stepped up my game over the week and made sure not to ruffle any feathers.

The thought of Abby was the only thing keeping me together most days. Whenever I felt myself slipping, I'd think of her face and her beautiful eyes gazing into mine when I held her in my arms. She brought me back from the edge every time.

Brad arrived on day fourteen to pick me up. I'd been given a change of clothing to dress into, clothing that belonged to me. I no longer needed to wear the dull and loose-fitting slacks and plain T-shirt the staff provided us with each day. The moment I was back in my own clothing, I felt transformed.

Brad stood next to Dr. Harland. They were both smiling at me like I was graduating from college. Apart from the concern that was running through my veins, it was embarrassing. Abby wasn't with Brad. I wasn't sure if that was a good thing or not. I never wanted her to see me in this place, but I was also afraid to be alone with Brad.

"You ready?" Brad asked me like he was picking up a kid from school.

"Yes," I said. I faced Dr. Harland and returned his smile, hopeful Brad would think I was playing along. "Thank you for your help, doctor," I said, forcing the words out.

"No need to thank me, Maia. I was just doing my job. I wish you all the best and hope that things improve for you and the family." He extended his hand to shake mine. I accepted and resisted the urge to tell him what I really thought about him.

Leaving Madison Ridge through the front door felt strange. I had imagined myself making a grand escape to flee back to Abby and take her away from her father, but now I was going along with him willingly. I knew I was walking into a trap. But what else was I supposed to do? London was dead, and I had no one else to ask for help. She was the only person in the world who might have taken me seriously.

Her death had plagued my conscience the moment I had found out about it. I couldn't shake the feeling that it was all my fault. She was killed for what she knew, and the man responsible was there to collect me.

We traveled home in silence. It was late in the day and would soon be dinner time. My stomach rumbled. It was accustomed to an exact timetable. At Madison Ridge, each meal was served at the same time every day, like clockwork. I wondered how much time it would take me to adjust back to the regular chaos of life. That was if I survived long enough for such a thing to happen.

I had no proof that Brad was going to kill me other than a gut feeling. But only a fool wouldn't listen to such a powerful instinct. I knew too much, and my memories hadn't been wiped the way they should have been. That made me the greatest liability to my husband. And soon, he was going to remove that threat to his life.

Over the last seven days, Dr. Harland's sessions had changed. He no longer tried to encourage me to forget the past. We just talked about anything and everything. There was no structure. He was running out the clock. It was like he knew it was a waste of time. Did he know what Brad was planning?

"How are you feeling?" Brad asked me when we pulled into the driveway.

"I'm fine. I just want to see Abby." Before he could say another word, I left the car. I didn't have a suitcase to carry. Just a small bag that held my polo midi dress. I was going to throw the thing in the trash the first chance I got. It would forever remind me of London and the fact that she was murdered because of me. Brad may have been the one who killed her, but it was my fault.

The thought of London made me want to call Fletcher and find out what he knew about London's supposed crash. I didn't know how much help he would be. He loved Brad like a brother and was loyal to the man. He wouldn't dare entertain the notion that Brad had anything to do with London's death. And the more I thought about it, the more I realized Fletcher had been acting a little strange on the phone when we spoke that night. Contacting him was a pointless risk. Besides, I had a daughter to scoop into my arms. It might be the last time I'd ever see her.

"Maia," Brad said from behind as I reached the front door. "About Abby."

I faced him with a wrinkled forehead. "What about her?" I asked, ready to rip his face off with my bare hands.

"She's not here. I've asked Claire and Richard to watch her for a few days. Just until you can settle back in."

I stared at Brad from a distance and did what I could to remain calm. He was keeping me from seeing her. He was depriving me of the one thing he knew I wanted more than anything else in the world. It was the ultimate bargaining chip, and he knew it.

"Okay," I finally said, not arguing. I couldn't argue. My goal was to stay composed. It was the only way to make him think I was safe to be around, that he had broken my soul. He had to believe I wasn't a threat to him, that I wasn't about to run off to the police and accuse him of murdering my friend.

Brad covered the gap between us and came within three feet of me. He said, "I know how badly you want to see her. I do, but Dr. Harland just suggested we let you settle in first. Then we'll bring Abby back home and get back to normal."

I closed my eyes and swallowed all the rage that was ready to explode from my mouth. When I opened my eyes again, I smiled and said, "If Dr. Harland thinks that's best, then I understand."

"That's good. Thank you." Brad brushed by me and unlocked the door. He guided me inside like I was too fragile to know how a door worked and asked if I wanted a glass of water. I said yes just to get him away from me for a second. Before he headed to the kitchen, he locked the front door using the key and placed it in his pocket.

I had no cell phone, and Brad held the keys. I'd gone from one prison to the next. Now, more than ever, I realized how much I needed London. She was the one person who never looked at me like I was fragile or broken. She had known the truth — or at least parts of it — and she'd been trying to tell me something before she died. I'd have given anything to go back to that moment and stop her from getting into her car.

Her absence filled my house with a heavy silence. Without her, there would be no one left to remember the real me. The version of me before the fear and the fog that Brad had built around me. Once I was gone, he could paint any picture he liked. No one would question him.

My only saving grace was that Abby wouldn't be here when Brad made his move. It wasn't much, but it was better than nothing. She'd dealt with more than enough torment for one lifetime.

Brad returned with the glass of water. I was still standing in our entryway. "Come on," Brad said. "Come sit down. We can watch some TV."

"Okay," I said, as he guided me to the living room. I felt like I was back in the common room at Madison Ridge, being escorted by an orderly. Except this man was more than just that. He was my keeper. An executioner who could drop his ax when it suited him.

We watched TV for a while, not making much in the way of conversation. Brad played with his cell phone as we sat there. All I could do was stare into space as I waited for my time to come. But he just sat there, using his phone like it was any other day of the week. If he was planning on killing me, we were alone in our house. It wouldn't be hard. What was he waiting for?

"Sorry," he said, seeing me staring. He shoved the phone into his pocket. "I can't give you your cell phone back just yet," he said. "Dr. Harland—"

"It's fine," I cut him off. It didn't matter if Dr. Harland had said it would be best if I didn't have a cell phone or the ability to see my daughter. Brad could make up any rule he wanted and use the doctor's name as a reason. There was nothing I could do or say to counter it. My only course of action for now was to comply and attempt to lure him into a false sense of safety.

My plans to find a way to threaten his life were still at the forefront of my mind, but I had no way to accomplish them. Not yet.

"That reminds me," Brad said. He fished something from his other pocket. Something familiar. It was my meds in a bottle. "Time for your next dose." He placed some tablets down on our coffee table beside my half-empty glass of water. Instead of three pills, there were now four. My dosage had been increased.

"Thanks," I said, sweeping the tablets into my hand. I threw them in my mouth and had a gulp of water. I gave Brad a smile, but that wasn't enough.

"I'm sorry to do this, Maia, but I have to be sure. Can you show me you swallowed the tablets?"

My smile wavered. Was he seriously going to do this? Apparently so. I opened my mouth wide, extending my tongue.

He took a quick look and nodded. "Thank you," he said, gesturing for me to close my mouth.

"That's okay," I said, making the words form. "I understand."

"Good," he muttered. "Well, I'd better go make us something to eat. You keep watching TV."

I maintained my grateful expression until he left. When I was positive he was out of the room and wasn't coming back, I removed the tablets from under my tongue and shoved them down the gap in the sofa's side. Brad was no professional. He hadn't thought to check the most obvious place I'd try to hide them. He was also no cleaner. He'd never find them in the sofa.

We ate a basic meal and watched some more TV. By nine, he suggested we both go to sleep. He wanted me to get a good night's rest. I wanted to ask why, but resisted. Instead, I asked him about his job.

"I've taken the next few weeks off. I just want to make sure you're okay."

"How thoughtful," I said, clenching my fists as we made our way upstairs. When we reached our room, he paused at the threshold. "I'm going to sleep in the spare room downstairs. I thought you could use some space. If you need anything, come find me. I'll check in on you during the night."

He kissed me on the forehead. When his lips touched my skin, it took everything in my power not to flinch and reveal how much I both feared and despised him. He may have been my husband, but that wasn't the way I saw him anymore. Sure, he may have killed a monster for our family, but he became one the second he committed the act. And that beast inside him had taken over and killed my only friend. Why couldn't he have killed Oswald, then handed himself in to the police? Why did he have to spend all this time trying to hide what he'd done?

Brad left me alone in our room. I immediately searched through our ensuite and discovered everything sharp had been removed, along with ninety percent of the medicine cabinet's contents. He'd thought ahead.

Brad had full control over my existence. The only way out was for me to end his. But killing him wasn't enough. I needed to get to the bottom of the truth and force him to admit to everything. I knew what had to be done.

CHAPTER FIFTY-FIVE

I waited a few hours before I made my move. I needed Brad to be asleep and lulled into thinking he had full control over me. He practically did, but he had no dominion over my thoughts, despite his best efforts.

I left my room and crept down the hallway, going past Abby's empty bedroom. If I pulled off the impossible, she would soon be back home with me at her side.

Brad's study door was closed as I walked by it, but I wasn't interested in wasting any more time in that space chasing down old passwords and broken watches. I needed to reach the kitchen and find something sharp. There was no way around this situation anymore. I had to take action and force him to tell me everything. And once I had achieved the impossible, I would put an end to him. It was me or him, and one of us had to go.

I would like to have found a better solution — something less violent — but my back was against the wall, and Brad had been the one to push me there.

He'd come across as caring and nurturing to anyone outside of our marriage, tending to my every need. But in reality, he now had complete control over my life. And soon he was going to rid himself of the burden that I had become.

Before Brad died, he would admit the truth to me. Every last detail. Once he was through confessing, it would all be over in a matter of seconds.

I found my way into the kitchen, keeping the light off. Only the glow of the moonlight and the displays on our appliances guided me. I walked to where the knife block was located. It was missing. Of course. I'd been away for two weeks. Long enough for Brad to clear the house of anything useful that I could use to harm him, he'd justify it to me as a means to stop me from hurting myself, but that wasn't the true reason for it.

Without a knife or something equivalent, I had no way to complete my plan. I couldn't make him talk without threatening his life. If I came out and asked him about London or Oswald, he could easily dismiss me and say I was unstable. Given I'd just gotten out of a psychiatric center, I'd have a hard time sounding rational.

Standing in the kitchen in the dark, I tried to think of another idea. I desperately needed something dangerous to use against Brad. Surely he hadn't cleared out the *entire* house. I paced around with a cloud of anxiety following my every step.

"Come on," I muttered, praying an idea would come to me soon. At some point during the night, Brad was planning on checking in on me. If he got up and saw me wandering around the kitchen in the dark, it wouldn't end well. I had to find a way.

I went through the rest of the kitchen looking for anything that could do the job, but it was no use. The best I could come up with was a meat tenderizer hammer. It was okay, but it wouldn't be enough. Brad would snatch it out of my hand in seconds.

He'd been thorough. I might as well have been locked up at Madison Ridge still. I tried both living rooms, looking for something that could be used in a blunt force manner, but I found nothing suitable. I couldn't exactly intimidate him with a paperweight or the Buddha statue we'd received from London as a gift from one of her many overseas trips.

The sight of the statue made me think of her again. London. Gone. Just like that. I would never see her smirking at me across a room, never hear her laugh at something wildly inappropriate, and never get the chance to ask what she'd been so afraid to say that night. The finality of it hit me all over again. There were no more tomorrows with her. No second chances. Just questions with no one left to answer them. Brad had obviously been following us and had seen London charging off. For some reason, he took that as a sign that he needed to end her life. It was my duty to find out why. I owed her that much.

After searching the lower floor for a weapon, I came up with nothing. Everything was gone, and all the doors were locked. I was ready to give up and go back to bed when a thought came to me. There was one place I hadn't tried: the garden shed. There was a machete in there. Last time I had been here, the padlock was missing. Something told me Brad would have replaced it by now, though, so I rushed back to the kitchen and took out the meat tenderizer hammer. I didn't know if it would do the job, but I had to try.

When I reached the back door, I twisted the handle and almost crashed into the thing. "Dammit," I muttered. Brad had locked the door from the inside as well. We used to keep the key in the lock, but it was no doubt with him. I wouldn't have been surprised if he kept the keys to each door around his neck. The man had become my warden. But Brad hadn't thought of everything.

I went back to the kitchen and took out a butter knife before returning to the door. For years, the back door to our yard had needed replacing. I had asked Brad a hundred times to fix it or pay someone else to do the job. Thank God he hadn't. I jammed the knife in where the latch was and popped it open in seconds.

I placed the knife down and moved outside. It was a cool and windy night, but I would not let a bit of cold weather slow me down. I had to do this. It was a tremendous risk, but Brad was going to strike sooner rather than later. I could see that glint in his eyes whenever he spoke to me. If I tried to bide my time, I would be in a position where I had no means to fight back.

I reached the garden shed and found the padlock back where it belonged. Fortunately, it wasn't anything my improvised hammer couldn't handle. At least, I hoped that was the case. Our cooking utensils were of high quality. The hammer was sharp and had some weight to it. I just had to have some faith that it would do the job.

With the meat tenderizer raised, I was ready to put it to work. A voice in my head said to stop, but I told it to shut the hell up. The time for reason was over. I had to end this.

I struck the padlock as hard as I could. The hammer bounced off the metal and sent a jolt of pain through my hand and wrist. The lock remained intact. I wouldn't get many more hits without Brad waking up, so I raised the hammer and brought it down on the lock. Again, all I got was pain and a racket. A third strike proved fruitless. "Come on, dammit," I muttered as sweat stung at my forehead. This had to work. I couldn't fail again.

On the fourth strike, the padlock broke. I cleared the shattered metal and opened the garden shed. It groaned. The night carried the sound. Then a glow of light came on downstairs in our house. Brad was awake.

"Oh, God," I let out as I hurried. I didn't have a flashlight on me, but the moon was full enough that I didn't need one. I ran a hand through the shed and found the machete where it was supposed to be. Brad hadn't expected this move from me. I took the weapon, still in its sheath, and closed the shed. The door made more noise. But without the padlock, the damn thing wouldn't stay shut, so I left it to sway in the breeze.

"Maia," Brad's voice boomed from inside. He was coming for me. I rushed to the back door and stepped off to the side where he wouldn't immediately see me, unsheathing the machete as I went.

I gripped the slashing tool as tightly as I could in my right hand and concentrated on slowing down my breathing as my heart crashed into my ribs. If Brad were dumb enough to come out here, I would make my move. Then, when I had him where I wanted him, he would answer my damn questions. He would die an honest man.

I held my breath when the back door opened; it was set back by a few feet. I was tucked tight to the side. He wouldn't see me until he came out. The door to the garden shed was banging in the wind and would hopefully make a decent distraction for me.

Brad stepped outside and went right past where I was standing. He was heading to the shed. I ducked low like I was a spy in a cheap movie and crept after him with the machete, ready to strike. The voice in my head tried to stop me again. It couldn't handle how intense this situation had become.

Brad reached the shed and stopped. He scratched at his head as I raised the machete. Part of me wanted to strike him down where he stood, but that wouldn't give me what I wanted. Not yet.

"Brad," I said.

He startled and spun around. His eyes went wider when he saw the weapon I brandished raised high. Even if he tried to run, I could slash him, and he knew it.

"Maia," he said with both hands in a defensive pose. "What the hell are you *doing?*"

"Don't move. I swear on Abby's life that I will use this. Do you understand me?"

He nodded with an open mouth and said, "Maia, please—"

"No talking unless I say otherwise. Nod if you understand."

Again, Brad nodded. I was in control. This was my show now.

"Good boy," I said. "It's time you and I had a little chat."

CHAPTER FIFTY-SIX

Brad looked scared for his life. After all, he was staring down the business end of a two-foot-long blade perfect for slicing gaping wounds in a person's body. He had backed himself against the garden shed and had nowhere else to go.

"What did you do to London?" I asked, keeping my tight grip on the machete's handle.

His eyes widened, and he shook his head. "Nothing. Maia, she died in a car crash two weeks ago."

I stared right through him. "I'm only going to say this once, Brad. If you lie to me again, I'll kill you."

"*Kill me?*" Brad asked, incredulous. "You can't be serious, Maia."

"Do I look like I'm playing? Now answer the question: what did you do to London?"

Brad shifted his weight as his eyes darted left and right. I kept the machete raised high, ready to put him down.

He took a breath in and slowly let it out. "I didn't do a thing to her. I swear."

I gazed into his eyes and studied him for a beat in the moonlight. I couldn't see a lie. How was that possible, given everything I knew? This had to be some kind of trick.

London rushed into my head. I remembered the way she spoke to Brad at the party. She saw right through him and tried to warn us all who he really was. I thought about it for a moment longer and realized that he was telling me a selective truth. That had to be how he'd been operating all this time. I had to dig deeper.

"How did she die?" I asked.

He shook his head. "Maia, this is all wrong. You should be asleep right now. Not threatening me with a machete."

"Don't tell me what I should and shouldn't be doing. You think you can control my every action, don't you?"

"No, I don't," he said with a furrowed brow.

"You're lying," I said, thrusting the machete toward his face. The blade was within a few inches of his eyes, slamming him back harder into the shed. "What did I say about lying?"

Sweat pooled on his forehead. "Okay, okay, you're right. I have been trying to control you."

A sneer came across my face. "How? Tell me everything, Brad. Why don't you start with my therapy?"

He closed his eyes and exhaled as if this was a long time coming. When he opened his eyes again, he didn't look away. "I've been controlling it from day one. I blackmail Dr. Corbyn to let me influence your sessions."

"Blackmail?"

"Yeah. He's been committing fraud for years with his practice. I used my firm's resources to find someone like him."

"Wow," I let out. I wasn't expecting that one. A chuckle escaped me as Brad confirmed what I had been debating in my head. "What else? This isn't the time to hold back."

He swallowed hard and continued. He told me how he had forced Dr. Corbyn to make me forget as much of the past as possible. Just as I had suspected, it was all about erasing events from before Abby was born, with a combination of therapy and medication. He had paid Dr. Harland to direct my therapy sessions at Madison Ridge in the same manner. Apparently, Harland and

Corbyn knew each other. But Brad realized he only had fifteen days to achieve his goals. When he realized it wouldn't be enough time to force me to forget, he paid Dr. Harland to release me.

"What did you want me to forget?" I asked.

This question sealed Brad's lips. "I can't tell you, Maia."

"Are you serious?" I asked, stepping closer to him. I placed both hands on the machete as it inched closer. The move pressed Brad tighter against the shed door.

"Can you put that down? We can talk about everything, I promise."

"We're talking now. How about you just answer my damn question? Tell me why you killed London. Tell me what she died for. Tell me what you want me to forget."

He shook his head again. "No. Not like this. I know what will happen if I do."

"That bad, huh? What did you do, Brad? What have you been so desperate to hide all these years?"

He closed his eyes, squeezing them tight. "I'm sorry," he whispered.

"Huh?" I let out, tilting my head. Half a second later, I discovered what he was sorry for. Brad's hands snapped up from his sides and seized my wrists. He twisted his entire body as he held my wrists and the machete out sideways away from his face. Before I could react, he slammed my gripped arms into the shed. I let go of my weapon after one crunch of my knuckles against the metal. The machete fell onto the grass and missed us both.

Brad's hands let go of my wrists and grabbed me by the shoulders. With little effort, he threw me to the ground. I landed with a thud with wild eyes as I flipped over and attempted to flee. He was going to kill me in the backyard and bury me here. Abby would never see me again. I couldn't let that happen, so I screamed for help as loud as I could while I scrambled to my feet and ran.

"Maia," he yelled after me as I charged for the house. There was nowhere else to go. I just needed to find a phone to call the police, or maybe a set of keys. Anything.

I burst inside with him right on my heels. He was faster than I expected as I dashed for the stairs. I was halfway up when his hands found my legs and tripped me over. I fell forward and collided with the steps. Before I could recover, he started dragging me down by one leg. I used the other to kick at him, but my strikes weren't enough.

This was it. This was how I would die. I only hoped that one of our neighbors heard the scream and called the police.

Brad pulled me the rest of the way down the steps and wrapped both arms around the front of my neck like he was catching me in a sleeper hold. He was going to choke me to death in our house, the one we had picked together. The one we had raised two children in.

But I didn't feel pressure around my throat. Instead, a familiar prick stabbed me in the neck. A moment later, the chemicals flooded my system. The son of a bitch had gotten me with a sedative, like he'd been carrying one around on his person just in case he needed to do this.

I tried to yell out, to say the last words I would ever speak, but it was too late. I fell into the abyss and passed out.

CHAPTER FIFTY-SEVEN

Now

"Keep going," Brad mutters. He sedated me at our house and dressed me in hiking boots and warm clothing. He's driven me far away from our home to somewhere remote and has dragged me up a secluded and non-existent trail on what looks like a mountain. I've never been here before.

I'm prodded again to move.

The night air is crisp and laced with the scent of autumn leaves. It will be the last thing I ever smell. Why did I push him to this? There were so many times when I should have stopped, when I could have decided I was done hunting for the truth. But I kept going. And now I'll pay the price for my pride.

I could try to fight my husband, but there's no point. He'd overpower me, but if I don't piss him off even more than I already have, maybe he'll give me a merciful death. It's the best outcome I can hope for, given what I know he's done.

"We're here," Brad says.

He's brought me close to the edge of a cliff. I glance down – it's a guaranteed end. This must be what he has planned. Make it seem like an accident. Given the clothing I'm wearing, no one will suspect a thing. Is this how he killed London and Oswald?

A sigh escapes me as I stare out into a dark void. The drop is almost invisible when the half-moon passes behind the clouds. I wonder if anyone will find my body. I hope so, for Abby's sake. I don't want her to think her mother has abandoned her.

"Turn around," Brad says.

"No," I reply. He wants to stare into my soul when he pushes me, the psycho. Well, I won't let his face be the last one I see. My last thought will be of my children.

"Do it," he shouts. His voice carries across the night, but it doesn't matter. I don't think there's anyone around for miles.

"No," I say again. But my defiance is soon met with two powerful arms that grab me by the shoulders. I'm spun against my will. All I can do is close my eyes and think of Imogen and Abby. Brad can take my life, but he can't have my thoughts.

"Open your eyes, Maia," he says.

I shake my head. I'll die the way I want to.

He shoves me to my knees and says, "Open your eyes. You need to see the truth."

Truth. The word forces me to think about the past two and a half weeks and everything I discovered. My life fell apart in record time, and all because I couldn't accept the lies Brad had built for me.

"Maia," he says, his voice stern.

"No," I say again. "I won't do it."

"Just open your eyes," he repeats, still holding my shoulders. "Then it will all be over."

I can't give in. That's what he wants. I might want to know what Brad is so desperate to show me, but my intrigue doesn't matter. He thinks he can control everything, but I won't give him my last thoughts.

Right as I expect to be thrown off the cliff, he lets go and takes several steps away from me. Without meaning to, I open my eyes.

Then I see it.

Alex Sinclair

The air escapes my lungs.

Nothing could have prepared me for this.

On the ground is the broken watch from Brad's study. The one that had belonged to Oswald Taylor.

I regain my lost breath and try to make sense of what is happening. Brad is standing to my side. He doesn't have a weapon and doesn't seem to be all that concerned that I could run away at any moment. I suppose he could easily chase me down. We are in the middle of nowhere in what looks like the early hours of the morning.

"Why are you showing this to me?" I ask.

"Do you know who this watch belonged to?" he replies, not answering my question.

With hesitation in my voice, I say, "Oswald Taylor."

He nods. "That's right. The same Oswald Taylor from the news article you've been obsessing over. And why do I have his watch?"

I close my eyes and try to steady my racing pulse. I open my eyes again as I exhale. "Because you killed him."

He sighs heavily, then shakes his head. "No, Maia. Because you killed him."

CHAPTER FIFTY-EIGHT

"What?" I spit, "Is that what you're going to tell the cops? That I killed Oswald? Is that why you brought me here, to frame me?"

Brad steps over to me and takes me by the elbow. He pulls me closer to the watch that is sitting on a small mound of dirt. "He's buried there," Brad says, staring at the ground.

"Oswald?"

"I put him in that hole four years ago. I drove up here all alone and buried his corpse. But I kept his watch and the shovel I used. Do you want to know why?"

"Because you're a psycho?"

"No, Maia. Something may have changed inside me that night, but I'm not psychotic."

"Then why, huh? Why did you kill him? Why did you kill London?"

Brad's lips part as if he is going to speak, but then he faces away from me.

"That's what I thought," I say.

Brad stares at the sky and mutters to himself. If the drugs weren't coursing through my veins, I would try to shove him off the cliff we are close to.

"You know what?" I ask. "I'm done with whatever this is."

"No, you're not," Brad says, refocusing on me. "I've spent so long trying to make you forget, but I can't do it anymore. I'm tired, Maia. I just want this to be over."

"So you're going to murder me as well? Is London buried here, too?"

He stares at me like I'm a rabbit caught in a trap, and he needs to decide if he's going to kill me or let me go. "You came so close," he says. "You almost did it on your own, but I can't keep the truth buried any longer. You'll find it, one way or another. It's just a matter of time. I'm sorry for this."

He reaches behind his back. I squint, thinking he is about to pull out a gun and shoot me where I stand, but instead, he retrieves a folded-up piece of paper. Brad holds it out to me.

"What the hell is this?" I ask.

"Just read it. Once you do, everything else will follow."

I try to ignore the piece of paper in his hand, but I know he'll end up forcing me to read it if I don't take it. I snatch it from him and open the document.

"This had better be good," I mutter. "I'm sick of your games."

"This isn't a game, Maia. Please, just read it."

"Fine. If it'll shut you up." I read Brad's paper. It's a police report that looks similar to the one Julia Taylor had on her. The tiny hairs on my body raise at the thought. This was what he was trying to keep me from seeing. This document was the reason I spent two weeks locked up and out of my mind on drugs.

I read the date and see that it is from five years ago. But it's not just any old date. It's the exact day Imogen died.

"Is this . . . ?" I ask.

"Just read it," he says. He no longer sounds cold and forceful, just exhausted. So I do. The words blur as my eyes pass over them, like my mind doesn't want to digest what I'm seeing. I force myself to keep going and don't stop until I get to the end. When I do, I'm frozen in place.

This can't be real. It has to be a fake. I read it again, but at half the speed.

According to the report, I was at Glacier Hollow State Park with Imogen. She had fallen into the lake when my back was turned. The second I saw her, I dove in after and called for help.

Oswald Taylor had been walking nearby. He heard me scream and jumped into the water without hesitation. He got to Imogen first and kept her head above water. He pulled my baby girl to shore and tried to save her using CPR while I called for an ambulance.

Emergency Medical Services arrived minutes later and took over, but Imogen had no pulse. They worked on her until they reached the hospital, but it didn't matter. She was already gone, long before then. She was declared dead on arrival at Upstate University Hospital.

The report ruled it an accident. No arrests were made. There was no foul play. Just a tragic, irreversible moment. Oswald Taylor hadn't murdered Imogen. He'd tried to save her.

"You've made this up," I mutter to Brad, shaking the paper. "It's fake."

"It's real. That's what happened that day."

"No, no, no. I was there. I saw him drowning her. I—"

I cut myself short as the memory comes to me. The distorted image I had of Oswald dragging Imogen into the water disappears. Instead, I see him taking my baby out of the lake with panic in his eyes. He places her on the shore and checks if she is breathing. He can't hear her tiny lungs working, so he starts CPR and yells at me to call for an ambulance. He clearly had been trained.

He works tirelessly on Imogen, who is wearing her favorite pink T-shirt, continuing CPR until the EMTs arrive. They try to save her life with their advanced medical equipment, but it's obvious to us all that Imy is beyond help. Too much water has filled her lungs. All because I hadn't been paying attention. All because I hadn't done my job as a mother and kept her safe.

They told me she had most likely been trying to retrieve her teddy bear that had fallen into the water. It could still be seen floating out in the lake.

"It was my fault," I cry to Brad as I collapse to the ground. The memory overpowers me. He drops by my side and holds me.

"It was an accident. It could've happened to anyone."

"No, I killed her. I killed our baby."

"It's okay," Brad whispers in my ear. "I've got you."

We stay like this for almost a minute until I regain the ability to think. "What happened to Oswald?"

Brad releases me and stands. He paces on the spot for a while with a hand on his forehead. "You were obsessed with this idea that someone had drowned Imy. You couldn't let it go. I tried to help you. I took you to therapy and blackmailed Dr. Corbyn to try and help you forget everything. I thought it was the only way you'd ever be able to move forward but instead of forgetting that day, you continued to twist reality until you were convinced that Oswald had killed her."

I shake my head, speechless.

"I tried to stop it. I did," Brad says.

"Stop what?" I ask in a shaky voice.

"What you did. You stalked him to Cliff Woods on the anniversary of her death. You had been following him for months. I'd caught you doing it several times. I should have done more, but I didn't want to lock you up again in another psychiatric center. All they did was pump you full of drugs until you were unrecognizable. I thought it would be different this time at Madison Ridge. I had more control. But I didn't have enough time."

The vein on Brad's neck pulsates as my hands shake.

"I didn't know what else to do," he says. "I tried to keep you home, but you always found ways to leave. Then on the anniversary of Imy's death, I stayed late at the office. I didn't want to come home and face it, or you. It was too much, but eventually I forced myself to leave before it got late. When I came home, you were gone. Fortunately, it wasn't hard to find you. By that point I had placed a tracking app on your phone. But I didn't need it. I knew where you were headed. I knew what you were going to do. You kept telling me your plan, again and again, but I didn't think you would actually do it. By the time I got there, it was too late."

Brad's last words echo through my head as more memories come flooding back. They squeeze my head like a vise and cripple my ability to function. I see that night in my mind as clear as day.

I followed Oswald Taylor on his night walk, the one he took every day at the same time. He was so predictable. I made sure no one saw me when I crept after him into Cliff Woods. I kept my distance, tracking his flashlight as he went while I stayed in the shadows. I waited until we were deep enough on the trail that no one else would interrupt. By that time of night, most people were safe at home, but not Oswald.

When the moment was right, I made my move.

I charged up behind him and struck him as hard as I could on the head with a rock. He fell and became disoriented. That allowed me to circle him like a shark with the bloody rock still in hand.

He saw me. There was a fear in his eyes when he looked up. He tried to speak and understand what I was doing, but I refused to give him a chance to talk his way out of what he'd done to Imogen. I struck him again. This time, he attempted to block my attack. He held up his arm to protect his face. The rock collided with his wrist and smashed his watch, so I struck again and again, releasing a year's worth of fury on this man who thought it was okay to murder my child. I didn't stop until he was dead.

When I'd exhausted myself, I glanced up from Oswald's body and saw Brad. I gave him a smile and said, "It's over." His face was filled with absolute disgust. He stared at me with a sickened, dark glare. The only time I've ever seen that expression again was at our anniversary dinner party during the game of Two Truths and One Lie.

Brad stares at me in the present as I finish reliving that night.

"I tracked your phone to the exact location where you did it. You were so determined to kill him. It didn't matter the proof I'd shown you or the things I'd said. You couldn't accept the fact that Imogen's death was your responsibility."

With an open mouth, I crawl to the broken watch on my hands and knees.

"I don't know why I kept it," Brad says. "For years it stayed hidden. You were going to therapy and were showing signs of improvement, but I needed to know if it was real so one day I did something crazy and showed it to you. It was a test to see how much you remembered. You looked at that thing like it was nothing and asked me how it broke. I made up some story that you accepted. I couldn't believe it. Still, it gave me hope for the future, that we could get back to normal."

I hold the watch in my hand and see in my head in full visceral detail as I smash Oswald Taylor again and again with a rock. His blood sprays all over my face. I can taste the metallic tang in my mouth.

"I don't understand," I let out.

"What?"

"What happened after? How did I get away with this?"

He shakes his head and swallows hard. "I covered it up. Everything. I'd driven to Cliff Woods, so I dragged his body out of there and put him in my trunk. You followed my every step like you were stuck in a blissful trance. You'd gotten your revenge, as you said. After I placed him in the trunk, I sedated you. It wasn't the first time I had been forced to do so. You constantly had episodes and outbursts. Anyway, when I returned to the spot where you'd killed Oswald, it rained. And I'm not talking a bit of drizzle. There was a major downpour. It washed it all away. Every drop."

I search my memories and see glimpses of what Brad is telling me. The sedative must have fractured some of those moments, because it's a struggle to see things clearly. But they are there. The elation that came after I'd killed Oswald sent a shudder through my core. I'd thought I was doing something noble, but instead I had murdered an innocent man. One who had tried to save my daughter's life.

I thought Brad was the monster, but it's me.

"I had to get rid of the body," Brad says, "but I also needed you to have a solid alibi. I was worried someone was going to ask you about it the next day and that you would confess everything, so I came up with a plan. That's where Fletcher came into play."

"Fletcher? He was part of this?"

"He owed me a favor for some legal trouble I got him out of a few years ago, so I called him."

"What do you mean?" I spit. "Tell me what Fletcher did."

"It doesn't matter. What's done is done."

"It does matter," I yell. "Please. Tell me everything. I want to know how you and Fletcher covered this up. I want to know how I got away with murder."

Brad stares at me with the same loathing I am becoming used to and says, "Fine."

CHAPTER FIFTY-NINE

Brad kicks the dirt at his feet as I wait for him to answer me. I need to know how he got Fletcher involved in the cover-up of a murder I committed. "Why did he help?" I ask, pushing Brad to speak.

"It wasn't easy," Brad starts. "I had to use what I had helped him with in the past."

"What do you mean?"

Brad runs a hand through his hair like the other things he told me were easier to tell me. "After I had the body taken care of, I called Fletcher. It was late, and I needed him to take you for the night without finding out what you had done. So I called in my favor."

"The legal problem?" I ask.

Brad nods. "He had a major tax problem. I made it go away. I brought you to Fletcher's and asked if you could stay with him for the night. No questions asked. I said if he did this for me we'd be even for the tax thing. You were out cold with the sedative, so you weren't going to say otherwise. Plus, I'd cleaned the blood off you. Fletcher agreed and set you up in a spare bed."

I squint and try to understand the insane story Brad is telling me. I have so many questions running through my mind that I don't know where to start.

"I gave you another sedative and left. Then I spent the next two hours scrubbing my car clean with plans to return in the morning and pick you up before you had a chance to say anything. It was the perfect plan to give you a credible alibi. The story was you'd had too many drinks at Fletcher's house and had to spend the night sleeping it off."

"What about you?"

Brad shrugs. "I wasn't thinking about me. I just wanted to keep you from going to prison. I knew I was kicking the can down the road, but I had to try."

"So what happened when you came to get me?"

Brad sighs. "I was too late. You'd woken up early and attacked Fletcher. When I came inside, he was about ready to call the cops. I used the only move I had left. I told him everything. What you did. How you did it. Every sorry part. Then I said to Fletcher that I'd tell the police he was in on it, that he helped plan the murder. After all, trace amounts of Oswald's DNA were in his home from the clothing you'd been wearing."

"You forced him into it," I utter. "You made him an accessory to a murder."

"I did what I had to, Maia. You killed a man. He's right here. That's where he's been for four years."

I yell louder, "I never asked you to cover anything up. You should have sent me to prison or the psych ward for the rest of my life. You thought you were saving me, Brad, but I was beyond saving. I still am."

Brad drops down beside me and places a hand on my shoulder. He whispers. "You're still worth saving."

I want him to pull me into his arms and tell me how everything will be okay, but then London comes into my mind. I remember the panic in her eyes right before she drove off. I shrug him off. "Did she know?"

"Did who know?"

"London. Did she know about this? Was that the secret she was so desperate to keep from me?"

"No. She didn't know. She wasn't part of this. Fletcher almost told her everything that had happened four years ago. But he changed his mind at the last second. It was too late, though. London knew he had a dark secret about us, so he made up some story that I had cheated on you back then. She believed him."

I stare ahead with a blank look on my face. "So she actually died in a car crash? She didn't die keeping a secret?"

Brad shakes his head. "I told you I didn't kill her, but I never thought she would do what she did. I'm sorry. It's my fault she's dead."

"And Fletcher's," I add.

"He didn't mean to—"

"Don't," I say, cutting him off. I crawl forward. I reach out, seeing London rushing to her car. I should have stopped her. My hand lands on the dirt mound where Oswald Taylor is buried. Without meaning to, I think of his wife, Julia. "She deserves to know," I say.

"Who?" Brad says in a hoarse voice.

I shake my head and stand. "Julia Taylor. She needs to know the truth. This has gone on for too long. I'm going to the police to tell them everything." I start down the path, but Brad intercepts me.

"Hey, wait just a second. What do you think will happen to Abby if you do this?"

The thought had already crossed my mind. "She can live with Claire, Richard, and Thea."

"While her parents rot in prison? What kind of life is that?"

"Not the one she deserves, but it's the one we've given her, isn't it?"

He doesn't stop me as I continue down the path. More comes to me about the morning after the murder. Still at Fletcher's home, Brad and Fletcher had been arguing and threatening one another. All the while, I could see Imogen smiling down on me. I had done the right thing. I had made the world a better place, except that it was all a lie my mind had dreamed up for me to believe.

Brad had taken me home and explained to me how I couldn't tell anyone — we had to keep this secret. I had nodded, as if on autopilot, and when we had gotten inside, something had overtaken me. A wild, insatiable hunger had filled me. I had grabbed Brad and dragged him to the bedroom. We had sex for the first time since Imogen was taken from us. Two weeks later, I had missed my period.

I had spent that time following every word Brad told me. I didn't leave the house. I gave him my cell phone. His word had been law. He had stopped telling me that what I had done was wrong. In fact, he had gone along with it, telling me I'd done the right thing. Then I had asked him to buy me a pregnancy test.

It had been positive.

"You're pregnant?" he had asked.

"Yes!" I had shouted. "We're going to have a baby." I had been overjoyed. I'd found a new purpose and a new reason to exist. Imogen was gone, but I would get a second chance at being a mother. Within a week, I had forgotten about Oswald Taylor — the blood and the rock — and had dived headfirst into what was more important.

Brad must have seen something in me change and had focused on that instead of the rest of it. He had even allowed me to go back to therapy. Dr. Corbyn had spent his time helping me to forget the past and focus on the future.

Brad now follows me as I trek down the path. "Wait for me," he says, pacing up to my side. "Let me help you. Let me drive you to the police."

"Do you mean it?" I ask.

"Yes. All I've ever wanted is to help you, Maia."

"Thank you," I said. "I know I've put you through a lot."

"It's okay," he says. "So when do you want to do this?"

"In the morning. We'll go to the police and tell them everything."

"Okay," he sighs. I can feel regret in his voice, but there is also a lot of exhaustion. The past five years have been absolute hell on him, and he only made it all worse by trying to hide the truth. Deep down, past his misguided obsession to cover up the awful thing I did to an innocent man and the hell he put Fletcher through by dragging him into it all, he's a good person. No one else will see that, though. But I do.

I could continue the lie. I could claim to do it for Abby's sake, but Julia Taylor deserves to know the truth. Her husband was a hero. He tried to save my little girl, and I beat him to death with a rock. Justice needs to be served, and the only way that will happen is if I go to the police and tell them everything.

When we arrive at the car, I reach for the handle and feel a sharp jab in the side of my neck. Before I can cry out, a hand goes over my mouth. The dark world fades to black.

CHAPTER SIXTY

Brad

I panicked. I should have known that the second Maia remembered everything, she would want to go to the police. I guess I was lying to myself thinking there was a way around this all. So I did what I've always done when she's put my back to the wall. I sedated her.

Showing her Oswald's grave was never going to end well, but that crazed look she had in her eyes when she was threatening me with the machete was the same one I saw four years ago when I found her standing over his dead body.

I had no option but to show her the truth. And now, I don't know what to do with her. I drove her back home after knocking her out again and removed the hiking gear I'd placed on her. I burned it along with the watch in the backyard in a barrel. I returned the shovel to the garden shed. There was no way anyone could trace it to Oswald's burial site. I'd bleached it clean. But the rest of it was now a pile of ashes. The watch took a while, but it's now a heap of melted slag at the bottom of the barrel.

I threw the police report in there as well, but it's only a copy. Maia could get another. That is, if I decide to let her go through with her dumb idea to go to the police. There's no sense in it. I realize Maia is riddled with multiple layers of guilt. I am, too, but why should we put Abby through more hell than we already have, and both be sent to prison? What kind of life will that be for her when she is old enough to understand what her mother and father have done?

She deserves better.

It's late morning, and Maia is sleeping in our bed. I'm sitting up beside her, stroking her hair as she rests. The sedative I gave her was a big one. I added to it with a double dose of propranolol, hoping the combo would make her forget part of what happened on that mountain.

I don't know what I'm going to do when she wakes up. I wish we could stay in this moment forever and forget the last two and a half weeks. I wish I could find those memories in her head and erase them from existence so we could move on. But I know that's impossible. I spent so long trying to make things right again.

It's time I made a difficult decision.

Abby is away with my sister for another two days. There's no chance of anyone barging in. If I'm going to do this, now is the time. Sobs fill my eyes. I've run through this scenario a hundred times in my head, but I can't bring myself to go through with it. She's my wife. I love her. Everything I've done, good or bad, over the past five years has been to protect her from herself, and for one good reason: I don't want to live without her.

But something has to give. I can't allow Maia to go to the police and destroy everything. I have to do this.

For Abby.

The pillow has been in my hands for some time. I just need to get this over with. I exhale and attempt to level my breathing. I've never killed anyone before. The thought takes me back to that damn game we played at our anniversary dinner. I didn't kill

Oswald, but I may as well have. I didn't do enough to stop Maia from going through with her plans to kill him. I didn't call the police after she beat his head in with a rock, and I made sure his body wouldn't be found anytime soon. I'm a monster, so it's time to do what monsters do best.

I ready the pillow. Maia continues to sleep, blissfully unaware. My hands shake as I place it above her face and close my eyes. All I have to do is press down and not let go until it's over.

"No," I yell, throwing the pillow away. I can't do it. I won't do it.

I lay down on the bed beside my wife and give up. Whatever happens when she wakes up, we'll face together. I won't hurt her anymore.

I hold her hand and rest beside her, feeling the weight of everything that's happened since Imogen drowned. That day and the rest that followed weren't Maia's fault. I just wish I could make her realize it.

I close my eyes. Sleep finds me and pulls me into a tranquil ignorance, if only for a few minutes.

"Brad?" Maia asks.

I open my eyes. It's time. I sit up and face her. "Hi, honey."

Maia gazes around the room, confused. "What time is it?"

I check my cell phone on the bedside table. "Almost lunch time. When do you want to do this?" I ask, referring to our inevitable trip to the police station.

"Do what?" she asks.

"You know," I say. "What we had planned. What we spoke about last night."

"At the party?" she asks. "I'm sorry, but I think I had too much wine last night. You'll have to remind me."

My jaw drops as a tingle runs over my skin. Does she seriously think it's the next morning after the party? Her expression is blank

289

and confused. There's no hint of what she learned last night. "You know what?" I say, "I think I was having a dream."

"Okay," she says, reaching for her cell phone. But it's not there. "Where's my phone?"

"Oh, I think I saw it downstairs. I'll go get it for you." I jump out of our bed and hurry to the door. If she truly has forgotten the past two and a half weeks, then I've got a few things to put back into place.

"Hey, you're already dressed," she says, seeing that I'm wearing jeans.

"Yeah, I woke up a few hours ago. I just came in here to see how you were doing. Guess I fell asleep, sorry."

Maia smiles at me. "Aw, you were checking on me. How sweet."

"You know me," I say with a forced chuckle. "Why don't you go have a shower while I find your phone?"

"That's a good idea," she says. "My head is killing me. Guess I overdid it last night."

"Yeah," I mutter. "Last night was something."

"Where's Abby?" Maia asks as I reach the door.

Shit. I forgot about Abby. With no other explanation, I say, "At my sister's. She stayed for the night, remember?"

Maia's brow twists. "Uh, yeah, that's right. Sorry, I forgot."

"Not a problem," I smile.

While Maia showers, I go about unlocking most of the doors and returning things to where they belong in the house. I had them locked away in the basement. The last item I handle is Maia's cell phone. I remove it from the Ziploc bag I had kept it in and rush upstairs. I place it on charge as Maia finishes up with her shower.

She gets dressed while I sit on the edge of our bed and think of every lie I will need to tell to keep this miracle going. It won't be easy, but I've done it before, and I can pull it off again.

Maia walks over to me. I wrap my arms around her waist as she kisses me on the forehead. "Have you had breakfast yet?" she asks.

"No," I lie. "How about I make you some waffles?"

"Sounds amazing."

I point her to her cell phone, testing the waters again. She takes it off charge and looks at the lock screen. If she has seen the date, it's not bothering her.

I stand and walk with my wife, holding her hand as we head downstairs for breakfast. We walk past my study. Maia doesn't glance at it and keeps beaming at me. She's happy.

As we reach the kitchen, she sees how tidy everything is. "You cleaned up for me?" she asks.

"Uh, yeah," I say, rubbing the back of my head. "You do so much around here. I thought you could use a break."

"Thank you," she says, pulling me into a hug. We kiss like there isn't a care in the world. Maia stares into my eyes with warmth in her heart and asks, "So, how did it go last night? Did I do anything embarrassing?"

"No, honey. It was great, and so were you. We all had a good time. Even London was on her best behavior and didn't drink that much. I suppose she was flying out early this morning."

"Flying?"

"On the trip she told us about? She's off on another one of her adventures."

"Oh, that. Right. Of course. So I guess it was a tremendous success then."

I continue to smile at my wife. I don't know how I will break it to her that London is dead, but I'll worry about that problem later. "It was a success, honey. If you ask me, things are going to work out for our family from here on out."

She smiles and kisses me again like a lovesick puppy. I don't know how this has happened, but we've been given a second chance. I won't squander it or let anything get in our way. In fact, I think it's time we moved away from Brookfield Terrace and started fresh.

For as long as I can, I will keep us going and never look back. I wanted to erase the past for Maia, but in the end, I think I erased it for myself, too.

There's no more suspicion in her eyes. No more lingering doubts. Whatever pieces of the truth had once threatened to unravel everything were now gone.

And as I watch her sitting across from me, eating waffles, I know in my heart that this is all I need. That this is how it's meant to be. And maybe, if I lie to myself for long enough, I'll believe it, too.

CHAPTER SIXTY-ONE

Maia

I woke up in our bed. "Brad?" I asked.

He opened his eyes and sat up to face me. "Hi, honey."

I gazed around the room, confused. "What time is it?"

Brad had checked his cell phone on the bedside table. "Almost lunch time. "When do you want to do this?" he asked.

"Do what?"

"You know. What we had planned. What we spoke about last night."

"At the party?" I asked. "I'm sorry, but I think I had too much wine last night. You'll have to remind me."

Brad's jaw dropped. "You know what?" he said, "I think I was having a dream."

I smiled and couldn't believe what I was seeing; Brad had thought I'd forgotten. He seemed convinced that I couldn't remember a single thing from the past two and a half weeks. We talked more, and I played along with his every word. He tested me a few times, even allowing me to see my phone after I had a shower. We went downstairs to the kitchen, where he lied to me about London. He made up some story about her going away on a trip. She was dead. I wondered how long he planned on lying to me about that.

I let him make me waffles and hold my hand like he didn't drag me up a mountain to a grave site to show me what I had done. I let him believe whatever version of reality he needed to. Because it was better this way.

For now.

When I had asked about Abby, and he said she was with his sister, I wanted to scream, but I kept my cool. Because I knew exactly how far Brad was willing to go when he felt the walls closing in. I wasn't afraid that he'd harm Abby, but I believed with every fiber in my being that he would take her away from me again and use my baby against me. So I had to play him. I had to be patient and still.

For her.

I laughed at his jokes. I kissed him with passion. I became the perfect wife and let him believe I was content, that everything that happened after the dinner party was a haze I didn't care to piece together.

But I remembered everything. And not just the past two and a half weeks.

I remembered Oswald and the rock. I remembered what Brad told me he did to the body after. I remembered the sedative burning through my veins as I reached for the door handle to the car at the bottom of the mountain.

And as if all that wasn't damning enough, I knew about the pillow.

I had woken up a few minutes earlier than he realized and had seen Brad holding the pillow in a way that told me he was grappling with a tough choice. I could feel the moment he almost crossed the line he'd no doubt danced along for years. But he couldn't do it. He couldn't kill me.

That was the difference between us.

I'd already crossed that line. And I'd made it to the other side.

He thought there was a version of us worth saving. But I wasn't there to be saved anymore. I no longer wanted to go to the police and tell them the truth. I was there to survive.

So I waited. I watched. I smiled and played the role he wanted me to play and would do so until the moment was right. Because eventually, he'd let his guard down again. And when he did, I wouldn't hesitate. I would finish this. I had to do whatever it took to keep Abby and me together. Nothing and no one could come between us. Not even the truth. My baby needed me. Now and forever. I wouldn't let Brad lock me away or convince me to forget the past with a haze of pills and therapy. Not again.

He had no idea what I was truly capable of. Soon, I'd make Brad pay for his part in London's death. She may have crashed the car herself, but it was his scheming and lies that were the catalyst. Seeing as he liked to play with all our lives like they were meaningless, I figured it was time to play a new game of Two Truths and One Lie. I would go first.

I once killed a man — truth.

My husband buried the body and covered up the crime — truth.

I had forgotten everything — lie.

THE END

AUTHOR'S NOTE

Writing this book was a complex, cathartic experience I won't forget. At its heart, this story is about memory and how it can protect us, deceive us, and betray us all at once. It's about the truths we bury to survive and the lies we tell ourselves to forget.

This book explores how trauma doesn't always scream. Sometimes it whispers and distorts the past until you no longer know what's real. I was fascinated by the idea that a forgotten truth can fracture a person's identity. What happens when you can't trust your own memories? When the version of yourself you've built turns out to be a house of cards?

To my incredible wife and children, thank you for your love, your patience, and your quiet understanding during the late nights and early mornings this story demanded. You've lived beside every draft and doubt, and your unwavering belief in me keeps me grounded.

I'm deeply grateful to my editor, Siân Heap, for her insight and sharp instincts that helped shape this novel into what it is. Thank you also to Senior Editor Kate Ballard and the team at Joffe Books for their hard work bringing this book to life.

To new readers and returning ones: I hope this book unsettles you in the best way. I hope it makes you question the narratives we build about others, and about ourselves. And if you find yourself haunted by one moment, one character, or one revelation, then maybe you're closer to the truth than you think.

And if you enjoyed *Two Truths One Lie*, I'd love to hear your thoughts. You can reach me on social media or through my website. Your support, messages, and reviews mean more than I can express.

Thank you for reading.
Thank you for remembering.
And thank you for playing the game.

Warmly,
Alex Sinclair

THE JOFFE BOOKS STORY

We began in 2014 when Jasper agreed to publish his mum's much-rejected romance novel and it became a bestseller.

Since then we've grown into the largest independent publisher in the UK. We're extremely proud to publish some of the very best writers in the world, including Joy Ellis, Faith Martin, Caro Ramsay, Helen Forrester, Simon Brett and Robert Goddard. Everyone at Joffe Books loves reading and we never forget that it all begins with the magic of an author telling a story.

We are proud to publish talented first-time authors, as well as established writers whose books we love introducing to a new generation of readers.

We won Trade Publisher of the Year at the Independent Publishing Awards in 2023 and Best Publisher Award in 2024 at the People's Book Prize. We have been shortlisted for Independent Publisher of the Year at the British Book Awards for the last five years, and were shortlisted for the Diversity and Inclusivity Award at the 2022 Independent Publishing Awards. In 2023 we were shortlisted for Publisher of the Year at the RNA Industry Awards, and in 2024 we were shortlisted at the CWA Daggers for the Best Crime and Mystery Publisher.

We built this company with your help, and we love to hear from you, so please email us about absolutely anything bookish at feedback@joffebooks.com.

If you want to receive free books every Friday and hear about all our new releases, join our mailing list here: www.joffebooks.com/freebooks.

And when you tell your friends about us, just remember: it's pronounced Joffe as in coffee or toffee!

www.ingramcontent.com/pod-product-compliance
Ingram Content Group UK Ltd.
Pitfield, Milton Keynes, MK11 3LW, UK
UKHW040653271025
8606UKWH00058B/1247